Ready *for* Love

The Gansett Island Series by Marie Force

Book 1: Maid for Love
(Maddie & Mac)
Book 2: Fool for Love
(Joe & Janey)
Book 3: Ready for Love
(Luke & Sydney)
Book 4: Falling for Love
(Grant & Stephanie)
Book 5: Hoping for Love
(Evan & Grace)
Book 6: Season for Love
(Owen & Laura)
Book 7: Longing for Love
(Blaine & Tiffany)
Book 8: Waiting for Love
(Adam & Abby)
Book 9: Time for Love
(David & Daisy)
Book 10: Meant for Love
(Jenny & Alex)
Book 10.5: Chance for Love,
A Gansett Island Novella *(Jared & Lizzie)*
Book 11: Gansett After Dark
(Owen & Laura)
Book 12: Kisses After Dark
(Shane & Katie)
Book 13: Love After Dark
(Paul & Hope)
Book 14: Celebration After Dark
(Big Mac & Linda)
Book 15: Desire After Dark
(Slim & Erin)
Book 16: Light After Dark
(Mallory & Quinn)
Book 17: Episode 1: Victoria & Shannon
Book 18: Episode 2: Kevin & Chelsea

Ready *for* Love

MARIE FORCE

ZEBRA BOOKS
KENSINGTON PUBLISHING CORP.
http://www.kensingtonbooks.com

ZEBRA BOOKS are published by

Kensington Publishing Corp.
119 West 40th Street
New York, NY 10018

All Kensington titles, imprints, and distributed lines are available at special quantity discounts for bulk purchases for sales promotion, premiums, fund-raising, educational, or institutional use.

Special book excerpts or customized printings can also be created to fit specific needs. For details, write or phone the office of the Kensington Sales Manager: Attn.: Sales Department. Kensington Publishing Corp., 119 West 40th Street, New York, NY 10018. Phone: 1-800-221-2647.

Zebra and the Z logo Reg. U.S. Pat. & TM Off.

First Zebra Books Mass-Market Paperback Printing: July 2018
ISBN-13: 978-1-4201-4689-9
ISBN-10: 1-4201-4689-0

10 9 8 7 6 5 4 3 2 1

Printed in the United States of America

Author's Note

Welcome back to Gansett Island for Luke and Sydney's story! As a wife and mother, this one really touched my heart. Sydney's losses are simply unimaginable, but thanks to Luke's devotion she might be ready to take a second chance on love. I so hope you enjoy their story as much as I enjoyed writing it. You'll also get to catch up on some of your favorite characters from the first two books and meet some newcomers to the island.

Ready for Love continues the story begun in *Maid for Love* and *Fool for Love*. Next up is *Falling for Love* with many more Gansett Island books currently available. The fun never ends on Gansett!

Writing about this family and their life on an island so much like my beloved Block Island has been about the most fun I've ever had as a writer. Thank you so much for embracing my fictional family and for all the lovely reviews you've posted. I appreciate your e-mails and Facebook posts more than you'll ever know. I always love to hear from readers. You can reach me at marie@marieforce.com. If you're not yet on my mailing list, join now at marieforce.com for updates on future books.

I'm grateful every day to have such wonderful, supportive readers and writing friends who make my life as an author such a joyful journey. Thank you from the bottom of my heart. And as always, to the family that puts up with me and all my eccentricities, you guys are simply the best.

xoxo,
Marie

Chapter One

"Are you ever going to say anything?"

Her familiar voice electrified Luke, startling him as he squatted in the dark beside her parents' porch.

The peal of laughter that followed her question reminded him of the happiest time in his life, when she'd laughed at all his corny jokes, before she'd gone away to college and met someone she liked better.

"Luke?"

He stood slowly, not sure if he was more relieved or mortified to have been caught watching her. "How long have you known?"

"Since the first time you came last summer."

Okay, mortified. Definitely mortified. Luke released an unsteady laugh. "And here I thought I was being so sly."

"As if I could ever forget the sound of your boat scraping against the beach. I used to listen for it every night."

The reminder of those unforgettable summer nights made his heart race. When he'd heard through the island grapevine that she'd arrived on a ferry earlier in the day, he'd told himself to stay home, to leave her alone. But knowing she was here, knowing she was just across the pond . . . Like the summer before, he'd been unable to stay away.

"I'm sorry," he said. "You must think I'm some sort of creep. I swear I'm not. It's just when I heard about what happened . . . to your family . . . I had to come. To make sure you were okay. Well, of course you weren't okay . . ." He ran his fingers through his hair. "Jesus, I'm screwing this all up."

She smiled, and he was relieved to see it reach her expressive eyes the way it used to, back when she smiled at him every day. He took it as a sign that she'd recovered, somewhat—as much as anyone ever could—since he last "visited" her a year ago.

"Do you want to come up?" she asked.

"Oh, I don't want to bother you or your parents—"

"They're off-island for a few weeks. Family reunion in Wisconsin."

"You didn't want to go?"

She wrinkled her nose. "I'd rather be here than anywhere else in the summer."

Somehow he worked up the fortitude to climb the five steps to the porch, his heart pounding so hard he wondered if it would burst through his chest. Keeping his hands in his pockets so she wouldn't see them tremble, he was unable to remember the last time he'd been so nervous. Speaking with the love of his life for the first time in seventeen years would make any man nervous, he supposed. "You always did love it here."

"It's my favorite place in the world."

"I wondered if you were going to come this year."

Her smile faded a bit. "I had some stuff I had to take care of before I could come out to the island." She gestured to the rocker next to hers. "Want to sit?"

"Um, sure. I guess. For a minute." Under the glow of the porch light, he took a furtive glance at her. He was relieved to see that she did, in fact, look a thousand times better than she had a year ago, just a few months after the accident. "Who's your friend?" he asked, referring to the gorgeous golden retriever who lay between their two rockers. The dog had taken a long, measuring look at Luke as he approached the porch but had remained silent.

"This is Buddy." She reached down to scratch his ears, and even as he clearly enjoyed the attention, the dog never took his solemn eyes off Luke. "We gave him to the kids the Christmas before . . . the accident . . . He loved them both, but he and my son Max had a very special bond. I thought poor Buddy would die himself of a broken heart after what happened. He whimpered and cried for months."

Luke's heart ached at the pain in her voice and at the image she painted of the devastated dog. "He wasn't with you last summer."

"I was still recovering from my own injuries, and we worried I'd trip over him or he'd knock me over without meaning to. He stayed with our neighbors at home for a few months. I'm so glad to have him back with me now. The poor guy has been through a lot."

So have you, Luke thought but chose not to say. As if she needed the reminder.

"I owe you the world's biggest apology," she said, startling him.

"I was the one stalking you. How do you owe me an apology?"

"You were *checking* on me. Big difference." She curled her legs up under her and turned to him. "The apology I owe you is for seventeen years ago."

"Oh. That."

"Yeah. That."

"Sydney—"

"Luke—"

He cleared his throat and folded his hands tight in his lap. This was far more excruciating than he'd ever imagined it would be—and he'd imagined it plenty of times. Thousands of times, to be honest. What he might say. What she might say. If either of them would have anything at all to say. "Sorry," he said. "Go ahead."

"What I did to you was unconscionable. I know it's no consolation, but I thought of you so many times. I wanted to write to you or call you or something, but what does one say in that situation? *I'm really sorry I left for the school year and never came back?* Would that have made anything better?"

"It helps to know you thought of me."

"Oh God, Luke, how could I *not* think of you? Those summers . . . The time we spent together . . . Other than when my kids were born, it was the most magical time of my entire life."

No, he decided, this was far more excruciating than anything he'd ever imagined. "If that's how you felt, then why—"

"I was an idiot."

Shocked by her bluntness, he gave up any pretense of trying not to stare at her. The thick strawberry-blond hair he'd loved running his fingers through was shorter than it used to be, but the summer freckles that had popped up on her nose after long days in the sun were still there. The bright blue eyes that had been so tragically sad last summer seemed to have recovered some of their sparkle.

"I had this idea, you know, of how my life should be. Who my husband should be. What he would do for a living. Where we would live. I was a snobbish fool."

"I suppose the boy you'd left behind on the island, who worked at a marina and never made it to college, didn't quite fit the bill." Luke tried like hell to keep the bitterness out of his tone, but after so many years of suspecting what had driven her away, hearing confirmation of what he'd most feared was hardly a balm on the still-open wound.

"I know there's nothing I can say to change what happened all those years ago, but I want you to know I regretted the way I treated you. I *always* regretted it."

Hearing that didn't help as much as he'd thought it would.

She looked down at her hands. "Sometimes I wonder if what happened . . . to me . . . was payback . . ."

"Don't say that. No one deserves what happened to you."

"Karma can be such an awful bitch," she said ruefully. "Maybe I asked for too much, you know?"

"I can't believe in a God or any higher power who'd take the lives of innocent children to pay their mother back for being cavalier with the feelings of an old boyfriend."

Sydney winced. "Cavalier. Ouch."

"What would you call it?"

"Horrible. I was horrible to you." She leaned her head back on the rocker and studied him. "You haven't changed at all. I'd know you anywhere."

"Your hair is shorter, but otherwise, you look exactly the same, too."

"Tell me you found someone else, got married, had a boatload of kids. Tell me it all worked out well for you."

"No wife, no kids, but a good life. A satisfying life."

"I ruined the wife and kids thing for you, didn't I?"

He fought to maintain a neutral expression, to not let her see the pain. "Don't give yourself too much credit, Donovan. You weren't all *that* important."

Her laughter danced through the night, making his heart flutter. "Whatever you say, tough guy."

He never had been able to fool her. "Could I ask you something?"

"Sure."

"Your husband . . . ?"

"Seth."

"You were happy with him?"

"That's a very complicated question."

Luke expelled a tortured moan. "Come *on*. Tell me it was worth it—at least for one of us."

They sat in uncomfortable silence for a long time. "Seth was a good man, a wonderful father, a devoted husband, and I loved him."

"But?"

She looked over at him, their eyes connecting with a powerful sense of awareness that left him breathless. "What I felt for him . . . It was different than what I felt for you."

He wanted to ask her what she meant by that. *How* was it different? Different better? Different more? Different less? But he couldn't seem to form any of those questions, so he had to settle for what she'd given him.

"I shouldn't be admitting these things, especially to you. See what I mean about karma?"

Luke shook his head. "The universe doesn't work that way. It just doesn't."

"Some days, it's hard to believe I didn't have it coming. I wasn't always a good person."

"You can't honestly believe that. A drunk driver killed your family, not you."

"That's what my counselor has been trying to get me to believe for fifteen months now."

"Getting any closer?"

"Good days, bad days."

"I hope seeing me won't make this a bad day."

"Seeing you is wonderful. I've wished for years to have the opportunity to tell you how sorry I was to have left without a word. Sometimes when we'd come for a summer visit with my parents, I'd think about going down to McCarthy's to see you."

"Why didn't you?"

"That would've been so unfair to you, for me to show up out of the blue like that after all that time, just so I could make myself feel better about being a shit to you."

"I would've liked to have seen you, to have met your kids. More than anything, I've missed my friend Sydney. The best friend I ever had."

Her eyes sparkled with tears. "I'm so sorry, Luke," she whispered. "I'm so very, very sorry. Can you ever forgive me?"

"I forgave you years ago. You were nineteen. You didn't owe me anything."

She reached over and rested her hand on top of his. "I owed you so much more than what you got from me after four magical summers together."

The brush of her skin against his brought back a flood of sweet memories, the sweetest of all memories. He turned his hand so hers was caught between both of his, and the emotion hit him so hard it took his breath away. Suddenly, it became urgent that he leave before he said or did something he'd regret. "It was good to see you, Syd."

"Thanks for checking on me."

Luke grimaced. "*Checking* is a much nicer word than *stalking*."

She squeezed his hand. "It touched me last summer to know you were here, that you cared, despite the way we left things. I hope you understand I wasn't ready yet . . ."

"Please. Of course I understand."

"Will you come back again?"

Startled by the question, Luke said, "Do you want me to?"

"I missed my friend Luke. I never stopped missing him."

Overwhelmed by her, he couldn't find the words.

"I can see I've caught you off guard. I've been doing that to people a lot lately. Ever since the accident, I don't see much reason to hold back. Life is short. What's the point of hedging?"

"No point, I guess."

"I don't mean to shock you."

"You haven't shocked me so much as given me a lot to think about."

"Do you accept my apology?"

He nodded. "Clean slate."

"That's far more than I deserve."

"The slate is clean, remember?"

She smiled at him the way she used to when she still loved him, and Luke swore his heart stopped for an instant.

He forced himself to release her hand, to get up, to walk down the stairs, to make his escape while he still could. He'd made it to the lawn on the way to the beach when she called out to him.

"Come back, Luke. Please come back again."

Luke waved to show he'd heard her and continued toward the shore on what used to be his well-worn path between her yard and the beach. His old rowboat, the same boat he'd had way back when, waited for him to make the trek across the salt pond to the same small house he'd once shared with his mother. Her illness had kept him tied to the island when Sydney and his other friends were leaving for college.

He'd never regretted giving those important years to

the woman who had raised him on her own, but he couldn't help but wonder what might've been different for him—and for Sydney—if he'd been able to accept the scholarship he'd been offered that would've made him a marine biologist. Would that profession have been good enough for Sydney? The Sydney she'd been back then?

Probably not. She'd married a banker. A guy who studied algae and pond scum probably wouldn't have made the cut. Either way, it didn't do any good to speculate now. What difference did it make? She'd made her decision a long time ago, and he'd had no choice but to accept it.

Except, as he rowed slowly across the vast pond, guided by the light of the moon and stars, he was filled with an emotion he hadn't experienced in so long he'd almost forgotten what it felt like: hope. She'd never forgotten him. She'd thought of him, missed him, regretted their parting. *God, what does that mean?*

She was no longer married. Her husband and children had been gone for more than a year. He could see just by looking at her that she was doing much better accepting the awful hand life had dealt her than last summer when the pain of her loss was still so fresh and new.

"Ugh," he said out loud as he rowed. "Don't go there, man. It was over and done with years ago. Leave the past where it belongs."

But even as he told himself there was no point, that pesky burst of hope refused to be ignored.

Chapter Two

Every morning since the accident, Sydney had woken to the ever-present physical reminders of her own injuries: aching hips and pelvis, throbbing in her left femur and the excruciating pain in her heart as she was forced to remember what she'd lost. The first few minutes of each new day were often the worst, so she always took a moment to absorb the pain and find the fortitude to keep going.

For a brief instant this morning, she couldn't remember where she was. That'd happened often since she'd woken in a pain-filled haze in the hospital, asking for her children, asking for her husband. As she'd done so many times since then, she forced the horrific memories from her mind and took a visual tour of the pleasant bedroom from her childhood summers on Gansett Island.

Filled with relief to be back on the island, she reached over to pet Buddy's soft fur, grateful as she was every day for his company and steadfast devotion to her. Before everything happened, she never would've allowed him on the bed she'd shared with Seth. Now he slept tucked against her every night, taking and giving comfort.

She'd come to the island filled with determination to make some decisions about her future. After the first agonizing Christmas without her family, she'd returned to work as a second grade teacher, thinking that getting back to her routine would help to jumpstart her life. It hadn't taken long to realize being around other children close in age to the two she'd lost was not at all the catharsis she'd hoped it would be.

Rather, it was sweet torture to look at the children in her classroom and be reminded day in and day out that her own beautiful children were gone forever. So she had soldiered through to the end of the school year and stood now at a crossroads with big decisions to make. She'd already told her school she wouldn't be back next year. The principal had urged her to take the summer, to think it over, to give herself some more time.

But she'd seen no point in holding up a job that someone else could do much better than she could. She saw no point in returning year after year to teach children the same age her son had been when his life came to an abrupt end. While she'd always loved the job and the age group she taught, it just wasn't possible to do it anymore. So she'd endured the party her concerned colleagues had given to wish her well, and emptied her classroom for the last time.

She would've left the next day for the island—the one place where she could find the peaceful calm she needed more than anything else at the moment. However, a court date for the drunk driver who'd hit them had kept her in Wellesley until late July, only to have the proceeding postponed at the last minute, until the fifth of September.

Her parents had fretted about her being alone on the island for the month of August, but she'd assured them she and Buddy would be just fine and had promised daily phone calls to check in with them. The promise had pacified them, and she'd sent them on their way to the reunion of her father's family they'd looked forward to in Wisconsin. They were heading to California from there, completing a lifelong goal to drive cross-country. After the long, dark winter that followed the accident, it was time for all of them to get back to living again.

Sydney had given herself this month to figure out what was next. Thanks to Seth's practicality and knack for growing money, she'd received a substantial life insurance payout after his death that, coupled with their savings, gave her a nice cushion. Maybe she'd go back to school or travel or move to a new city where no one knew her. The entire world was open to her. It was just a matter of deciding what she wanted and where she wanted to be.

According to her counselor, making plans was a sign of recovery. Sydney wasn't sure she wanted to hear that. How does a mother ever "recover" from losing her babies? After Max was born, someone had given her an embroidered pillow with the saying, "A child is your heart walking around outside your body." If that wasn't the truth! And then when Malena came along, Syd had given away what was left of her heart. Losing them wasn't something she expected to ever "get over."

But life had an irritating way of marching forward, of forcing the living to get on with it even when it would be so much easier not to. For a while, after the accident, she'd entertained the darkest thoughts of her life, had flirted with the notion of ending it all, of putting a stop to the relentless pain any way she could. Only knowing that she couldn't—and wouldn't—do such a thing to her grief-stricken parents had kept Sydney from going too far down that tempting path.

Turning over in bed, she took a moment to study the photo of Seth and the kids that she'd placed on the bedside table. Sometimes it was still so hard to believe they were really gone forever and not off somewhere together, due home any time now.

She shifted her gaze to the view of the pond in the distance. Not much had changed since the summer mornings of her youth: scores of boats at anchor, activity and bustle in Gansett's vast salt pond. As she had during many of those long-ago mornings, she wondered if Luke was out on the water or working on the docks at McCarthy's Gansett Island Marina the way he had since he was a boy.

Seeing him last night had brought back so many precious memories. It was no surprise to her that he was as stunningly handsome at thirty-six as he'd been at nineteen. Perpetually tanned skin, silky dark hair that fell over his forehead, soft brown eyes, lips made for kissing . . .

For so many years, he'd been at the center of her life, even though she'd seen him only during the summers. Her parents hadn't approved of the passionate love between two teenagers, so she and Luke had been forced to do a lot of sneaking around to be together.

It pained Sydney to realize as an adult, with the hindsight of so much time gone by, that she'd allowed her parents' views to influence hers. She'd let social status and money, and things that didn't matter in the least, drive her decisions. When she thought about what she'd done to a decent, kind young man who'd deserved so much better, she was ashamed. Even all these years later, even after she'd apologized to him, she was ashamed of how she'd treated him.

That wasn't to say, if she had it to do all over again, she would change anything. Her decisions had led to Seth, Max and Malena, and she could never, ever be sorry about having had any of them in her life. Yes, she was sorry her decisions had caused such pain for Luke. She would always be sorry about that, but she was wise enough now to know that all the regrets in the world couldn't change the past. All anyone had was right now. Today.

"What shall we do with this bright and glorious day, Buddy?"

The dog barked and then stretched on the bed.

Sydney laughed. "I figured you'd vote for the beach."

Sydney drove back to the house after a few hours at her favorite hideaway beach. Buddy rode shotgun, head out the window, tongue lolling in the breeze. Before Seth had worn her down and convinced her that kids shouldn't grow up without a dog, Sydney wouldn't have described herself as a dog person. That, too, had changed. Sometimes she wondered how she ever would've survived the last fifteen months without Buddy's loving presence.

She'd purposely sought out a secluded stretch of beach where he could play in the surf without any of the disapproving glares they would've gotten at the town beach. There'd been a time, not that long ago, when she might've been one of the glare givers. Not anymore.

Approaching the house, she slowed when she saw a black SUV parked in the driveway. Even in the peaceful Boston suburb where she lived the rest of the year, she would've had a moment of trepidation about a strange vehicle outside her home. But since nothing bad ever happened on Gansett Island, Sydney pulled up next to the vehicle and cut the engine.

Her childhood friend Maddie Chester—Maddie McCarthy now—got out of the SUV and waited for her.

Sydney let out a squeal of pleasure at the sight of her old friend and rounded the car to hug her. "Oh! Look at you!" Syd pulled back to rest a hand on Maddie's pregnant belly. "Oh, Maddie!" They hugged again, both with tears on their faces.

"It's so good to see you, Syd."

"You, too." Maddie had hair and eyes the color of caramel and a figure that resembled a pinup girl. "You look so good! When are you due?"

"Not until November, if I don't explode before then." She tugged on a lock of Sydney's hair. "I love it shorter."

"Thanks. It's much easier at this length." Sydney appreciated that Maddie didn't lead with the grief. She'd received her friend's cards and letters, and contacting her this summer had been at the top of Syd's to-do list. "I'm sorry I didn't call last summer."

"No apologies necessary." Maddie waved her hand. "But I heard you were back, and I had to see you. I hope it's okay that I just showed up."

"Of course it is!" Sydney linked her arm through Maddie's and led her inside. Buddy followed close on their heels. "Can I get you a drink? I'm sure I have something that's caffeine-free."

"Ice water would be great."

Sydney introduced Maddie to Buddy, fixed the water and a diet cola for herself, and led Maddie to the back porch. "Tell me everything! I heard you married Mac McCarthy of all people—only the island's most eligible bachelor. You devil! Do tell!"

Maddie's face turned bright pink the way it used to when Sydney would whisper to her about having sex with Luke on the beach. Some things, it seemed, never changed. She and Maddie had scooped ice cream together for three summers and had formed a tight bond, even though

Sydney was a few years older. Before the accident, Syd had made it a point to see Maddie every summer when she brought the kids to the island to visit their grandparents.

"I'm sure you've heard the story."

Syd smiled. "Not from you."

"Well, Mac had just arrived from Florida for a visit with his parents. He stepped off the curb on Main Street, and I crashed right into him on my bike."

"I heard you got the worst of the injuries."

"Ugh, I was a scabby mess for *weeks*. While I recovered, he took care of me and Thomas—he was just nine months then—and he's been taking care of us ever since."

"So I see," Sydney said, raising an eyebrow and nodding to Maddie's rounded belly.

Maddie giggled. "He's so amazing. I'd love for you to meet him."

"I knew him way back when. I'd see him around the marina when I met Luke there. If I remember correctly, he was quite handsome."

"He's even more so now."

"I thought the same about Luke when I saw him last night. Amazing how the men out here age so well."

Maddie's mouth fell open. "You saw Luke? Where?"

"Right here." She filled Maddie in on Luke's "visits."

"That's so sweet," Maddie said. "How he came all those times just to check on you."

"It was far more than I deserved after the way I left him without a word."

"I'm sure he understood."

"I don't think he did. I apologized, but that's hardly adequate after all these years."

"Will you see him again?"

"I don't know. I hope so. We were always such good

friends before anything else. I missed him for a long time after it ended between us."

"As I recall, it never really ended."

"Not the way it should have, that's for sure."

Maddie reached for Sydney's hand. "How are you? Really? I've thought of you so often."

"I'm doing okay. Today has been a good day. Yesterday was a good day. Two weeks ago, I had a really bad day. It happens. Not as often as it used to, but still . . ."

"I suppose it's to be expected."

"That's what I'm told."

"I hope we can spend lots of time together while you're here. I want you to come to my house and see Mac and meet Thomas—" Maddie stopped herself, and her face flushed. "I'm sorry."

"For what?"

"I shouldn't have . . . You may not want to see Thomas."

"Oh, Maddie, of course I want to meet your son. I'd love to."

Maddie's eyes filled. "I think about Max and Malena all the time. They were so beautiful and so well behaved."

Sydney smiled even as her throat closed at the reminder of her children. "I was proud of them."

"With good reason. So will you come over sometime soon? Have dinner? Mac's sister Janey is getting married at the end of the month, so it'll be a fun time around here. I hope you'll be part of it all."

"I wouldn't want to intrude."

Maddie stood to go. "Don't be ridiculous. There're so many McCarthys, one extra person would hardly be a hardship."

Sydney got up to hug Maddie. "Those McCarthys are lucky to have you."

"We're lucky to have each other. Call me?"

"Promise."

After Maddie left, Sydney fed Buddy and prepared a pasta dinner with some grilled shrimp she'd picked up at the grocery store the day before. She made a salad, opened a bottle of white wine and sat at the kitchen table that overlooked the pond. At home, dinnertime was one of the more difficult parts of her day. It reminded her of just how alone she really was. Often she didn't bother to cook, resorting instead to a sandwich or a can of soup. What was the point in cooking for one?

Here on the island, removed from the daily grind of her routine, being alone didn't feel quite the same as it did in the too-quiet house that had once teemed with activity and the shrieks of children. Sure, her children were present here, too, in the house they'd loved to visit each summer, but it was different. She could breathe here.

Sydney cleaned up the kitchen, poured a second glass of wine and took it to the porch to watch the sun set. Long after the sky went dark and the activity on the pond stilled for the evening, long after she finished her glass of wine and the crickets began to sing, Sydney stayed on the porch, rocking back and forth as Buddy slept at her feet.

She told herself she wasn't waiting for Luke. He hadn't made any promises about coming back. They'd said everything they needed to say the night before. What was left to say?

Just as she was about to head inside, she heard the unmistakable sound of his boat scraping against the beach. A smile tugged at her lips, and her heart began to beat fast with anticipation. He'd come back.

Chapter Three

All day, Luke had vowed to stay away. After their conversation the night before, he had the closure he'd longed for. He had the satisfaction of her apology, of knowing she'd suffered over what she had done to him, that she hadn't left him behind and never thought of him again while she moved forward with another man. What more was there to say?

Apparently, a lot, he thought, laughing softly to himself as he pulled the boat onto the beach, announcing his arrival to her. Would she be waiting? When she asked him to come back, had she meant the very next night? Those were the questions that had tormented him all day as he went about his work at the marina, guiding boats, collecting payment, and shooting the shit with Mac, Mac's father, "Big Mac" McCarthy, and the other old men who hung out on the docks. Just another busy summer Sunday at McCarthy's.

At midday, Mac had asked him if everything was okay.

Taken aback by the question, Luke had nodded, surprised to realize Mac had picked up on the disquiet that had overtaken him. Not that Luke was ever one to run on at the mouth, but Mac said he seemed distracted.

That was one way of putting it. Yes, he'd been distracted by thoughts of freckles dancing across a sunburned nose, the light timbre of her voice, the laughter he'd missed so much and the feel of her hand in his, her fragile bones and pale skin such a sharp contrast to his much larger hand.

Now, despite all his plans to the contrary, he was back for more. The thought that he could be setting himself up for an even bigger disappointment than he'd suffered before nagged at him. At the end of the month, she would leave the way she always did. She would return to her life on the mainland while he stayed behind to weather another isolated winter on the island. Since Mac had moved back to the island and started a small construction business, Luke stayed busy working with him in the off-season.

But still . . . the idea of spending time with her this summer and then watching her leave again . . . Shaking off those unpleasant thoughts, he gathered up the gift he'd brought for her, and calling himself fifty different kinds of fool, he headed up the overgrown path that led to her yard. No matter what he might want to believe, he never had been able to stay away from her. From the moment he first saw her scooping ice cream in town, he'd been drawn to her like a moth to flame. Why should now be any different?

Emerging from the reeds that lined the shoreline, he looked for her on the porch and was filled with relief when he saw her in the rocker, almost as if she'd been waiting for him. "Don't go there," he muttered. "She's sitting where she sits every night. It's got nothing at all to do with you."

"Talking to yourself?"

Startled, he looked up to find her standing now and gazing down on him from the porch with mischievous laughter dancing in her eyes that soon slipped from her lips. The melodic sound stopped him dead in his tracks as hundreds of memories of long-ago moments besieged him. No one had ever gotten him to laugh at himself the way she had. She'd poked and prodded and cajoled him right out of his shell.

Luke had always been quiet and reserved, content to sit back and watch life go by rather than actively participate. Until he met Sydney. Until she forced him to participate. With her, he'd been more open, more spontaneous, more talkative than he'd been with anyone else. After she left him, he'd retreated right back into that shell, where he'd remained ever since.

"Luke?" He snapped out of his thoughts to find her laughter had faded to concern. "Are you coming up?"

"If you're sure you want the company."

She gestured to the stairs. "I'm sure."

As he took the stairs to the porch, his hands felt clammy and his heart raced, the way it had all those years ago when he'd been a teenager in the throes of first love. Nothing at all had changed since then. The realization left him staggered. He still loved her as much as he ever had. Despite everything that'd happened, despite the pain she'd caused him, he still loved her.

"Are you all right, Luke?"

For the second time that day, someone looked at him with concern. Apparently, he was doing a piss-poor job of hiding the fact that seeing her again had rocked his world.

Rather than try to explain his odd behavior, he withdrew the gift from behind his back. "For you."

Her eyes lit up with surprise and delight. "You brought me something?"

"Don't get too excited," he said, suddenly wishing he'd brought her a real gift rather than the dead starfish she unwrapped with reverence.

"Oh, Luke. You remembered." She ran a finger over the starfish. "I always loved them."

"Yes, I remembered." What an understatement! He remembered every damned thing they'd ever talked about, every damned moment that had ever transpired between them. Yes, he remembered.

"It's beautiful. Where did you find it?"

"I saw it on one of the rocks by the marina at low tide and climbed down to get it."

"It makes me so sad that such a glorious creature is dead."

Her sadness gutted him. God, what had he been thinking bringing her, of all people, something dead? "I'm sorry. I wasn't thinking." He started to reach for the starfish, but she hung on to it.

"Why are you sorry? It's a very thoughtful gift."

He wanted to shoot himself for putting that pensive look on her gorgeous face. "I didn't mean for it to make you sad."

"The damndest things make me sad these days, but then, I also find joy in things that might not have touched me before, such as a gift from an old friend who remembered how much I love starfish." She went up on tiptoes and kissed his cheek. "Thank you."

Luke stood frozen in place. The quick and spontaneous gesture, so typical of the Sydney he'd once known, left him riveted and thankful for the dark shadows on the porch that hid his instant reaction to her touch. It had been a mistake to come here when he wanted her more than his next breath. It was a mistake to restart something that couldn't go anywhere, something that had the power to crush him all over again.

"I'm sorry," she said, tuning in to his dismay. "I shouldn't have done that."

"Don't apologize. It's my fault. I shouldn't have come."

She stared up at him with those clear blue eyes that had never contained an ounce of guile. "Why?"

He glanced at the floor, summoning the strength he'd need to walk away—this time for good. "I can't do this. I really thought I could, but I can't."

"What can't you do, Luke?"

"I can't come here and pretend to be your friend when that's not what I want."

She winced, and her eyes shone with tears.

Luke hated that he'd caused her more pain. Like she hadn't already had more than enough.

"I understand," she said stoically. "I hurt you so badly. Why would you want to be my friend anymore?"

Luke uttered a softly spoken swear that was so far out of character for him, he could see he'd shocked her. "That's not it. You apologized, and I meant it when I said I forgive you."

"Then why can't we be friends?"

As if attached to a string controlled by someone other than him, Luke's hand reached out to caress her soft cheek. "Because what I want from you goes far beyond friendship, and you're not ready for that."

"Luke," she whispered, gripping his wrist. She turned her face into his hand and pressed a kiss to his palm.

A tremble zipped all the way through him. Nothing had ever electrified him the way her touch did. With great reluctance, he withdrew his hand. "I'm sorry. I wish I had it in me to be around you and not want more, but I can't do it."

"When it first happened," she said tentatively, "the accident . . . I never imagined I'd get to a point where I'd be ready . . . to try again. With someone else. But now, it's been more than a year, and it doesn't seem quite so impossible to imagine anymore."

"Syd," he said, shaking his head. "I look good to you because I'm familiar, because you once had feelings for me, but I couldn't bear to be your rebound guy or your transition guy, or whatever I'd be."

She finally dared to glance up at him, and what he saw in her eyes and on her face made his heart stagger. "Just because things ended the way they did between us doesn't mean I didn't still have feelings for you, and I would never use you to prove a point to myself or anyone else. You mean too much to me, and after what I did to you once before . . ." Her voice faded.

"What're you saying?"

"I don't want you to go."

Luke told himself to get the hell out of there while he still could, but somehow his legs didn't seem to get the message.

She rested her hands on his chest. "I don't know for sure that I'm ready for what this might be. All I know is I don't want you to go."

Against his better judgment, his hands landed on her hips and drew her closer. He really hoped she couldn't feel what her nearness did to him. The last thing he wanted was to scare her off by giving away how desperately he wanted her. As his arms went around her, she relaxed into his embrace, and he was reminded of how they'd once fit together so perfectly. The sweetness of the memory, the familiar scent of her hair and the hopelessness of the situation made him ache.

He held her tight against him, all the while telling himself it was unwise. This was a recipe for disaster for him—and maybe for her, too.

"Syd," he said, drawing back from her. "I'm going to go. I want you to really think about this. You need to be sure you're ready." He framed her face and urged her to meet his gaze. "If we start this up again . . ."

"What?" she asked, breathless.

"The last time you walked away from me, I was a kid without any options. I'm a grown man now, and I wouldn't let you get away so easily."

Her lips parted as if she had something to say, but then her eyes fluttered closed.

Luke couldn't resist the urge to brush a soft kiss over those perfect lips that had dominated his fantasies for such a long, lonely time.

The moment their lips connected, her eyes flew open.

"Think long and hard, Syd. Be sure it's what you really want. Be sure you're ready."

"Luke—"

He rested a finger over her lips to quiet her. "If it's tomorrow or next week or next summer or two summers from now, doesn't matter. I'll be here, and you'll always be welcome. If you never feel ready, that's okay, too."

"That's crazy," she said. "You can't wait forever for me."

"I already have. I've never met anyone I like better than you. After a while, I stopped looking." He kissed her forehead because he didn't dare kiss her lips again. If he did, he might not be able to stop kissing her. "You know where to find me."

Before he could let the possibility of never seeing her again set in, he got out of there. Without looking back, he went down the stairs, across the yard and into the reeds. Only when he was rowing his boat across the pond did he breathe again. What the hell had he just done?

Chapter Four

Sydney passed the week after Luke made his offer feeling like she was wading through quicksand. The lethargy that hung over her reminded her in some ways of the days and weeks that followed the accident. Aimlessness overtook her. She had trouble deciding what to eat or how to spend her days and was back to sleeping far too much.

Buddy was worried about her. She could see it in his solemn eyes as he watched her every move.

Sydney was getting sick of herself by the time Maddie called and invited her to a girls' night out with her sister Tiffany, sister-in-law Janey, and some of their other friends. Sydney's first inclination was to say no as the idea of showering and doing her hair and putting on makeup and choosing clothes seemed overwhelming.

But then Buddy nudged her and let out a soft whimper. He seemed to be asking her to do it for him.

"All right, Buddy. If it means that much to you."

He barked and wagged his bushy tail.

For the first time in a week, Sydney laughed. She

showered and shaved her legs and found a cute sundress that showed off the light tan she'd acquired while walking Buddy.

She brushed her hair until it shone and put on makeup that highlighted her eyes. As she wielded the mascara wand, her breath caught at the memory of Seth teasing her about how different she looked when she wore makeup. He preferred her au naturel. She took a moment to absorb the blow. Seth had been such a good and decent man, as well as funny and cute. He'd been so full of life and plans that sometimes it was still hard to believe he was really gone.

When Maddie arrived a short time later to pick her up, Sydney felt like she looked as good as she ever would. She'd done her best to shake off the rough moment with the mascara. It occurred to her then that the rough moments were happening less and less often. Oddly, that made her sad.

While she knew it was healthy to be recovering from the initial burst of horrible grief, she also felt guilty. What right did she have to be getting on with her life when her children would never have *any* life? When sweet, wonderful Seth was gone forever?

"You look gorgeous, Syd," Maddie said, hugging her.

"So do you." Maddie had worn a gauzy maternity top over white capri pants.

"I look like a beached whale," Maddie said with a snort.

"A very pretty beached whale."

"Gee, thanks."

Sydney gave Buddy a pat on the head and a kiss to the snoot. "Be a good boy while I'm gone."

He sat and watched with those solemn eyes as she went out the door with Maddie.

"He's so adorable," Maddie said. "Such a good boy."

"He never used to be." A shaft of pain lanced through Sydney as she remembered the Buddy from before the accident. "He was a holy terror—into *everything*. We used to joke that he was deaf to the sound of my voice and Seth's. Max was the only one he minded. The two of them were joined at the hip. After . . . he lay outside Max's room and cried for six months."

"God," Maddie said. "The poor guy."

"One day, I woke up, and he was sleeping next to me. He's been my dog ever since. Not once since Max died has Buddy done anything even slightly naughty or mischievous. He's been on his best behavior, which is sad in its own way." Sydney glanced at her friend and saw tears in her eyes. "I'm sorry. I don't mean to be a Debby Downer."

"Oh please, you're not at all. I just feel so sorry for Buddy—for both of you. I can't begin to understand what you've been through."

"I'm doing better. We both are." Despite the torment of the last week, the torment of Luke's offer, Sydney couldn't deny she was better than she'd been. Much better. But was she far enough along that she was ready to take another chance on love? That was the great unknown. Until she was sure, how could she gamble with her heart or Luke's? Especially when she'd done such tremendous damage to his heart once before.

"Did I dredge up bad memories?" Maddie asked as she drove them into town to meet the others.

"Not at all."

"What've you been up to all week?"

"I've been taking it easy. This past school year was particularly exhausting." She wanted to tell Maddie about what had transpired with Luke, but she just couldn't bring herself to share.

"I can't imagine being responsible for twenty seven-year-olds. One two-year-old is killing me."

Sydney laughed. "It does wear you out after ten months. I'm sure I'll miss it, though."

"Miss it? What do you mean?"

She told Maddie about her decision to leave her job—and why.

For a long moment, Maddie was quiet and pensive. "So what'll you do now?"

"Not sure yet. I'm hoping to figure that out this month while I'm here."

"You should stay out here with us permanently. This is your favorite place, after all."

Sydney chuckled at Maddie's shameless campaigning. "It's nice to feel wanted."

"We'd keep you plenty busy. You'd be surprised how much goes on around here in the winter these days."

"You'll be plenty busy this winter with a new baby."

"That's true," Maddie said. "I can barely manage the one I have. I can't imagine how I'll handle two." She gasped. "God, I'm sorry. I just keep putting my foot in my mouth."

"Can we make a deal? Right now?"

Still looking stricken, Maddie nodded.

"Can we please keep it real? What you said is something anyone would say with a two-year-old and a new one on the way."

"I don't mean to be insensitive."

"You're not being insensitive. It's your life right now, and I don't want you to walk on eggshells with me. If you think it, say it. Please don't filter yourself because something bad happened to me."

"I hope you know I don't mean to complain. I'm so blessed, and I know that."

"Don't ever take those blessings for granted."

"Did you?" Maddie asked hesitantly. "Take your blessings for granted?"

"Don't we all sometimes? I was always grateful for what we had, but I don't know if I appreciated it quite the way I should have. When I think of the kids, sometimes all I can remember is hollering at them for getting mud on my floor or getting after them about leaving their toys all over the place."

"That's stuff every mother says to her kids."

"I know, but it's more than that. You'll see when your kids get a little older. You get sucked into life and work and school and friends and birthday parties and sports, and the days go by in such a whirl of activity. Weeks would pass, and I'd feel like the only conversation I had with Seth was about Max's T-ball team or whose turn it was to help with homework."

"I can see how that happens. There're days when it's all Mac and I can do to get Thomas fed, bathed and in bed before we're ready to drop ourselves. I can't remember how I ever did it by myself."

"I'm so glad you found a great guy, Maddie. No one deserves to be happy more than you do."

"Aww, thanks. That's so sweet of you to say. Do you think, you know, you might ever . . ."

"Venture into dating again?"

Maddie nodded. "I don't mean to pry. I just can't imagine you alone the rest of your life. You've always been such a people person. I was so painfully shy when we were kids, but you were Ms. Sociable."

"I've become a little more introverted—that happened even before the accident. But I'm not big on the idea of being alone forever, so I suppose I'll wade back into those shark-infested waters eventually." She thought of Luke and what he'd said to her a week ago. "Maybe sooner rather than later."

"Are you keeping secrets? Has your nocturnal visitor continued to come by?"

"Not in the last week or so." She stared out the window, wanting to tell Maddie about Luke's last visit but afraid to put words to the torment it had caused her.

Maddie pulled into a parking space behind the Beachcomber, cut the engine and turned to Sydney. "What aren't you telling me?"

Sydney hesitated but only for a second. Who was she kidding? She was dying to tell someone about what'd happened. After she relayed the story, Maddie stared at her. "Say something, will you?"

"What'll you do?"

"I don't know. Part of me wants to run to him and *live* again, you know? But the other part doesn't want to take advantage of a good guy who's already been hurt enough by me in one lifetime. What right do I have to do that to him?"

Maddie took a moment to think that over. "It seems to me that by making the offer he did, he's willing to take the risk."

"He'd be crazy to take a chance on me. My life is a mess at the moment."

"It's not a mess. It's in transition, and you're smart to not want to start something you might not be ready for."

"But?"

"You already know he's a good guy. You know what you'd be getting."

"True."

"Do you still love him, Syd?"

She'd asked herself that same question a thousand times over the last week. "Oh God, I don't know. Part of me suspects I never stopped loving him. I thought about him far too often over the years. Even when I was married, I thought of him. I hate to say that because it sounds so disloyal to Seth, and I don't want to be disloyal. But I can't deny I thought of Luke."

"Well, he left it up to you and didn't put a time limit on his offer. So you could let it ride for the time being."

"Which is more or less what I've decided to do."

Maddie raised an eyebrow. "More or less?"

"I can't deny I'm tempted. Just being near him makes me all fluttery and weak-kneed the way I was with him at seventeen."

Laughing, Maddie said, "Girl, you're in serious crush."

"Is that why I've been so *miserable* all week?"

"Absolutely." They got out of the car and walked arm in arm toward the iconic hotel. "When Mac moved into my place to take care of me and Thomas after he knocked me off my bike, I had the most god-awful crush on him. I wasted far too much time listing all the ways it would never work rather than contemplating how it might work perfectly."

"What changed your mind?"

"Mac did. He can be *very* convincing when sets his mind on something."

"I can't see Luke doing that. He's much more reserved, and he made it clear he won't be pursuing me. He put the ball firmly in my court."

"That doesn't mean he won't try to convince you to give him a chance."

As Sydney stewed over that possibility, they arrived at the Beachcomber lounge, where a trio played live music.

The small dance floor was crowded with couples and just about every seat at the bar was taken.

Mac's sister Janey, Maddie's sister Tiffany, Abby who owned Abby's Attic, and several other women Maddie knew from her job at McCarthy's Gansett Inn waited for them. Maddie made the introductions, and the others put Sydney immediately at ease. She had no doubt Maddie had fully briefed her friends on Sydney's tragedy, but unlike the social gatherings at home where Sydney usually felt like a pariah since the accident, here she was far more comfortable.

"Janey," Maddie said as she sipped a club soda, "you have to tell Syd how you and Joe got together."

After much hooting, hollering, and catcalling, Janey waved her hands to quiet the others. She was tiny and blond but seemed to make up for her lack of height with a larger-than-life personality. "I was engaged to someone else," Janey began. "I'd been with David, a medical student in Boston, for thirteen years."

"Can you even *believe* that?" Maddie asked.

Amazed, Sydney shook her head. "That's a long courtship."

"Too long, as it turned out. I caught him in bed with another woman."

Sydney gasped. "No way! What did you do?"

"After I ran away from David's Boston apartment, my car broke down. I called Mac's best friend, Joe, who has always been like a fifth brother to me, and he came to my rescue."

"In more ways than one," Tiffany said with a snort, and the other women howled with laughter.

Janey's face turned bright red. "Turns out," she said,

"Joe had been secretly in love with me for *years*. We've been together ever since."

"That's such a great story," Sydney said.

"You left out a few very important parts," Maddie said with a pointed look for her sister-in-law. "They'd only been together a short time when Janey realized a lifelong dream of getting accepted to veterinary school at Ohio State. Joe owns and operates the Gansett Island Ferry Company, so Janey naturally assumed he wouldn't be able to go with her to Ohio."

"I just couldn't do another long-distance relationship," Janey said ruefully, "so I made the supreme mistake of breaking up with him."

Maddie started laughing, an infectious sound that quickly spread around the table. "He carted her right out of our wedding reception and let her know there was *nothing* he wouldn't do, nothing he wouldn't give up, nowhere he wouldn't go to be with her. *So* romantic! And, he proposed—*in bed*!"

Janey stuck her tongue out at Maddie. "You had to get that in there, didn't you?"

"That's the best part! They're back from their first year in Ohio, and how was that, exactly?"

"*Sublime*," Janey said with a dreamy smile that was met with more whoops from her friends.

Satisfied with the retelling of the story, Maddie sat back and crossed her arms, sending Sydney a rather calculating look. "It's interesting, isn't it, Syd, that Janey thought she was doing what was best for *him*, and it turned out *she* was the best thing for him."

Maddie McCarthy, it seemed, was a whole lot less subtle than Maddie Chester had once been. Sydney raised her wineglass in toast to Maddie. "Touché."

Maddie waggled her brows at Sydney, and then her expression suddenly changed. "Now *what*, do you suppose, *they* are doing here?"

Sydney looked over to see Mac, Luke and another guy who she assumed was Joe, pulling up stools at the bar.

"Checking on us, no doubt," Janey said, even though she lit up with pleasure at the sight of Joe.

Sydney's heart skipped into overdrive as she feasted her eyes on Luke, startled to realize she'd missed him terribly during the long week since she'd last seen him. How was that *possible*? She'd had exactly two conversations with him in seventeen years!

"Mmm," Tiffany said. "That Luke Harris is some kind of sexy." She added a predatory growl to her statement that set Sydney's nerves on edge.

Oh my God, she thought. *I'm jealous!*

"Need I remind you, dear sister, you're married," Maddie said. "Besides, I heard Luke is seeing someone."

While Sydney bit back a groan, Janey pounced. "*Who* is he seeing? I've never known him to date anyone!"

"That's not true." Maddie cast another sly glance at Sydney. "He and Syd went out for years back in high school."

"Is that so?" Janey said. "Well, you must've ruined him for all other women."

Sydney winced at the teasing comment that struck far too close to home. She was saved from having to reply when the three sinfully good-looking men ambled over to their table carrying bottles of beer and wearing predatory grins. Well, two of them were grinning. The third one looked as undone as she felt.

She made an effort to breathe normally as she took in every detail of the white button-down shirt he wore with the sleeves rolled up over strong forearms. Not that she was looking too closely, but he had what looked like a shark's tooth on a leather string around his neck. Something about that slash of white against his tanned skin was ridiculously sexy.

Sydney felt a stirring deep inside that she recognized as desire. It'd been so long since she'd felt anything other than devastation that the emotions Luke awakened just by walking toward her were overwhelming, to say the least.

While Mac and Joe said hello to the women and shook hands with Sydney when Maddie introduced them, Luke, being Luke, hung back. Within a minute, Maddie was seated on Mac's lap, and Joe had dragged Janey off to dance.

"So much for girls' night out," Maddie muttered as she leaned into her husband's loving embrace. "What've you done with our son?"

"He's with my parents," Mac said with a suggestive wink as he rested a hand on her pregnant belly. "Having a sleepover."

Maddie flashed him a seductive smile. "Is that so?"

"Uh-huh," he said, laying a lingering kiss on her.

Sydney was about to escape to the ladies' room when Luke leaned down to whisper in her ear.

"Dance with me."

Chapter Five

Tongue-tied, Sydney stared up at him. "Um, sure. Okay." She started to get up and tripped on the chair leg.

Luke reached out to steady her, and their eyes met. A hum of awareness rippled between them.

Sydney had no doubt everyone at her table as well as the entire bar full of people were staring at them as Luke wrapped his hand around hers to lead her to the dance floor.

Naturally, the musical trio picked that moment to switch the tempo to something slow and sultry. Sydney wondered if Luke had paid them to do that. She expected they'd be awkward and fumbling with each other, but Luke brought her smoothly into his arms and moved them around like they'd been dancing together forever. His fingers on her neck sent shivers rippling through her.

Absorbed in the clean scent of soap and citrusy aftershave, Sydney had to remind herself to keep breathing. She'd forgotten how much bigger than her he was, but she hadn't forgotten the tenderness he'd always shown her or the gentle way he'd held her. The way he did now, as if she was the most precious thing in his world.

She fixated on the shark's tooth hanging from the leather cord around his neck, all the while resisting the urge to reach up and touch it. "Did you find the shark's tooth or buy it?"

"Found it." He drew her in even closer to him, and Sydney had no choice but to rest her head on his chest. His heart hammered under her ear, and she was relieved to know she wasn't the only one affected by this dance.

"So how've you been?" he asked.

"I've been good. How about you?"

"Great."

"Oh. Really?"

"No," he said, laughing softly. "I've been crappy."

Sydney raised her head to look up at him. "You have?"

With his dark eyes fixed on her, he nodded.

"Me, too," Sydney confessed.

"In case you were wondering, I didn't know you'd be here tonight."

"I could tell you were surprised to see me."

"Pleasantly surprised." His fingers slipped from her neck to her shoulder, laying a path of sensation as they went.

All too soon, the song ended, and Luke drew back from her. "I could use some air," he said. "Care to join me?"

Even though she knew it would be all over the island by morning that they'd gone off together, Sydney took his outstretched hand and went with him to the hotel's dark porch. They stood looking down at the busy street as well as the breakwater that formed the harbor and the ferry landing, where a lone boat waited to make the first trip to the mainland in the morning.

The air coming in off the water was warm, but Sydney's

skin prickled with goose bumps that had nothing to do with the temperature and everything to do with the man standing beside her.

"I missed you this week, Syd."

She turned to him, about to take a step she wasn't entirely sure she was ready for. "I missed you, too." Running her tongue over her lips, she ventured a glance up at him. "I thought a lot about what you said."

Tucking a strand of hair behind her ear, he said, "And?"

"I have no idea what I'm doing right now. I'm a bad bet."

He put his arms around her. "So you've said."

How did he manage to do that so smoothly? How did he manage to make her feel surrounded by him yet totally safe?

Almost as if he couldn't resist, he dipped his head and kissed her.

"Luke—"

"Hmm?" He kissed her again. "Did I mention how gorgeous you look tonight?"

Sure enough, her knees went weak, and she reached for him. At first he just pressed his lips softly to hers, letting her know the next move was up to her. When she realized what he was doing, that he was giving her the power to decide for both of them, she couldn't resist running her tongue gently over his bottom lip.

That drew a tortured groan from deep inside him.

Encouraged, she did it again, this time letting her tongue venture a little farther into his mouth. Everything about his embrace was familiar, yet new, too. His taste, the texture of his lips, the way he held her so close. She tempted and teased, but still he held back.

"Luke," she gasped.

"What, honey?"

"Kiss me back. Will you please kiss me back?"

"Gladly."

While Syd waited breathlessly to see what he would do, he sprinkled soft kisses on her face before returning his attention to her mouth. Once again he began softly, gently, as if he was making sure she was with him before he went any further.

By the time she felt the first tentative brush of his tongue over her sensitized lips, she was on the verge of begging him for more. The tangle of tongues and teeth and breathless passion went on until Sydney wasn't sure how she remained standing.

"God," he whispered. "Syd . . ." He cupped her cheek and went back for more.

As they strained against each other, trying to get closer, her nipples pebbled and brushed against his chest. His free hand slid down her back to align her with his erection.

Approaching voices on the porch startled them apart.

Breathing hard, they stared at each other in the darkness, stunned to discover everything they'd once felt for each other was still there, lying dormant, waiting for the opportunity to remind them of what they'd shared so long ago.

"Will you come to my house for dinner tomorrow night?" he asked.

Overwhelmed by the passionate kiss, Sydney continued to stare at him.

"It's still your choice, Syd."

"I ah . . . I don't know. I just don't know." She recalled the story Maddie and Janey had shared earlier. Janey had done what she thought was best for Joe, which had turned out to be the exact *wrong* thing for him.

"What don't you know?" Luke asked. "Talk to me."

"I'm afraid."

His fingers spooled through her hair the way they used to when they made love on the beach. "Of what, honey?"

"Hurting you again. I have to go home after Labor Day. After everything that happened between us before—"

"Clean slate, remember?"

"I can't promise I won't hurt you again. I wish I could, but I can't."

"Remember what I said the other night about being a boy with no options the last time we were together?"

She nodded.

"This time, I'm all grown up with my eyes wide-open to what might happen."

"Still . . ."

With just the tip of his index finger to her chin, he compelled her to look at him. "I've been warned, Syd." He kissed her softly, sweetly, with none of the urgency he'd shown earlier. "Come to dinner and bring Buddy. No pressure. No expectations. Just dinner."

"I—"

He rested a finger on her lips. "Come if you want to. Or not if you don't feel up to it. Either way, it's up to you."

"You can be very charming when you put your mind to it."

His smile transformed his entire face. Sydney remembered the punch of that discovery the first time around. "Is that so?"

"Uh-huh."

"I'd better get you back inside before we start a five-alarm Gansett scandal."

"Probably already too late."

"Sorry about that," he said with what sounded like genuine regret.

She could tell she caught him off guard when she went up on tiptoes to kiss his cheek. "I'm not. It was well worth it." Before he could reply to that audacious statement, she left him to rejoin her friends.

Sydney spent the entire next day debating Luke's invitation. She went through the motions of cleaning the large Victorian house, changing sheets, grocery shopping, walking Buddy. One minute, she was going to Luke's for dinner. The next minute, she'd talked herself out of it.

By four o'clock, she had worn herself out.

"It's just dinner," she told Buddy.

He stared at her, almost as if he was calling her out on her bullshit.

"Did I tell you he kissed me?"

Buddy continued the ruthless stare.

"It was a good kiss. A *really* good kiss." She went upstairs with the dog trailing behind her. "If I go over there, it'll happen again."

Sydney stretched out on the bed.

Buddy jumped up and settled next to her.

She ran her fingers through his silky hair. "I want to go," she whispered. "Does that make me a bad person?" Sydney realized she was actually expecting Buddy to answer her. Rather, he let out a deep sigh, as if her pontificating annoyed him. "I know what you mean, Buddy. I'm sick of me, too."

Sydney watched the ceiling fan for a long time. "All right. I'll go, but only if you come with me."

He extended his paw.

Smiling, Sydney took it and gave it a shake. "Deal."

As the sun dipped low over the pond, she grabbed a bottle of wine and the brownies she'd baked and headed for the car with Buddy tagging along at her heels.

Driving the familiar roads that led to Luke's house brought back a slew of memories of his old pickup, of late nights and summer breezes, of first love and heart-pounding desire.

Sydney couldn't remember the last time she'd been so nervous. At least she hadn't fretted over what to wear. She'd chosen a denim skirt with a white T-shirt and sandals. Luke was the most casual person she'd ever known, so there was no point in dressing up for him. He'd never been impressed by style or flash.

She pulled onto the long dirt road that led to his house at the end. As she navigated the final turn, the nerves she'd battled all day resurfaced. *What am I doing? He didn't say what time. What if he's not even home?*

His warmly lit house came into view. At least he was home. She turned in next to the dark green pickup truck that was parked behind the house. Before she could chicken out, she opened the car door.

In a move that reminded her of the Buddy she'd once known, he jumped over her and sprinted off into the darkness. "Great," she muttered, gathering the wine and brownies and starting after him.

"This guy belong to you?" Luke asked, grinning as he waited for her with Buddy panting next to him.

Sydney swallowed hard and tried to ignore the goose

bumps that broke out over her skin at the sound of his deep voice.

"He doesn't get out much," Sydney said.

"He and I have that in common."

"Still a homebody?" she asked as he gestured for her to follow him on the lighted pathway to the door.

"Some things never change."

And that, Sydney decided, was comforting.

"I wasn't sure what time—"

"I didn't think you'd come—"

He turned to her, smiling. "I'm glad you came."

"So am I." She handed him the wine and brownies.

"You didn't have to bring anything."

"Yes, I did."

"Come in." He ushered her into the modest ranch-style house with the million-dollar water view.

Sydney had once spent a lot of time there, and the memories came flooding back when she saw that hardly anything had changed. Luke's mother had been welcoming and supportive of their relationship, whereas her parents had been disapproving and judgmental, so they'd spent much more time here than at her house.

She glanced around at the worn but comfortable sofas, the overflowing bookshelves and elaborate telescope, which was new.

"I know—I need to redecorate," Luke said. "Somehow I never got around to it."

"I've always loved how cozy this room is."

"Especially in the winter with the woodstove going." He gestured for her to follow him to the kitchen. "What can I get you to drink?"

"What're my choices?"

"Beer, soda, wine, water."

"Wine sounds good."

He offered the chardonnay she'd brought and a pinot noir.

Syd chose the chardonnay, and as she watched him open the bottle, she couldn't deny the pull she felt drawing her to him. But was it the comfort? The history? The familiar? Or was it something all new? She wasn't entirely sure, so she focused on the meal he was in the midst of preparing. "What're you making?"

"My own invention—cut-up meat, vegetables and potatoes, dump them all in foil with either teriyaki or barbecue sauce, and put it on the grill. Voilà. Dinner."

"That's fabulous."

"And easy."

"I'm all about easy." As soon as the words left her mouth, her face heated with embarrassment that was exacerbated by his low chuckle.

"I'll keep that in mind."

Needing something to do with her suddenly fidgety hands, Sydney picked up the knife. "What can I do?"

Curling his hand around hers, he relieved her of the knife. "Not a thing. You're my guest."

A zing of attraction zipped through her at the feel of his hand on hers. "That doesn't mean I can't help."

He gestured to the stools at the counter. "That's exactly what it means."

"All right," Syd said as she settled on one of the stools. "If you insist."

"I insist. So how was your day?"

She couldn't exactly admit she'd spent most of it trying to decide whether or not to come for dinner. "Housework," she said. "Nothing exciting. How was yours?"

"Busy. Typical summer day at McCarthy's. Boats coming and going. Big Mac playing Wiffle ball with the kids on the dock." As he spoke, he chopped potatoes and peppers. "Dogs, families, bikes, grills, the usual chaos."

Sydney smiled at the picture he painted. "Is Mr. McCarthy still working?"

"Every day, even though he hardly needs to with me and Mac running the place."

"It's working out well? With Mac?"

Luke shrugged. "He's great. Just like his dad. Nothing really changed." He opened the antiquated fridge and withdrew a plastic container. "What's your pleasure? Chicken or steak? Teriyaki or barbecue?"

Sydney contemplated the choices. "I'll go with chicken and barbecue."

"Then I'll do steak and teriyaki. We can share if you want."

"Perfect." Despite the attraction that complicated everything about this evening, Sydney realized she was more relaxed than she'd been in months.

"Come on out with me while I grill." He stepped around the counter and led the way through the dining room to the deck.

Sydney followed with Buddy trailing just behind her.

"I was hoping we could eat out here if the fog held off," he said.

The evening remained clear and warm, ideal for alfresco dining. "Such an incredible view," she said as she lowered herself onto one of the comfortable lounge chairs. Whereas her parents' house overlooked the pond, Luke's place faced the ocean with the pond just across the way.

"I like it."

The statement was so typically Luke, to reduce a million-dollar view to three small words, that it drew a smile from her.

He put the foil pouches on a sleek stainless-steel grill

and closed the lid. "Stay put for a sec." Carrying the platter inside, he returned a minute later with a bottle of beer and settled on the lounge chair next to hers.

Deciding there was no chance of scraps for the moment, Buddy plopped down on the deck.

Sydney curled her legs under her and turned so she could see Luke. His dark hair was as silky as she remembered, his skin brown from the sun, his hands strong and efficient. As she studied him, Sydney felt a subtle change taking place within her, a reawakening of sorts. She was suddenly more aware of the sizzle of food cooking on the grill, the scent of the sea and fresh-cut grass, the slight dampness in the warm air, the chill of the glass in her hand and the sharp sting of desire.

"What're you thinking?" he asked.

"That this is nice, being here with you again."

He reached across the gap between their chairs and took her hand. "It's great to have you here."

Once again, his touch set off a tingling reaction that had her full attention. "Are you happy with your life, Luke?" She wasn't sure where the question came from, but she really wanted to know.

"I'm content."

"Is that the same thing?"

Pondering his beer bottle, he shrugged. "I'm not *un*-happy."

"Do you ever think about doing something else?"

"Not so much anymore."

"You had so many things you wanted to do."

"Life happens."

Sydney knew his ailing mother had kept him on the island when he should've been leaving for college. "Are you ever bored?"

He released a short laugh. "Nope. There's always something to do. We're straight out at the marina in the summer. Last winter, Mac and I renovated a couple of kitchens and a bathroom. Keeping this place up takes some work. I stay plenty busy."

"Would you ever consider living somewhere else?"

"Depends."

"On?"

He glanced at her, his eyes dancing with mischief. "Who's asking me to relocate."

Chapter Six

As Sydney absorbed that statement, Luke got up to check the grill.

He moved the pouches around and then turned to her, leaning against the rail that surrounded the deck. "What's with the twenty questions?"

"I'm sorry. I'm curious about your life."

"No need to be sorry. Not much has changed. I'm still the same simple guy I always was. I don't need a lot to be happy."

She'd once loved that about him—desperately. He was unlike anyone else she'd ever met, and that was still true.

"What do you need?" he asked. "To be happy again?"

"I'm trying to figure that out."

He returned to the other lounge chair and sat facing her. "I give you so much credit."

"For what?" she asked, perplexed.

"Trying to figure it out. So many people who'd been through what you have would've given up."

"I came close," she confessed. "It was pretty rough for a long time after."

"I can't imagine. When I heard what'd happened, God, I just . . . I *ached* for you."

The emotion behind his softly spoken words touched her deeply. "Thank you."

"I didn't mean to upset you."

"You didn't. It's part of who I am now."

"I admire who you are now even more than I admired who you used to be—and that was quite a lot."

"I'm a work in progress," she said with a laugh, hoping to lighten the mood.

He flashed that potent grin. "Aren't we all?"

"Don't try to fool me. You're not in progress. You're all grown up."

"I'd like to think so," he said, his eyes shifting to the water, "but sometimes I wonder."

"About?"

"Whether there might be *more*." He brought his eyes back to focus on her. "You know?"

The intensity she saw in his gaze caught her off guard. "What do you want that you don't have?" she managed to ask, even though she suspected.

"Someone to share this view with. Someone to keep me warm on cold winter nights. Someone to talk to."

"You don't like to talk," Sydney said, teasing him even though his words and the yearning she heard in them moved her.

"I like talking to you."

The statement hung in the air between them, charged and heavy.

"I like talking to you, too."

"I think I talked more when I was with you than I have in all the years since."

"Luke—"

He seemed embarrassed by the confession, as if he'd said more than he'd meant to. "Ready to eat?"

* * *

After the delicious—and filling—dinner, Luke invited her to take a walk on the beach.

Sydney hesitated, not certain it was wise to revisit the place where they'd often made love.

"It's okay if you don't want to."

"It's not that, it's just—"

"Believe me, I know."

"Did I ruin that for you, too?"

"Nah. Nothing could ruin the beach for me. I'm there almost every day." He extended a hand to her. "Come with me?"

Sydney couldn't think of a good reason not to, so she took his hand and swallowed the swell of emotion that came with taking the familiar pathway to the stairs.

Luke kept a firm grip on her hand as she followed him down steep stairs that brought back so many memories.

"I used to wonder if your mother knew what we were doing down here."

Luke guided her off the stairs and onto the beach but didn't release her hand. The tide was out, leaving them a wide expanse of beach. "She knew."

"Why do you say that?" Sydney asked, shocked and embarrassed as they passed the groove in the dunes where they'd hidden from the world as teenagers.

"Because I told her."

"You *told* her? Are you *crazy*? Who tells their mother that stuff?"

Shrugging, he laughed at her dismay. "We talked to each other about everything. Don't forget—she was only twenty years older than me. She wasn't so far removed from her own teenage years that she couldn't remember what it was like to be in love for the first time."

"It's a good thing I didn't know then that you were telling her everything."

"Why's that?" he asked, his face alight with amusement she could barely see in the waning daylight.

"First of all, you wouldn't have gotten any more, and second, I never would've been able to face her."

"Don't be silly. She loved you."

"I loved her, too. I was so sad to hear she'd passed away."

"It was a rough time. She died far too young."

"Yes."

"I never regretted staying here with her, if you wondered."

"It never occurred to me that you would. I know how close you always were. Of course I didn't know just *how* close . . ."

Laughing, he released her hand to bend and pick up a flat stone that he sent skimming across the calm surface of the water. "You were close to your mom, too."

"Not as close as you were to yours. I'm almost thirty-six, and I've still never had a conversation with her about sex."

Luke picked up a stick that he tossed for Buddy, who ran into the small waves to get it. "I bet she knew what we were up to when we were kids."

"Which is probably why she went to such great lengths to keep us apart."

"They couldn't stand me."

"Oh, Luke, they didn't dislike you. They hated seeing me serious about a boy when I was so young. I imagine I would've been the same way with my kids."

"You would've been more tolerant after what we went through."

"Maybe."

"Do you ever think . . ."

"What?"

"About having more kids. Someday."

The query sent a ripple of anxiety through her. "I'm getting kind of old to start all over again."

"You're a regular senior citizen."

She tried to give him a playful shove but ended up with his arm tight around her, engulfed in the scent of soap and citrus that was so Luke. He'd never been one to wear the expensive cologne Seth had favored.

"So do you think about it?" Luke asked.

"I have. At times. I just can't imagine what a freak show I'd be, worried all the time that something would happen again."

"It wouldn't."

"How can you be so sure?"

"Do you know anyone, anyone in your whole life, who's had what happened to you happen to them?"

"No," she said softly. "I can't say I do."

"Neither do I. You're all done with epic tragedy. Now you get to live in peace, knowing the worst that life has to offer is behind you."

She hadn't thought of it that way before and had to admit the idea brought comfort. "I sure hope you're right."

"Want to take the boat out on the pond?"

Startled by the sudden change in conversation, she looked up at him. "Now? It's getting late."

"Perfect for stargazing."

She remembered how he knew every constellation and the story behind each one.

"We can do it another time," he said.

Sydney decided she wasn't ready to go home. Not yet. "Now is fine."

"You're sure?"

She nodded, and they turned back the way they'd come. With the light of a half-moon guiding them, they climbed the stairs and crossed the yard to the path that led to the pond and Luke's old rowboat. He helped her in and got her settled before he lifted Buddy into the bow. Pushing the boat off the sand, Luke hopped in and reached for the oars.

Sydney let her head fall back as she studied the sky above and enjoyed the smooth glide of the old wooden boat through the flat-calm water. She brought her eyes down from the heavens to study the play of muscles visible through Luke's T-shirt as he rowed.

"I love it out here at night," he said after a long period of comfortable silence. "It's so busy all day, but then the sun goes down and it becomes the calmest place on the island."

"That's because all the boaters are in the bars."

He chuckled. "True. Ready for some stargazing?"

"Whenever you are."

Luke let the oars go idle and arranged two cushions on the floor of the boat. He guided her to sit between his legs, resting against his chest with his arms around her. "Comfortable?"

"Very." And yet so *un*comfortable, too.

"Let's see what you remember." He pointed to a constellation.

She tipped her head back to use his shoulder as a pillow. "Orion."

"Good," he said, trailing a finger over her neck. "How about that one?"

Sydney swallowed hard as his touch sent goose bumps cascading down her arms and legs. "Big Dipper."

"A-plus."

Sydney laughed, even though he was making her crazy with what he was doing to her neck with just the tip of his finger against her skin. "Those are the easy ones."

"All right then, how about that one?"

"Cassiopeia."

"I'm impressed."

Sydney turned her head so she could see him. "I had a good teacher." She reached up to touch his face, which was warm and smooth. "You shaved."

"Huh?"

"After work. You shaved."

"Yeah, so?"

"You always shaved in the morning."

"Still do, most of the time."

"Why the change in routine?"

"Because," he said, nuzzling her cheek, "if I was lucky enough to get this close to you tonight, I didn't want to burn your soft skin."

"Oh," she said, breathless as his lips found the sensitive spot just below her ear. "That was nice of you."

"You smell so good. Just like I remember."

Sydney tilted her head to give him better access to her neck.

His arms tightened around her, bringing her even closer to him.

She reached back to bring his mouth down on hers.

The night before, on the deck of the Beachcomber, he'd been all about restraint. Tonight, he devoured.

Sydney twisted in his arms, needing to get closer, and the boat took an unsteady dip.

"Whoa," Luke said, laughing.

Buddy whined from his post in the front, and Sydney couldn't believe she'd forgotten where they were.

Luke shifted to steady them and brought her into direct contact with his erection. "Sorry," he muttered.

Sydney wrapped her arms around his neck and pressed against him, drawing a deep groan from him.

"What do you say we take this somewhere more comfortable?"

"Yes," she said, still breathless from the passionate kiss. "Please." When she started to return to her seat, he stopped her.

"Stay," he said. "Right here." He arranged her so he could keep her close but still row.

The movement of the boat, the play of his body wrapped around hers as he rowed and the feel of his lips on her neck combined to make her burn for him. She rested her hand on his leg. Almost as if it had a mind of its own, her hand traveled from his calf to his knee, relearning him as it went.

"We'll be going in circles if you keep that up," he said gruffly.

She withdrew her hand. "Oh."

"That wasn't a complaint."

Sydney smiled at the restraint she heard in his tone. Being with him like this reminded her of those long-ago summers when she'd had not a care in the world beyond finding a way to spend as much time with him as she possibly could. The carefree feeling was a welcome change from her reality of late.

The moment the boat bottom scraped against the shore, Buddy bolted.

"He doesn't have his sea legs," Sydney said, taking the hand Luke offered and stepping out of the boat.

"Yet." He tightened his grip on her hand and tugged

her into his arms for another of those drugging kisses that stole her breath and left her weak in the knees.

As much as it pained her to admit, no other man had ever made her weak in the knees. Only Luke. Sydney reached up for a handful of soft dark hair as her tongue tangled with his.

He tore his lips free, grabbed her hand and headed for the path. And then they were running, laughing, breathless. Sydney slid on the dew that had collected on the grass and stumbled. He caught her and twisted to cushion her fall. They landed in a hard thump with her on top of him, encased in strong arms.

"Are you okay?" she asked, still breathing hard.

His fingers tunneled into her hair, drawing her into another kiss. "Better than I've been in seventeen years."

"Luke . . ."

"Kiss me, Syd."

Right there on the lawn under the moon they made out like the teenagers they'd once been, but with the wisdom of knowing how precarious life and love and desire could be.

Even though she burned for him, he did nothing more than kiss her and hold her and whisper sweet words in her ear that sent more goose bumps to her arms and legs and everywhere in between.

He kissed her as if he'd never get enough, and then he shifted them so she was under him. His kiss slowed from wild and unrestrained to gentle and sweet, which was no less powerful. Sprinkling kisses on her face, eyelids, nose and lips, he looked down at her. "This wasn't what I was thinking when I suggested something more comfortable."

She caressed the cheek he'd made smooth for her. "Works for me."

"Mmm," he said against her lips. "Me, too."

"I should probably go home," she said many minutes later.

"Probably," he said but made no move to let her up.

Feeling brazen and full of her own power, Sydney slid her hands under his T-shirt and stroked the warm, soft skin on his back.

He trembled and pushed his erection into the V of her legs. "I told myself I shouldn't rush you," he said, his lips light against her neck, "that we should go slow and take our time, but God, Syd, I want you. I've never stopped wanting you."

"I want you, too. I hope you know that. I just . . . I don't think . . ."

He kissed her gently, a light touch of his lips to hers. "You're not ready."

She shook her head. "I'm sor—"

"Don't apologize. Please don't." More soft, sweet kisses. "We've got the rest of the summer."

Sydney closed her eyes, content for the first time since her life had been shattered, content to let him surround her with his warmth, his comfort, his overwhelming appeal and yes, his love. She had no doubt he still loved her. It was in every look, every touch, every kiss.

"I'm going home after Labor Day," she reminded him.

"I know." He trailed kisses from her collarbone to her ear. "Tomorrow night," he said, "we'll go out to dinner."

Chapter Seven

The phone woke Sydney the next morning, and she was startled to see it was after nine. Clearing her throat, she reached for the bedside extension.

"Do *not* tell me you're still asleep when I've already been up for three hours," Maddie said.

"Okay, I won't. I can't remember the last time I slept past eight."

"Were you out late last night?"

Sydney smiled, remembering the evening she'd spent with Luke. "Maybe."

"Get your butt out of bed and get over here for some coffee and muffins right out of the oven."

"Can't say no to that."

Maddie rattled off directions to her new home. "Hurry! I want every detail."

Sydney got up to let Buddy out. She debated a quick shower but decided to wait until later. Before her date. With Luke. A flutter of anticipation had her placing a hand over her belly. Last night had been amazing, and she couldn't wait to see him again later.

Buddy rode with his head out the window on the way

to Maddie's house and once again bounded out of the car ahead of her when they arrived. Sydney wondered if he, too, was starting to recover a bit from his terrible grief.

Maddie waited for them on a deck she'd decorated with comfortable outdoor furniture and pots full of bright, fragrant blooms.

"This is some spot you've got here," Sydney said, admiring the rolling meadow that led to the water in the distance.

"We got married right there," Maddie said, pointing to the yard.

"I bet it was beautiful."

"It was. I'll show you the pictures." She gestured for Sydney to follow her into the spacious contemporary that was scattered with the toys of a busy little boy.

The two women stopped short when they found Maddie's son, Thomas, hugging Buddy, who was making noises Sydney had never heard before. She rushed over to him. "Buddy? What is it, sweet boy?"

Maddie scooped up Thomas.

"He sad," the boy said, a solemn expression on his cherubic face.

"Are you sad?" Sydney asked as tears filled her eyes. "Does Thomas remind you of Max?" She wouldn't have expected the blond, blue-eyed toddler to remind the dog of Max, who'd been much older than Thomas when Buddy arrived in their lives. Not to mention her son had had his father's dark hair and eyes. Maybe it was just because Thomas was a smaller person, like the boy Buddy had loved and lost.

Sydney hugged the wailing dog until he eventually settled. Looking up at Maddie, she said, "I'm sorry. He's never done anything like this before."

"Please don't apologize," Maddie said, subtly brushing at a tear.

Thomas wiggled free of his mother's embrace and toddled over to pet Buddy.

The dog licked and sniffed the boy, who stayed patient and still while Buddy investigated him.

"Thank you for making friends with Buddy, Thomas," Sydney said when she could speak over the giant lump that had formed in her throat.

Maddie knelt next to Thomas. "This is Mommy's friend Syd. Can you say hi?"

"Hi, Syd," Thomas said.

"I hope you don't mind first names," Maddie said. "I don't stand on formality with him."

"I didn't with my kids, either."

"They should be okay," Maddie said of Thomas and Buddy, who were bonding over Thomas's squeaky toys. "Let's have some coffee."

Still rattled by Buddy's reaction to Thomas, Sydney patted Buddy's head and kissed his nose. "Be a good boy."

"Good boy," Thomas said in the serious tone that made Sydney smile.

"He's adorable," she said to Maddie as she stirred cream into her coffee. The house boasted a wide-open floor plan that allowed them to sit in the kitchen but still keep an eye on Thomas and his new friend.

"Thank you. Sometime you have to see the way he flips out when Mac gets home. It's hysterical. The two of them are joined at the hip."

"Is there anything sexier than a man who loves another man's child the way he would his own?"

"Not that I can think of. He's been amazing with

Thomas since day one. Until he met us, he'd never changed a diaper in his life. Now he can do it in his sleep—literally."

Sydney smiled at the picture she painted. "Your home is beautiful. I'm so happy for you, Maddie."

"Sometimes I want to pinch myself to believe it all really happened."

"Are you still working?"

"Four days a week. I'd do more, especially this time of year, but Mac wants me to take it easy. He's telling everyone this is a high-risk pregnancy."

Alarmed, Sydney said, "Is it?"

"No! He's being ridiculous."

Sydney cracked up. "Sorry, but that's funny."

"Do me a favor and don't tell him that. He's already out of control." Maddie placed a plate of warm muffins on the counter. "So, how was last night?"

"It was great. Being with Luke is . . ."

"What?"

"Comfortable, and yet I'm very *un*comfortable, too."

Maddie raised an eyebrow. "Is that so?"

"Mmm. It's still very hot between us. Like it always was."

"And that's bad how?"

Sydney cut a blueberry muffin in half. "It's not *bad*. It's just, you know, I feel kind of guilty."

"Because of Seth."

Sydney nodded and took a moment to get herself together when her throat closed. "I loved him," she said in a near whisper. "I hope you believe me when I say that."

"Of course you did. You married him, had children and a life with him."

"It was a good life. I was happy with him. But it was different between us than with Luke."

"What was different? You've lost me."

Sydney felt her face heat with embarrassment. "Sex."

"How so?"

"It was sweet and nice with Seth, but with Luke . . . it was wild and kind of earth-shattering. I don't know if it would still be that way, but it was back then." Sydney released a long, deep breath. "I sound like a horrible person even saying that."

"No, you don't. You would've been a horrible person if you'd continued to sleep with Luke after you were married. That's what horrible people do."

Sydney smiled. Leave it to Maddie to cut to the chase. "I used to think my feelings for Luke took on such mythic proportions because everything about our relationship was new and exciting and a bit forbidden."

"And now?"

"I'm not so sure it was any of those things. Seeing him again, I've begun to realize it was *us*. That what we had was that special thing they write about, but I was too young and stupid to know it at the time."

Maddie reached across the counter to squeeze Sydney's hand. "Oh, Syd."

"I walked away from him like he meant nothing to me. How could I have done that to him, Maddie? It ruined him. *I* ruined him."

"If he wasn't capable of getting past that, I doubt he would've been looking at you the other night like he wanted to take you home and keep you in bed for the next year."

Sydney's face heated. "He was not."

"Was too." Maddie refilled their coffee and glanced at Thomas, who was reclined against Buddy, sucking his thumb. "Did he kiss you last night?"

Sydney popped a bite of muffin into her mouth. "Maybe."

"That's *not* an answer."

"Well, somehow we ended up rolling around on his lawn."

"Shut up!"

"You asked."

"Sydney, listen to me. Are you listening?"

She nodded.

"He's moved past what happened before. If he hadn't, if he *really* hadn't, he wouldn't have invited you into his home and he certainly wouldn't have been rolling around on his lawn with you."

"You're sure about that?"

"Positive. You're the one who needs to get past what happened before. And don't waste your time comparing him to Seth. That's not fair to either of them, and it won't change anything. You did what was best for you at the time. There's no sense rehashing history."

"I know you're right."

"I remember when you left that last summer you were here. You were concerned about whether you and Luke wanted the same things out of life. He'd given up his scholarship and was content to stay here. He was never going to set the world on fire with ambition or make a lot of money. Those things were very much on your mind then."

"I was focused on all the wrong things. Maybe he never set the world on fire, but he sure did set *me* on fire. Still does."

"That's so exciting."

"Sometimes I wonder if it's the comfort. Am I attracted to him—again—because it's comfortable? Because I know he won't crush me? Or is it more than that?"

"You thought about him for seventeen years. That has to count for something."

"True."

"Don't overanalyze it. Just enjoy it. After all you've been through, you deserve some joy. If being with Luke brings you joy, there's nothing wrong with that."

Being with Luke had always brought her joy.

"You've got plenty of time to figure it out."

"I have to be back by September fifth," Sydney said, her blood going cold at the thought. "Sentencing for the guy who hit us."

"Oh God, Syd. Do you have to be there?"

"Someone has to represent Seth and the kids. I try not to think about it, but it's like my life is on hold in many ways until that's over."

"You've got a few weeks until you have to face that. In the meantime, you've got a sexy guy who sets you on fire."

Sydney nodded in agreement and took the conversation in a lighter direction, but she still worried over whether she was entering into a relationship with Luke for the right reasons or because being with him was so damned easy.

When things had calmed down at the marina later that afternoon, Luke backed his truck up to the marina's main building and pulled out the hose. He washed the grime and salt off the outside and was vacuuming the inside when Big Mac ambled up to him.

"Are you sick or something?"

"Very funny."

"The only other possible explanation for this unprecedented event is a hot date."

"Maybe. Maybe not."

Big Mac stood up to his full six-foot-four-inch height and dropped the sunglasses down his nose so he could take a good long look at Luke over the top of them. "Try pulling that evasive act on someone who hasn't known you since you were knee-high to a grasshopper."

Luke wilted a bit under the older man's scrutiny, the same way he had at eight when he'd hung around the marina, hungry for even a second of Big Mac's time and attention. And Big Mac, being Big Mac, had taken the fatherless boy under his wing and kept him there ever since. "And your point is?"

"Rumor has it you're seeing that Donovan girl again."

"So what about it?"

"I just hope you're being careful. That's all."

Luke ran a damp cloth over the dusty dashboard. "I am."

"You sure about that?"

"Why don't you say what's on your mind," Luke said, fighting off exasperation.

"Don't mind if I do." Big Mac leaned against the truck. "I remember how it was last time. That summer she didn't come back."

Luke could still recall the agony. No other word could do it justice—pure, unadulterated agony.

"I don't want to see that happen again."

"It won't," Luke said with more confidence than he felt. He'd do whatever he could to make sure it didn't.

"She's been through an awful thing. People come out the other side of something like that changed."

"I can't see how it wouldn't change a person."

"See to it she doesn't use you to put the pieces back together and then move on like she did last time."

"Now wait just a second—"

Big Mac held up a huge hand. "I'm sorry. I don't mean to overstep."

"You didn't. You can't overstep with me. You know that." Luke dropped the rag and rested his hands on his hips, fighting a range of emotion that included anger, fear and a bit of despair. "I hear what you're saying, and I appreciate why you're saying it." Luke paused, took a moment to get himself together and then looked up at the man who meant the world to him. "Am I a chump for giving her another chance?"

"Nah," Big Mac scoffed. "You're only a chump if you ignore the handwriting on the wall telling you history is about to repeat itself."

Luke responded with a brisk nod.

Big Mac squeezed Luke's shoulder. "Have a good time tonight." He walked away but left the weight of his concerns behind.

Turning back to the truck, Luke stared into the cab for a long time before he finished the job.

Chapter Eight

Big Mac's concerns stayed with Luke the rest of the day and into the evening as he showered and shaved. Wiping the steam from the mirror, he took a good long look at his reflection. He'd never had any trouble attracting female attention, but no matter how many women he met, there'd never been another Sydney Donovan. For years he'd actually made a concerted effort to connect with other women, but it just hadn't happened. After a while, he'd stopped bothering and accepted he was fated to love just one woman in his lifetime.

"Maybe I am a chump," he said. "How many guys would give a woman a second chance after what she did to me?" Even as he said the words, however, he couldn't seem to work up the energy to be mad with her or to resent her for something that'd happened when they were little more than kids. Still, the worry nagged at him and took something away from the thrill of knowing he was going to see her again—soon.

Remembering how much Sydney liked seafood, he'd made a reservation at the Lobster House. He dressed in pressed khakis and a button-down shirt he left untucked.

After rolling up the sleeves, he put on the shark's tooth she'd admired and slid his feet into leather flip-flops. This was about as fancy as it ever got for him. He hoped it was good enough for her. He hoped *he* was good enough for her.

As much as he'd loved being close to her last night, the niggling doubts had him wondering if they were moving too fast. After all she'd been through, after all she'd put him through, maybe they were on a road to ruin. A wise man would dial it back a notch. He liked to think of himself as a wise man, but being around Sydney again made him question whether he was as wise as he thought.

Still, taking it back a few steps might be the best idea until he knew more about her plans for the future and whether or not they included him. He vowed to go slower tonight, to keep the physical contact to a minimum. That last part was crucial, because the minute he touched her, any resolve he might have would disappear. He had no doubt about that.

The ride to her house was as familiar to him as anything on the island. While there were only three miles between their homes, a world of difference separated them. His was small and cozy, while hers was large and sprawling.

When he arrived, Buddy came running out to greet him.

Luke squatted to give the dog his full attention. "Hey, boy."

He was rewarded with an enthusiastic lick to the face that made him laugh.

"Sorry about that," Syd said from the doorway.

Luke looked up as she stepped outside wearing a yellow dress that showed off her light tan. She'd worn her hair up, leaving her shoulders bare. A memory of trailing kisses over her collarbone the night before stole the breath from his lungs. Maybe he was a chump, but he couldn't help wanting her with every fiber of his being.

"I think he likes you," she said of Buddy, drawing Luke out of his thoughts.

"He's a good boy."

"Let me put him inside so we can go." She called for the dog and led him into the house.

Through the screen, Luke could hear her talking to Buddy, giving him orders to behave while she was out. He smiled as he watched her kiss the dog's face and pat him on the head.

She came outside carrying a small purse and sweater.

Luke leaned back against the clean truck and watched her come toward him.

"What?" she asked, her eyes darting over him in a show of nerves that touched him.

"Just admiring the view."

She smiled and shook her head as if she thought he was full of it.

Forgetting all his resolve, he reached for her. "I missed you today."

Looking up at him, she ran her tongue over her lips, and he went hard as stone. "I missed you, too."

Tugging gently to bring her even closer, he watched her eyes go wide when she encountered proof of his arousal. He bent his head to kiss her softly. Her lips tasted like strawberries, and even though he hadn't intended to linger—hell, he hadn't intended to *touch* her—he couldn't help but run his tongue over her plump bottom lip to get a better taste. "Mmm," he said.

With her arms encircling his neck, her mouth opened under his, encouraging him to take more, and Luke was lost. Nothing else could compare to the way he felt when he was with her, and as he kissed her, it became clear to him that there was absolutely nothing he wouldn't do to feel this way every day for the rest of his life.

"Syd," he said, his lips still resting against hers.

Her fingers combed through his hair, sending desire rippling through him like a live wire. "Hmm?"

"Dinner." He kissed her again, softly, gently.

"Oh. Right." She let her arms drop from his shoulders but continued to stare at him with a befuddled expression that made his blood boil.

It took all the fortitude he possessed not to scoop her up, carry her inside and take what he wanted more than anything, what he knew she'd willingly give. Only the thought of what he might see in her expressive eyes afterward stopped him from acting on the urge. He couldn't bear to see regret or guilt or anything other than the pure joy he would feel, so rather than scoop her up, he opened the passenger door to his truck and ushered her inside.

"It smells so clean in here."

"It's always like that," he said with a grin.

She laughed, and just like that, his mood lightened.

He got in the driver's side, and before he could buckle in, she reached for his hand. "Thanks for cleaning your truck for me."

"No problem. It needed it anyway."

After he put on his seat belt, he took her hand again, linking their fingers as he drove them the long way around the island.

"Where are you taking me?"

"To the Lobster House with a sunset thrown in."

"Oh, yummy. My favorite."

"I know."

Over winding roads, he drove to the northernmost point on the island, where a lighthouse stood watch and the sun flirted with the horizon.

"Best spot on the island to watch the sunset," Syd said, taking it all in.

"I love it here."

"I remember that."

He glanced over to watch a blush spread over her cheeks. Releasing her hand, he ran a finger along her cheekbone. "I know what else you're remembering."

She shot him a seductive look. "And what's that?"

He took off his seat belt and leaned toward her. "You're thinking about all the times we came here to make out." His lips brushed against her ear, and he watched the goose bumps form on her arm. He'd always loved getting that reaction from her. She was so sensitive. So much for his vow to take it back a notch, to protect them both from too much too soon. Who was he kidding? He could no more resist her than he could resist breathing. "Syd . . ."

"Yes?"

He had to know. He *needed* to know. "Do you feel it, too?"

Her breath seemed to catch in her throat as she looked at him. "Feel what?"

"*Everything.*" How else to put it?

She ran her fingers over his jaw. "Yes."

Overcome with relief that he wasn't in this alone, Luke gazed into her eyes. "I'm worried we're moving too fast."

"We probably are."

"So we should—"

"Enjoy it." She framed his face with her hands and kissed him. "We should enjoy it."

"For how long?" He hated that he needed to ask.

"I don't know the answer to that. I wish I did, but all I can give you is right now. I'd understand if that wasn't enough—"

Luke kissed the words off her lips. "Do you promise you'll talk to me about your plans? That you won't leave me out of it?"

"The way I did before."

"I'd rather not go through that again."

"I promise I'll talk to you."

He twirled a lock of strawberry-blond hair around his finger. "Then it's enough. For now."

"Most guys never would've given me a second chance."

"I'm not most guys."

"Believe me, I know that. Why did you give me another chance?"

Continuing to play with the strand of hair, he shrugged. "I've never felt everything with anyone else."

"Luke," she whispered, reaching for him. She drove him wild with her teasing tongue and soft lips.

They'd be late for their reservation, but Luke didn't care about that. Not when the woman who'd haunted his dreams was back in his arms. He ran his hand up from her ribs to cup a breast that was fuller than he remembered and felt her nipple harden against his palm.

"Maybe we should skip dinner," she said, her voice husky and sexy.

Luke forced himself to think with his brain and not the part of his anatomy that burned for her. "Dinner first."

"I won't tell anyone you didn't buy me dinner first."

"I'll know," he said, disentangling himself and starting the truck. He was surprised to notice it had gotten dark while they lost themselves in each other.

"Thank you," she said so softly he almost didn't hear her.

"For what?"

She reached for his hand and brought it to her lips. "For not rushing me, and for knowing what I need even when I'm not quite sure."

Luke squeezed her hand and brought it to rest on his leg as he navigated the twists and turns on the way into town. Approaching Sweet Meadow Farm Road where Mac and Maddie lived, Luke was blinded by the headlights of another car that had crept over the center line.

"Holy shit," Luke said, swerving to avoid a collision. *"What the hell?"*

Sydney screamed and pulled her hand free of his.

For a brief moment, Luke feared he would lose control of the truck but managed to keep it on the road as the other car passed in a flash of light and throbbing bass.

Breathing hard, Luke pulled the truck to the side of the road and looked over to find Sydney curled into a ball in the passenger seat. When he rested a hand on her shoulder, she flinched. "It's okay. We're okay."

Her moan was barely human. *Oh God.*

Luke released his seat belt and moved closer to her. He was almost afraid to touch her but more afraid not to. "Everything's okay, Syd. Come here, baby. Come to me."

She turned into his embrace, and sobs shook her entire body.

"I'm so sorry," he said. His lips brushed over her hair. He wished now he'd been less of a gentleman earlier. If he'd taken her home rather than heading for town, the wound on her soul wouldn't have been ripped open again.

Her gasping sobs broke his heart, and her tears wet his shirt. "It's okay, honey." He wondered if he said it often enough she might actually hear him. They sat there for a long time, Luke's mind racing with thoughts about what he should do. He was afraid to let her go long enough to drive them home.

Fishing the phone out of his pocket, he continued to speak softly to Sydney while he used one hand to send a text to Mac, asking him to come. While he waited and hoped Mac hadn't shut off his phone, Luke rubbed Sydney's back and told her over and over again that they were okay, that everything was okay.

Mac appeared out of the darkness ten minutes later.

Moving closer to Sydney, Luke signaled for Mac to stay quiet and drive the truck. Luke could see the questions in his friend's eyes, but thankfully Mac didn't ask as he slid into the driver's seat.

"My place," Luke whispered to Mac because it was closest. Returning his focus to Sydney, Luke held her against him on the short ride home. When they got there, Luke freed her from the seat belt and scooped her up to walk inside. He sat on the sofa with her on his lap and kept his arms tight around her.

She clung to him, crying softly and shaking with sobs. Looking helpless and uncertain, Mac watched over them.

Luke closed his eyes and tightened his hold on Sydney, rocking her the way he would a small child who'd had a bad dream. His poor Syd had been through a nightmare, and their close call had clearly triggered horrifying memories.

After a long while, he felt her sag against him when sleep claimed her. He stood and carried her into his bedroom, settling her into bed and waiting to be sure she would stay asleep before he pressed a kiss to her forehead and went to talk to Mac.

"What the hell happened, man?" Mac asked when Luke joined him in the kitchen.

"A near collision with an asshole who was driving too fast on the curves. Brought it all back for her."

"Shit," Mac muttered.

"Thanks for coming. I was afraid to let go of her for even the few minutes it would've taken to get here."

"No problem at all. Do you think it would help to have Maddie talk to her? They go way back."

"Maybe. She needs to sleep for a while."

"What about you? You have to be freaked out. What can I do for you?"

"Can you go to her place and get her dog? He's a golden named Buddy. She wouldn't want him to be alone all night."

"Will he come with me?"

"I hope so. If you call him by name, he'll know you're a friend."

"Do you have her keys?"

Luke walked with Mac to the truck to get Sydney's keys from her purse. "I'm not sure which one it is."

"I'll figure it out."

"Thanks, Mac."

Luke stood in the driveway and watched his truck disappear from view. Turning back to the house, he headed straight for the kitchen to unearth a bottle of whisky he kept for an occasional indulgence. The burn of the liquor coursing through him settled his nerves. Now if he could just do something about the trembling in his hands.

He put down the glass and walked down the hallway to the bedroom, turning the hall light on so he could check on her. She was curled up on her side in the middle of the bed, still asleep. The poor thing had worn herself out.

A flurry of doors closing in the driveway drew Luke back to the living room fifteen minutes later. He wasn't surprised to see Mac and Maddie returning in two vehicles. When Luke opened the door, Buddy seemed to know where he was needed and disappeared into the bedroom.

Mac handed Luke a bag of dog food and a leash.

"Thanks," Luke said.

"Is she okay?" Maddie asked. "What happened?"

"She's asleep," Luke said. Once again, he related the story of the near miss on the road. His hands grew damp as he remembered the heart-stopping moment when he'd been certain they were going to crash or roll over or worse.

"Oh God," Maddie said. "Poor Syd—and you. Are you okay?"

"I'm fine. Just a little rattled by the whole thing. She was doing so well."

"Until something brought it all back again," Maddie said. "Do you want me to stay? In case she wakes up?"

Luke shook his head. "You need to get home to Thomas."

"Janey and Joe are with him. They were at our house when Mac got your text." Maddie rested her hand on Luke's arm. "I can stay if you think you might need some help tonight."

As much as Luke feared Sydney waking up and re-membering what'd nearly happened, he had a feeling she might not want extra people around for that, even her close friend. He wondered if she'd want *him* around for that. Well, she was stuck with him, and somehow he'd get her through it. "I'll have her call you in the morning, okay?"

Maddie nodded. "If you're sure."

He was sure of nothing. "Thanks for the offer."

"Call me in the middle of the night if need be. I'll come." She gave Luke a quick hug that caught him off guard for a moment before he returned the embrace.

Mac reached out to squeeze his shoulder. "We're a phone call away if you need us."

Overcome by their support and friendship, Luke nodded. "I might not be in tomorrow. If that's okay."

"You certainly don't have to ask. Remember that whole 'make you a partner in the business' thing last year?"

"I still forget sometimes," Luke said with a small smile. "Old habits die hard."

"Business owners come and go as they please. Don't worry about tomorrow. I'll be there all day."

"Thanks again for coming earlier and for getting Buddy for me."

"Anytime."

While he and Mac had known each other all their lives and had always been friendly, they'd never been *friends* until they started working together every day.

With a new wife and young family, Mac had been hesitant to take on the responsibility of running the marina on his own. So Big Mac offered to make Luke a partner. After Luke had been assured that none of the other four McCarthy siblings had any interest in the business, he'd accepted Big Mac's offer of forty percent. Luke and Mac each had forty, and Big Mac retained twenty in case one of his other kids changed their mind and wanted in.

Luke still had to remind himself every now and then that he actually *owned* a big chunk of the profitable marina where he'd worked since he was fourteen. Flipping off the porch light, he closed and locked the door, leaning against it for a moment to collect himself.

Sydney Donovan was in his bed. Too bad it had to happen this way.

Chapter Nine

Sydney woke with a start, unsure of where she was. As usual, Buddy was snuggled up to her, but so was someone else. The pillow smelled like Luke, clean and fresh and citrusy. She was in Luke's bed. With Luke and Buddy. The whole thing rushed back to her like a horror movie—the bright lights, the truck swerving, Luke's cry of distress. After that, it all went murky.

"You're okay," Luke said softly. "I'm right here."

Comforted by the sound of his voice as much as his words, she turned to him, groaning when the hips and pelvis she'd injured in the accident fifteen months ago protested. "What time is it?"

He checked the illuminated face of his watch. "Two thirty."

"How'd we get here?"

"You don't remember?"

"Not much after . . ."

He smoothed a hand over her hair and kissed her forehead. "You were upset, so Mac came and drove us here."

She winced at the thought of her friend's husband seeing her unglued. "Where did Buddy come from?"

"I sent Mac to get him. I knew you wouldn't want him home alone all night, and I figured he might bring you comfort when you woke up."

"Thank you for thinking of that." She brushed a hand over his face. "You had a special night planned. I'm sorry—"

Leaning a finger on her lips, he stopped her. "Please don't apologize." He hugged her tight, and she rested her face against his chest. His skin was warm, and the light dusting of chest hair was soft against her face.

Steeped in his familiar scent, Sydney closed her eyes and absorbed the comfort of his embrace as his heart beat fast under her ear.

"Want to talk about it?" he asked after a long period of silence.

She closed her eyes even tighter, trying to stem the flood of new tears.

"You don't have to," he said, sounding alarmed.

"I don't remember much about it," she said. "We'd been to Portsmouth, New Hampshire, to see Seth's parents. I'd had a bad cold for a week and was sleeping on the way home. Someone told me later I survived because of the position I was in. I only remember Seth screaming, which woke me up. He said . . ." Her voice hitched, and for a moment she couldn't speak.

Luke held her tight against him. "You don't have to tell me, Syd. Not now. Not ever if you don't want to."

"He said the same thing you did tonight. The exact same thing. That's the last thing I ever heard him say."

All the air left Luke's body in one big exhale. "Oh God. I'm so sorry. I didn't know—"

She tipped her face up to kiss the words off his lips. "How could you? What else does one say in that situation?"

"I wish I'd said something else."

"The car hit us from behind. We were stopped in traffic, and Seth must've seen him coming in the mirror. There was nothing he could do, nowhere to go. The kids were killed instantly. Seth died later, in surgery. I don't remember anything after he screamed until I woke up in the hospital five days later."

"I'd give everything I have to keep you from having to relive it, to go back to when we were at the point watching the sunset."

"Please don't beat yourself up, Luke. It's not your fault. I live with it every day of my life."

"Tell me about them," he said. "About Seth and the kids. If you feel up to talking about them."

Sydney took a deep breath and gave herself permission to remember. Thinking of them brought a small smile to her face. "Seth was the eternal optimist. Nothing ever got him down. He was full of plans and ideas and grand schemes that usually involved making money. That was his gift—investing and growing money. Everyone we knew sought his advice. I used to say the stock market was his mistress." She laughed at the memory.

"He loved to cook—and not just regular food, but gourmet dishes that would make your mouth water just thinking about them. He played the piano and loved rugby, although he didn't play anymore after the kids were born because he was afraid of getting hurt and not being able to care for them."

"How'd you meet him?"

"Through my college roommate. They were cousins. Since they were both in school in Boston, he came to visit her a lot. At first I didn't like him all that much. His eternally upbeat and happy disposition grated on my nerves.

I figured he had to be fake or medicated or something, because no one is ever that happy all the time."

"But he was?"

She nodded, smiling as she thought of her late husband. "Over time, I came to realize that was how he was wired. Nothing bothered him, and *everyone* liked him. He asked me out a hundred times before I finally said yes."

Sydney looked up in time to see a flash of naked pain cross Luke's face. "What're you thinking?"

"That when you said yes to him you were saying good-bye to me, and I didn't even know it."

The pain she heard in his voice made her sad. "Maybe," she said, dropping soft kisses on his chest, "I was saying 'good-bye for now' to you."

"You really believe that?"

"I'm beginning to."

"Tell me about the kids."

She knew they needed to have this conversation if they had any chance of moving forward together, but that didn't make it any easier. "Max was brilliant. All mothers say that about their kids, but in his case, it was true. He taught himself to read before kindergarten, and we were talking about having him skip third grade because he was so far ahead of his age group. He loved the Red Sox and video games, even though we didn't let him have them at home. Seth took him to Fenway Park every summer, and they watched the games every night. There was nothing he didn't know about that team."

Luke ran his fingers through her hair, offering comfort as he listened.

"Malena was all girl—ballet and nail polish and frills and bows. She drove her brother insane wanting him to play with her dolls and trying to dress him up for tea parties. She was in kindergarten, often in trouble for talking in class. We suspected she'd be a handful as a teenager. But she was sweet and kind and generous. Always fighting for the underdog and befriending the kids no one else liked."

"I'd love to see pictures of them sometime."

Sydney tilted her head back so she could see him. "I'd love to show you."

"Thank you for telling me about them. I know it's not easy for you, but now I feel like I know them a little bit."

Another thought occurred to her, making her hurt the way she did every time she thought of it.

"What, Syd? What is it?"

"I never saw them after. By the time I came to, they'd all been buried. My parents and Seth's took care of everything."

"That might've been for the best, don't you think?"

"The shrink assured me I didn't want those images in my head. He said I was better off remembering them the way they'd been in life."

"But?"

She appreciated he understood there was more to it. "I feel guilty I wasn't there for them. That's weird, right?"

"You were badly injured yourself. There was nothing you could do for them but get better so you could keep their memory alive."

His softly spoken words went straight to her heart. "That's such a sweet thing to say. Thank you for that."

"I'm feeling a little out of my league here, but then again, I always did with you."

Surprised to hear that, she said, "Why?"

"Come on," he said, laughing. "You were far too good for me. Still are."

"That's not true. I was never, ever good *enough* for you."

"We can agree to disagree."

"I don't know how you can say I was too good for you when I walked away from what we had without a word."

"All right, if you insist. I'll agree you're not good enough for me, but I'm willing to overlook your deficiencies."

Astounded, Sydney let her mouth fall open, which made him laugh. And then he leaned in to take advantage of her open mouth, chasing the thoughts from her busy mind.

His lips moved gently over hers, as if he was afraid to scare her away by taking too much.

She wrapped her arms around his neck, and let her tongue wander into his mouth, seeking him.

That seemed to spark something in him, and his kiss went from gentle to fierce. All of a sudden, he pulled back. "I'm sorry," he said, breathing hard. "I shouldn't have done that."

"I wanted you to."

"Syd, I want you so much. Not just tonight, but every night. The last thing I want is to rush you or push you into something you're not ready for."

"I set us back a bit tonight, huh?"

He pushed himself up on an elbow. "No, baby," he said, brushing the hair back from her face. "It's not your fault. It'll take the time it takes. Look how far you've already come."

"Sometimes it seems like I haven't come very far at all. Other times, I feel closer to my old self again, which of course makes me guilty. How can a mother ever feel like her old self again when her children are gone forever?"

"Trust me—I saw you last summer. You're a thousand times better than you were."

"That's right," she said, smiling. "You were 'visiting' me back then."

"I couldn't stay away."

She reached for him, and he snuggled into her embrace, his lips brushing against her forehead. Sydney smoothed her hand over his hair, comforted by his warmth, his scent and his calm, quiet demeanor.

"Luke?"

"Hmm?"

"Will you make love to me?"

His entire body went still, and she swore he stopped breathing.

"It's okay if you don't want to," she said after an uncomfortable moment of silence.

He took her hand and directed it to the front of his gym shorts.

Sydney gasped when he pressed her hand against his erection.

"It's not that I don't want to," he said in an unsteady tone.

"Oh." She took advantage of the opportunity to stroke him and felt him grow even harder. She'd never forgotten what it'd been like with him—the thrill, the connection, the overwhelming passion. "Then what?"

"Syd," he said, his eyes closed and his face tightened with tension as she relearned his length and width. His hips seemed to have a mind of their own as he pushed against her hand.

"Tell me."

"When we do this, I want it to be about us."

"Who else would it be about?"

He opened his eyes and met her gaze. "It's not about us tonight. And that's okay. That's what you needed. But when we do this, it has to be for the right reasons. We've already had one chance and managed to screw it up. I don't want to screw it up again."

Sydney withdrew her hand and shifted onto her back. "I should go home."

He stopped her. "No. Stay here with me. Stay for as long as you want. We'll get there." Cupping her cheek, he turned her face toward him and kissed her. "And when we do, it'll be worth the wait."

"You're sure of that?" she asked with a smile, anxious to diffuse the tension she felt coming from him.

"I've had *years* to think about what I'd do if I ever got a second chance with you."

The intensity behind the statement made her shiver with anticipation. "Is that so?"

"Uh-huh." He trailed kisses from her throat to her ear. "As much as I love being with you like this again, I never would've wished for it to happen the way it did. I hope you know that."

"I do. I know that." She rested her head on his chest. "I love being with you again, too."

"Being in a bed is a novelty for us."

Sydney laughed. "Remember all the crazy places we did it?"

"I remember everything."

"You really do, don't you?"

"Every minute. So you'll stay awhile? Spend some time with me? Let me take care of you?"

She studied his handsome face for a long moment before she said, "Yes, Luke. I'll stay with you."

Chapter Ten

The next time Sydney woke, she was alone in the big bed and bright sunlight was working its way through small cracks in the blinds that covered the windows. She looked around the room, which was tidy but short on frills, like the man who occupied it. Outside she heard Buddy barking the way he did when he was engaged in a fierce game of fetch.

She glanced at the clock and shot out of bed when she saw it was almost noon. Luke was probably waiting for her to get up so he could take her home and get to work. Her dress from the night before was impossibly wrinkled from being slept in, but it would get her home. After a quick trip to the bathroom, she rushed outside, where Luke was throwing a tennis ball for Buddy.

As Buddy flipped himself over in his haste to grab the ball, Luke laughed. Watching him, Sydney remembered the tender way he'd cared for her the night before, how he'd encouraged her to talk about the family she'd loved and lost, and how he'd put her needs above his own, the way he had even as a boy.

"Hey," Luke said. "You're up."

"I'm so sorry. I've made you late for work."

Walking over to her, he said, "I took the day off."

"Because of me."

He kissed her nose. "We work seven days a week this time of year. I can't tell you when I last had a full day off, so I was due. No worries, honey."

Sydney could tell she surprised him when she put her arms around his waist and went up on tiptoes to kiss him.

"What's that for?"

"To thank you for last night. You got me through a rough spot, and I appreciate it."

He wrapped her up in a tight hug. "I was glad to be there for you. Now, how about some coffee and something to eat? You have to be starving after not eating last night."

"Coffee would be great, but then I should go. You probably have things to do."

Drawing back to look down at her, he touched his lips to her forehead. "I thought we agreed you were going to stay with me a while."

Sydney looked up at him. His face was freshly shaven, his hair still damp from the shower, and his serious dark eyes were intensely focused on her. "I thought you meant just last night."

"I meant for as long as you want to be here."

"Oh."

He reached for her hand and linked their fingers. "Let's start with coffee and go from there."

She followed him inside, where he poured coffee and insisted on making her an omelet and toast. Sydney was lingering over a second cup of coffee when she asked Luke about her purse.

"I'll get it for you." He went into the living room and returned with it.

"Thanks." She checked her cell phone and let out a gasp. "Oh God. My mother's been calling all morning." Sydney called her mother back as Luke got busy cleaning up the kitchen.

"Sydney!" Her mother's voice was frantic. "*Where have you been?* Why haven't you answered your phone?"

Syd closed her eyes, summoning fortitude. "I'm so sorry. My phone fell out of my purse in the car last night. I didn't notice until now."

"Your father and I were about to call the airlines!"

"I'm sorry you were worried. How was the reunion?" She talked to her dad next, and by the time they hung up, her parents were reassured that Sydney was doing fine on the island. She put her head down on the counter for a second to regroup.

Luke's hands landed on her shoulders, kneading away the tension. "Everything okay?"

"It's normal, isn't it? After what happened, it's normal for them to hover over me to the point of suffocation, right?"

"I suppose so."

She tipped her head to encourage him to continue the divine massage. "I know they don't mean to smother me, but I wanted to jump for joy when they left on their trip. If they come back before the end of August, I may very well shoot myself."

"I'll lock up the guns."

Sydney laughed and then moaned when he worked out a tight knot.

"Will you tell them?"

"About what?"

"That you're seeing me again."

"Eventually."

"Will it be an issue?"

Even though she wasn't at all finished enjoying the massage, she turned so she could see him. "Not for me."

"So if your parents flip out that you're dating the marina guy again, you'll be fine with that?"

"I imagine they'll want me to be happy."

"And if they don't approve?"

Sydney wrapped her hands around his and waited until his gaze met hers. "It won't matter."

"You say that now."

"Trust me when I tell you I love my parents, but I'm not under their thumbs. Not anymore."

He nodded, released her hands and went to finish the dishes.

Sydney followed him and wrapped her arms around him from behind, resting her face on his back. She held him until she felt the tension begin to leave him.

"You need to call Maddie. She was here last night, and she's worried about you. She's called this morning hoping to talk to you."

"I'll call her. After that, can we run by my place so I can get some clothes and a toothbrush?"

"Sure."

"Are we okay, Luke?"

"Of course we are."

He said what she wanted to hear, but she wondered if he meant it. Once again her parents were coming between them, and this time they were more than a thousand miles away.

Luke drove her home to pack a bag and collect Buddy's toys. She made them a picnic lunch that they took to the beach in front of Luke's house. Buddy chased the seagulls and flirted with the waves, running back to the safety of the blanket when the waves got the better of him.

Sydney laughed at his antics, patting him on the head to reassure him every time he returned to her. "He's a big baby," she said. "Although it's such a relief to see him being playful again."

From the blanket, Luke chucked the tennis ball and sent the dog flying down the beach. "That ought to give us three or four minutes."

"For what?" Syd asked.

Smiling, he slipped a hand around her neck and drew her into a kiss that started out soft and sweet but turned hot and wild.

They were interrupted when a spit-soaked tennis ball landed with a plunk on Luke's back.

"Ugh," he said, pulling back from her. "Gross, man."

Buddy barked, demanding Luke throw the ball again.

"All right, hold your horses." Luke put some serious muscle behind the throw this time and sent the ball even farther down the beach.

Buddy took off like a shot.

"Now," Luke said, turning back to Sydney, "where were we?"

She opened her arms to him. "Right about here."

"Mmm, I love it here." He left a trail of kisses from her collarbone to her ear.

"Luke?"

"What, honey?"

Her hands slid over his shoulders to his back and muscular backside. "If we were to, you know, do what we used to do here, would it be about us?"

Groaning, he recaptured her mouth in another torrid

kiss. "Not here," he said when he came up for air. "I want a shower and a bed."

"You're no fun anymore."

He grunted out a laugh. "Gee, thanks."

"Now where did Buddy go?" She called for the dog.

"Is that him?" Luke pointed. "Way down there?"

"Yes! What's he doing?"

"I'll go get him," Luke said, kissing her quickly. "Don't go anywhere."

"Hurry."

Sydney shivered at the almost predatory look he gave her before he jogged down the beach to where Buddy was working on something he'd found on the sand. She hoped it wasn't gross or smelly, because she really didn't want to have to give him a bath. Not right now. Not when she and Luke had better things to do.

She reclined on the blanket, letting the afternoon sun warm her face. *Am I really going to do this?* Did all widows feel guilty and torn the first time they made love with another man after losing their husband? "Seth would want me to be happy," she said. "That was all he ever cared about." But would he want her to be happy with Luke, the only other man she'd ever loved?

Of course she'd told Seth about Luke and how she'd left their relationship unfinished. She didn't think Seth had seen Luke as any kind of serious threat to him or their marriage, but then he hadn't known how often she'd thought of her first love or how bad she felt about leaving him without a word.

"Seth is gone," she said, almost as if she needed the reminder as Luke ran back to her with Buddy trotting along beside him. Luke was tall and had the kind of muscles men earn from years of hard physical work rather than hours in the gym. He had just the right amount of dark chest hair, and watching him come toward her with intent in his eyes sent awareness zinging through her that landed in an ache between her legs.

All he'd ever had to do was look at her in that particular way, and she was his.

"He found a dead bird and a garbage bag," Luke said.

"Yuck. He didn't actually eat the bird, did he?"

"I think it was more about giving it a proper burial."

Sydney looked closer to find Buddy's paws and nose caked with sand. "Fabulous."

Luke held out a hand to help her up. "I'll squirt him off in the yard."

Buddy's bath turned into a three-way water fight when Luke trained the hose on Sydney rather than the dog. She fought back, wrestling him for the hose and getting doused again with icy water that had her gasping.

"I guess we can skip the shower," Luke said with another of those heated looks that made her knees weak. "For now." He toweled Buddy dry and sent the dog inside for some food and water. "Your turn," he said to Syd, using a sun-warmed beach towel to dry her face and shoulders.

By the time he dragged the towel over her belly, Sydney was about to combust. "Luke." The single word carried a world of need.

He ran the towel over his own body, dropped it to the ground and reached for her. "Are you sure, baby? Really sure you're ready?"

She went up on tiptoes to kiss him. "I'm sure." Sydney was startled—and even more aroused—when he scooped her up and carried her inside. He kicked the bedroom door shut so Buddy wouldn't follow them.

As he deposited her on the bed, his gaze traveled over her reverently. "I can't believe you're really here," he said. "And that we're really about to do this."

"In the middle of the day, no less," she said, smiling at him. "Scandalous."

He stretched out next to her. "Very."

"Your bed will be all wet if we don't lose the bathing suits."

"Is that your way of saying we should get naked?"

"If you want to," she said with a nonchalant shrug that made him laugh.

"I want to." He kissed her and tugged on the string that held up her top. "I *really* want to."

Luke watched her breasts spring free of the top and had to remind himself to keep breathing. He'd imagined this scene so many times, but his fantasies hadn't come close to the reality of having her with him again. Everything about her appealed to him—from the silky softness of her strawberry-blond hair, to the freckles that danced across her tiny nose to the pretty pink nipples that pebbled, waiting for him to lavish them with attention.

He wanted her so badly he was almost afraid to touch her, almost afraid to let her see the full extent of his desire. Reminding himself this was a bigger deal for her, he pressed a much darker hand to the quivering white skin of her belly.

"You're even more beautiful than I remembered," he said as he bent his head to taste her nipple.

She gasped and squirmed beneath him, which only

made it harder to hold on to the control he knew would be so essential to her this first time. Next time, he could lose control. Not this time, though. This time she needed tender and sweet.

Sucking her nipple into his mouth, he held her plump breast in one hand and let the other slide down over her belly to cup her through her bathing suit. The heat of her core radiated through the fabric, and his cock strained against the confines of his own suit.

He gave her other breast the same attention, reveling in the pants and moans that told him she was with him and not locked in the past. Kissing his way from her breasts to her belly, he nuzzled her center, breathing her in.

"Luke," she said, her voice unsteady.

He tugged at the suit bottoms, getting her to raise her hips so he could remove them. When the garment cleared her feet, he tossed it over his shoulders and smoothed his hands over her legs, inching them apart as his lips followed his hands. She was so sweet and soft and everything he'd remembered but so much more, too.

The thatch of curls at the juncture of her thighs identified her as a true redhead, reminding him of the awe he'd experienced the first time he made that discovery as a boy. The man was no less awestruck. Just above the hairline, he noticed a thin white scar. Curious, Luke traced a finger lightly over it. "You had surgery."

"Two C-sections."

Since he didn't want her thinking of anything but him and them, now wasn't the time to ask the questions that cycled through his mind. Instead, he dipped his head and ran his tongue over her core, teasing and tempting.

Her legs fell open, and her hips surged off the bed.

Luke slid a finger into the slick heat between her legs

and drew the throbbing center of her desire into his mouth, running his tongue back and forth. He added a second finger and took her to the precipice before backing off and doing it again.

"Luke!"

"What, honey?"

She was panting, and goose bumps dotted her sensitive skin. "Stop teasing!"

Laughing softly, he went back for more, and this time he took her all the way. She came with a sharp cry of completion that had Buddy scratching at the bedroom door and barking.

"Should I let him in?" Luke asked.

"No," she said breathlessly. "He'd freak out even more."

While he gave her a minute to recover from the powerful orgasm, Luke shed his bathing suit and started to reach for a condom in the bedside drawer.

"It's okay," Syd said, stopping him. "I'm safe if you are."

Luke's heart skipped a happy beat. Sex without a condom? Sex with *Syd* without a condom? This might go down as the very best day of his life. Speaking of going down, was she, *oh my God . . . "Syd."*

With her hand to his chest she urged him to lie back and let her have her wicked way with him. And wicked didn't begin to describe the sensation of her hot, wet mouth closing over the head of his cock. If she continued to do that—

He all but launched off the bed when she sucked— hard—and stroked him at the same time. This was going to be over in about two seconds if she kept that up. "Stop. Syd. *Stop.*"

She looked up at him with the eyes of a vixen, and he'd never loved her more.

"Come here." He sat up, reached for her and brushed the hair off her face, which was flushed from the sun as well as the orgasm. Arranging her so she straddled him, he ran his hands from her shoulders to her hips and back up again, noting her slight grimace. "Are you okay?"

"My hips need a second to adjust," she said, wincing.

"Stop me if anything hurts."

"I will." With her hands on his face, she urged him into a deep, carnal kiss that made him want to beg. Sliding his hands down her back, he cupped her soft buttocks and used his legs to position her. "You're sure we don't need a condom?"

She bit her lip and nodded, sliding back and forth over his erection. When had she turned into such a temptress? His Syd wouldn't have thought of such things. But the last thing he wanted to think about right now was where—and how—she might've learned to tease and tempt a man. He held her hips and began to enter her, letting her set the pace, despite what it cost him to remain still.

Her head fell back as she slowly took him in, gripping him like a tight, hot velvet fist.

Nothing in his life could compare to this. Nothing. "God, Syd, I missed you. I missed this."

She wrapped her arms around his neck, pressed her breasts to his chest and settled into a rhythm that had him fighting off a fast finish.

He looked up, met her gaze and was floored by what he saw there—love and trust and peace. "Kiss me."

Her mouth came down on his, slick and warm and tasting of strawberry lip balm. If she continued to rub her tongue against his that way, she would finish him off.

"Luke," she whispered against his lips, "I'm going to . . . *Oh*." Her head fell to his shoulder, and she came apart.

He held off as long as he could, riding the waves of her release. When he finally let go, he exploded, coming harder than he had since the last time with her. While sex with other women had been satisfying, sex with Syd was a religious experience, and he wanted to worship her for the rest of his life.

A sniffling sound caught his attention.

"Syd, baby, look at me." With his hands on her face, he forced her to meet his gaze. The tears in her eyes broke his heart. "Did I hurt you?"

"No, no," she said. "I'm sorry. I'm fine. Really."

Except she didn't look fine. Not at all. "Talk to me."

She shook her head, and tears spilled down her cheeks. "I don't know why I'm crying. I'm so happy to be here with you. I couldn't have done this with anyone but you. I hope you know that."

He knew she meant it as a compliment, but the comment filled him with fear. "I don't want to be your bridge guy."

Her brows furrowed. "What does that mean?"

"If you're on your way somewhere else—"

"There's nowhere else I'd rather be. No one I'd rather be with."

"For now."

"For as long as it works for both of us."

"And then what?"

"I don't know that, and neither do you."

"Don't tell me what I know," he said, his tone harsher than he'd intended.

"Are we really doing this? After we just made love?"

Her eyes filled again, and that broke him. He lifted her off him and arranged her so her head was on his chest and his arms were wrapped around her. "I'm sorry. I shouldn't have said that. It's just the thought of losing you—again—makes me crazy."

"I'm here, Luke. I'm not going anywhere for a while yet."

He wondered if she remembered saying those exact words to him once before.

Chapter Eleven

They dozed the afternoon away. For once, Sydney's racing mind had quieted, and she gave Luke credit for that. It was hard to be around him for any period of time and not be drawn in by the calm that surrounded him.

Most of him, anyway. The part of him that was anything but calm pulsed against her back, letting her know he was ready for more.

Sydney laughed softly. She couldn't remember the last time she'd been so carefree or relaxed. "You're insatiable."

His hand shifted from her belly to cup a breast. "Only with you."

"Were there many others?" She had no right to ask, but she hoped he hadn't been totally alone.

"A few. Here and there. Nothing serious." His thumb moved back and forth over her nipple, sending an electrical current to her sex and making her squirm against him. "No one like you."

"Luke." She started to turn over to face him, but he stopped her.

He pushed his erection into the cleft of her bottom. "Stay. Like this."

Sydney's entire body hummed with tension and desire, as if she hadn't already been thoroughly satisfied— multiple times—in the last few hours. Waiting to see what he would do had her holding her breath in anticipation.

His hand traveled slowly from her breast to her hip and down her leg. He curled his fingers under her knee and drew her leg back to rest on him. As he placed soft, strategic kisses on her neck, his fingers traveled up the inside of her thigh, making her quiver.

She arched her back into him, seeking him.

Finding her slick and ready, he buried his fingers inside her and pressed his erection into the cleft of her ass.

Sydney gasped at the dual sensations. Sex with him had always been earthy and almost primitive. They'd tried everything at least once—more than once, if they'd liked it. Without ever exchanging a word on the subject, he somehow knew what it took to make her scream.

Acknowledging that he was the only man who'd ever known her so well made her feel guilty and disloyal. But his tender ministrations gave her no time for thoughts of anything but right here. Right now.

As he slid his fingers in and out of her, he continued to pump against her ass. Until he shifted his focus to the tight bundle of nerves at her core, and she climaxed so suddenly that she cried out her pleasure in a keening moan that came from her toes. She was still in the throes of it when he moved her onto her hands and knees to enter her from behind.

Sydney gasped and fought to accept the length and width of him. He filled her so completely, so thoroughly.

"Is this okay?" he asked.

"Yeah."

"Nothing hurts?"

She shook her head.

He held her hips carefully and pressed into her hard and fast.

She rested her head on folded arms and gripped the sheet to keep from flying off the bed.

Using his knees, he urged her legs even farther apart as he slowed the pace. If he was out to drive her crazy, he was doing one hell of a job. Then she felt his hands on her bottom, smoothing over the cheeks in a gentle caress that made her legs turn to jelly. Her breath got caught in her throat when his finger slid into the cleft, teasing, pressing, exploring.

Sydney came again, screaming as the powerful release rocketed through her.

Luke slipped an arm under her hips and surged into her one last time, grunting as he let himself go. He collapsed, half on her, half off, his lips pressed against her back as they recovered.

For the longest time, they lay there joined, cooling, breathing, throbbing with aftershocks.

He nuzzled her hair aside, his lips brushing against her ear. "God, Syd," he said so softly she almost didn't hear him.

She nudged at him, encouraging him to let her up.

He withdrew from her and shifted onto his back. Gathering her close, he kissed her forehead. "We'll make it work this time. One way or the other, we'll make it work."

Sydney closed her eyes tight against the rush of emotion. She wanted another chance with him, but first there was something she needed to tell him.

"Maddie called while we were in the shower," Sydney said, catching the heated look he sent her way when she mentioned the shower. Just when she'd been certain they'd worn themselves out, he had proven otherwise, taking her fast and rough against the wall. She'd never had so much sex in her life, and even though she was tender in a few interesting places, she was enjoying every minute with him.

"What'd she have to say?"

"She left a message that she and Mac are going with Joe and Janey to the Tiki Bar at McCarthy's tonight. Something about a guy playing there they want to see."

"Owen Lawry. He comes through a couple of times every summer. Plays the guitar and sings. He's really good. You want to go?"

"I wouldn't mind getting out for a bit."

He turned away from the grill and came over to where she stood looking out at the sunset. Putting his arms around her from behind, he nuzzled her neck. "Because I've worn you out?"

Sydney laughed and covered his hands with hers. "Partially."

"What's the other part?"

"Maddie was worried when I talked to her earlier. She wants to see that I'm okay."

"And are you? Okay?"

Sydney turned to him and slipped her arms around his neck. "I'm fine."

"Are you feeling, you know, guilty at all?"

"Some. My therapist said I should expect that the first time."

"If it makes you feel any better, I'm a little guilty, too."

"Why?"

"I'm so damned happy to have you back in my life and in my bed, but I know how difficult this step is for you."

Sydney reached up to brush the hair off his forehead. "I'm glad I took the step with you."

Luke hugged her. "So am I."

She drew back to look up at him. "There's something I need to tell you."

His entire body went rigid. "What?"

Taking a deep breath, she tried to calm the nerves that suddenly gripped her. "Remember when we talked about whether or not I want more kids?"

He nodded. "What about it?"

"Well, the thing is, I can't have any more. Not naturally, anyway."

"Oh."

"I know I should've told you sooner. It just didn't seem like the right time the other day. But I wanted you to know."

Luke looked over her head at a point off in the distance.

"I'd understand if that changes things for you—"

He brought his gaze back to meet hers. "It doesn't change anything."

"You must want kids of your own someday."

"I haven't given it that much thought, to be honest. I've never come close to being married, so it hasn't been an issue."

"You'd only have kids if you were married?"

"I didn't know my own father, so I'd never want a kid of mine to grow up that way. Marriage seems to seal the deal."

"You should think about this, Luke, and be sure how you feel about it."

He drew her into a hug. "If I had a choice between five kids with someone else or no kids with you, I'd pick you." He brushed a soft kiss over her lips. "I pick you every time."

Overwhelmed by him, Sydney rested her forehead against his chest.

"Were you worried about what I might say?"

She nodded.

"That's good."

Looking up at him, Sydney laughed. "Why?"

"It means you care."

"I do care."

He kissed her nose and then her lips. "I know you do. Come on, let's eat."

Luke and Sydney arrived at the marina just as Big Mac was pulling the garage doors closed on the dockside restaurant.

"What're you still doing here?" Luke asked him.

"Linda had a thing with the ladies, so I stuck around to have a beer with Owen."

"Syd, you remember Mr. McCarthy, right?" Luke said.

She extended a hand to the older man, who enclosed hers between both of his. "Nice to see you again, Mr. McCarthy."

"That's Big Mac to you, and it's good to see you, too. I was so sorry to hear of your terrible loss."

"Thank you."

"Good day off?" Big Mac asked Luke.

"It was. Thanks for the time."

"You don't have to thank me. In fact, take tomorrow, too. We're slow this week."

"Are you sure?"

"Absolutely. Everyone needs downtime once in a while."

"I won't say no to that."

"I'm heading home. They're all down at the Tiki Bar. Have a good time tonight."

"We will." Luke reached for Sydney's hand and escorted her to the bar Big Mac had installed off the main pier in another of his successful schemes to expand the business.

Maddie waved to them from the corner of the crowded outdoor bar.

On the way past the small stage, Luke waved to Owen, the blond surfer dude with an incredible voice, who loved to boast of his vagabond existence in an old van with an even older guitar.

Owen stopped singing when he saw Luke but kept strumming his guitar. "Is that Luke Harris? With a *girl*? Did hell freeze over since I was last here?"

Luke flipped his friend the bird, which drew laughs from the table in the corner. He looked over at Sydney in time to catch the blush that flamed her cheeks.

The group made room for Luke and Sydney. Maddie dragged Syd down to the chair next to hers and gave her a big hug.

"How're you doing?" Maddie asked.

"Better. Thank you—both of you," she said, including Mac.

"Anytime," Mac said.

"What's a guy gotta do to get a beer around here?" Luke asked, looking around for a waitress.

Mac gestured to the bar. "It's quicker to help yourself tonight."

"Anyone need anything?" Luke asked.

"We're good," Joe said. "Just got a new round."

Luke leaned over to Sydney. "Wine?"

"Actually, light beer is looking good to me tonight."

"You think you know a girl," Luke said with a smile for her as he made his way through the crowd to the bar. He found Big Mac's best buddy, Ned, the island's number one cab driver, leaning against the bar. "How goes it, Ned?"

"Not bad. Madhouse tonight."

"Always is when Owen's here."

"Pretty girl grew up to be a lovely woman."

"What's that?"

"Yer girl," Ned said, nodding toward the table.

"Oh. Yeah. She sure did." Luke tried and failed to get the bartender's attention. Didn't she know he partially owned the place? Not that he'd *ever* play that card.

"Had me a girl like that once," Ned said in an odd moment of introspection. "Even had red hair like yer girl."

Astounded by the revelation, Luke stared at the old man with the wild white hair and bushy beard. He wore a faded red T-shirt and khaki shorts—an outfit that was dressed up by Ned's usual standards. "What happened?"

"Same thing that happened to you—she picked someone else."

Luke wasn't sure how to reply to that. "Is she still with him?" he asked, deciding that was the safest of his many questions.

"Nah. Ended more than twenty-five years ago."

"So why didn't you go after her?"

Ned shrugged. A toothpick danced around his mouth. "She knows where I am."

"Is she here? On the island?"

"What'll it be, Luke?" the bartender asked before Ned could reply.

"Two light beers, please."

"Coming right up."

Luke turned back to Ned. "Well, is she? Here?"

"Yep."

"You ever see her?"

"Only from a distance."

"Who is it?"

"Ya ain't gettin' that outta me, boy," Ned said with a snort.

The bartender delivered the beers, and Luke paid her. Turning back to Ned, he said, "Let me tell you—from experience—everything is better the second time around. If you still think about her, go see her. You never know what might happen."

"Suddenly yer the wise one, eh?"

Luke shrugged. "I wouldn't say that."

"She gonna break ya heart again?"

"Hope not."

"She's looking for ya. Better get back to her."

Luke shifted his gaze to the table. When his eyes met Sydney's, he returned her smile.

"Whoo, boy, ya got a bad, bad case," Ned said with a howl of laughter.

"I sure do."

"Hope it works out for ya this time."

"Me, too. Maybe it'll work out for you if you give it a shot. What've you got to lose?"

"Eh," Ned said, shrugging. "Bygones."

"Whatever you say. See ya later."

"Look out fer yaself, boy. Don't wanna see ya crushed by her again."

The comment stopped Luke short. "That's not going to happen." But as he returned to the table, Luke wondered who he was trying to convince—Ned or himself.

Chapter Twelve

Owen played his way through a song list of summer tunes that everyone sang along to: "Summer Breeze," "Sister Golden Hair," "God Only Knows," and "Peaceful Easy Feeling." Under the table, Luke kept a firm grip on Sydney's hand and felt her tense when Owen launched into "Southern Cross."

Luke glanced over to find a faraway look on her face.

Sydney caught his eye and offered a small smile. "Seth's favorite song."

"You want to go?"

"No, it's okay. Just took me by surprise."

It had caught her when she was actually having a good time, and Luke was sorry to see the sadness creep back into her expression. He tightened his grip on her hand and felt her relax when the song ended.

Owen took a break and wandered over to join them. He plopped down at the table, all his formidable charm focused on Sydney. "So tell me the truth: How much did he pay you to come out with him tonight?"

Startled by the question, Sydney laughed. Even though

the joke was at his expense, Luke was grateful to Owen for making her laugh.

"I'm actually rather cheap," Syd said with a sly smile that made Luke's blood boil and earned an appreciative grin from Owen.

While the rest of the group cracked up at her comment, Owen studied her with new respect and a hint of interest.

"Down, boy," Luke said, attempting a menacing scowl.

"It's like that, is it?" Owen said.

"You're damned right it is."

"Who is this guy?" Owen asked Mac and Joe. "And what've you done with quiet, unassuming Luke Harris?"

Joe slipped an arm around Janey. "Happens to the best of us, my man."

"Y'all are falling like dominoes around here," Owen said with a shudder. "Remind me not to drink the water."

"You're still playing at the wedding, right?" Janey asked.

"Wouldn't miss it for the world, sweet pea."

Janey rewarded him with a bright smile. "You were Joe's only request."

"I'm doubly honored, and I understand I'll be sharing the stage with the eminent Evan McCarthy."

"Well, I had to ask my brother, too, but you're the headliner," Janey said to laughter from the others. "Just don't tell Evan that."

"Ohhh, blackmail," Mac said. "I never get any dirt I can use on her."

"If you lived a pure, pristine life like I do, I wouldn't always have truckloads of dirt on you," Janey said haughtily.

Joe snickered, and Mac held up his hand. "Whatever you're dying to say, Joseph, stifle it. That's my baby sister."

"It's so nice to be out like this," Syd said, and the

others focused their attention on her. "Sorry. Didn't mean to blurt that out."

Maddie gave her a one-armed hug. "Don't apologize to us. We're thrilled to have you with us."

For Owen's benefit, Sydney said, "I was widowed fifteen months ago."

"Sorry to hear that."

"Thank you."

"Had you been out at all?" Mac asked. "Before you came here?"

"Don't ask her that," Janey said with a chastising look for her brother.

"What? It's a perfectly innocent question."

Sydney smiled at their sibling banter. "It's fine. I went out exactly once, and it was a disaster of epic proportions."

"Okay, now I have to hear this," Janey said, settling in for the story.

The others chimed in with agreement, and Luke had to admit he was curious, too.

"After I went back to work, I started seeing this one guy everywhere—in traffic, at the gas station, in the grocery store and at the coffee shop. After we'd seen each other a few times, he was behind me in line getting coffee one day, and he leaned in and said, 'We really have to stop meeting like this.'"

The guys groaned at the cheesy come-on.

"I hope you didn't fall for that," Luke said.

"Well, he had a charming smile, so I took pity on him. He asked me out to dinner, and I figured why not? I gave him my number, and we made plans. He picked me up, took me to a nice place, did the gentlemanly thing with the doors and all that."

"I can't imagine how this goes from polite to disaster," Maddie said.

"It was the wine," Sydney said with that mischievous smile Luke loved so much.

"What about it?" Maddie asked.

"He ordered soda water with lime, and when I ordered a glass of chardonnay, he got this really weird look on his face. I asked him if everything was all right. He says, 'I didn't realize you were a drinker.'"

The entire group erupted with laughter.

Sydney held up a hand, clearly enjoying her moment in the spotlight, and Luke's heart contracted. She was so beautiful when her eyes sparkled with mirth. "You haven't heard the best part," she said. "I told him I'm *not* a drinker. I just like a glass of wine with dinner. He got really quiet and closed his eyes. I had no idea what he was doing. Then he opens his eyes, and says, 'I talked to Jesus, and he said it's fine for you to have a glass of wine with dinner.'"

Luke stared at her as if he'd heard her wrong, while the others hooted with laughter.

"What the heck did you say?" Janey asked, wiping tears from her eyes.

"I asked him to thank Jesus for me, and then I closed my eyes for at least as long as he had closed his. Then I opened them, and I said, 'I talked to Jesus, too, and he said this date is over.' I got up and walked out. The restaurant called me a cab, and that was that."

"Fabulous," Joe said. "Good for you."

"You never heard from him again?" Mac asked.

"Oh, I heard from him. The phone calls started at eight the next morning and kept up until I mentioned the words *restraining order*."

That earned her another round of laughter.

"And that was my only foray into dating."

Luke slipped an arm around her and kissed the top of

her head. "Jesus told me to give you all the wine you can drink."

As the others cracked up, Syd rewarded him with a big smile. "And for that I shall be eternally grateful."

Luke thought his eyes were surely deceiving him when Grant McCarthy strolled into the bar.

"Mac, Janey," Luke said, nodding to the doorway.

"What the hell?" Mac said, grinning. "Janey, look who it is."

Janey let out a piercing shriek when she saw her second oldest brother coming toward them wearing a big smile for his siblings. She launched out of her seat and into Grant's welcoming arms. "What're you doing here already? The wedding isn't for another two weeks!"

"The only reason I'm allowed to come home is for your wedding, brat?"

"We're not supposed to call her that anymore," Mac said dryly.

"And how's that going?" Grant asked.

"Not so well," Janey said with a scowl for Mac.

"When did you get in?" Joe asked, shaking hands with Grant.

"On the last boat. Mom and Dad said you guys were here."

Luke introduced Grant to Sydney.

"I think we might've met years ago," she said.

"I remember. Nice to see you."

Grant shook hands with Owen and hugged Luke. "Good to see you."

"You, too. How are things in Lala Land?"

"Fake, pretentious and utterly decadent."

While the others laughed at Grant's description of Hollywood, Luke took a moment to study his old friend. Of all the McCarthy brothers, Luke had always been closest to Grant, even though the two of them didn't have a damned thing in common.

Grant had been the smartest kid in their small island school, and no one had been surprised when he grew up to be an Academy Award–winning screenwriter. Since moving to Los Angeles more than a decade ago, he'd been back to the island only a handful of times—most recently for Mac and Maddie's wedding last summer.

Grant hugged Mac and made a fuss over Maddie's round belly. "Thank you for taking the pressure off the rest of us, big brother."

Mac sent his wife a salacious smile. "My pleasure."

"*Mac*," Maddie said, smacking him.

"What? It *was* my pleasure."

"Shut up."

As Grant laughed at their banter and joined the group, Luke thought his friend looked tired and maybe a little sad.

Since he was sitting next to them, Luke saw Janey place a hand over Grant's. "You've heard about Abby," she said quietly.

Grant replied with a short nod, his jaw tightening with tension.

"Is that why you're here?"

Grant seemed to rally for Janey's sake. "I came for your wedding, brat." He kissed his sister's forehead. "Don't worry about me."

"What'll you do?"

"Whatever I can," Grant replied grimly.

On the way home, Sydney told herself to relax and not to freak out every time a car came at them from the other direction.

Luke reached for her hand. "You okay over there?"

"Trying to be."

"We're almost there. Just another minute. Hang on."

Sydney cradled his hand between both of hers. "Sorry to be so skittish."

"Don't be sorry. It's understandable. Did you have fun tonight?"

"I sure did. Maddie is campaigning hard for me to move here permanently."

"Is she now?"

"She says it's a lot more fun in the winters than it was growing up. Of course that's because she has Mac now."

"I've never seen him so happy."

"What was going on with Grant? He got really quiet."

"His ex-girlfriend Abby got engaged recently. She owns Abby's Attic in town."

"Oh, I love that store. Max and Malena used to drag me in there at least once every summer."

"Grant and Abby were together forever, sort of on-again, off-again recently. I never heard what happened, but something went bad last summer when he was here for Mac's wedding. Next we heard, she was dating the new doctor."

"LA is a long way from Gansett Island."

"So is Boston," he said.

Sydney looked over at him. "Not that far."

"All depends on your perspective."

"Maddie asked me to help with the baby's nursery."

"You feel up to doing that?"

"It'll be fun. Maddie knows decorating is one of my hobbies. In fact, before the accident, I'd been thinking about leaving teaching to give it a whirl full-time."

"Is it something you might still want to do?"

"Maybe. I'm told I have a knack for it."

"I should hire you to update my place. I haven't touched a thing since my mother died."

"No, *really*?" she said, smiling.

He laughed at the face she made at him. "You're itching to get your hands on it, aren't you?"

"I always thought you could better highlight the amazing views."

"That's a very diplomatic way of saying it needs everything—furniture, paint, updated appliances, new bathroom."

Syd fanned herself and shivered dramatically. "Don't toy with me this way."

Luke pulled up to the house and killed the engine. "That's all it takes to make you hot? Clearly, I've been going about this all wrong."

"Going about what?"

He leaned over to plant a kiss on her neck. "Convincing you to stay here with me permanently."

"Luke, I—"

Cupping her face, he turned her to receive his kiss.

Her hand pressing on his chest brought him back to his senses.

"Is that what you want? For me to stay here permanently?"

"Of course it is, but only if it's what you want, too."

"I'm not . . . I can't . . ."

"You're not ready to decide anything yet."

"No," she said.

"That's okay. We don't have to worry about any of that now." He kissed her again. "In the meantime, knock yourself out here and at Maddie's."

"You have no idea what you're saying."

Laughing again, he said, "Yes, I do."

"No, you don't. Seth used to go ballistic when he'd

come home to a whole new living room." She glanced at him, pained. "Sorry. I don't know where that came from."

"It came from your life, and you don't need to apologize or feel like you can't mention his name around me."

Sydney placed her hands on his face and drew him into another kiss that had them both breathing hard by the time they came up for air.

"I've had to wait hours and hours," he said between kisses. "I had to keep my hands to myself in front of our friends. I can't wait another minute."

"Then let's go put you out of your misery."

They met at the front of his truck for another heated kiss. Luke slid his hands down her back and shocked her when he suddenly lifted her and hooked her legs around his hips.

"Nice move," she said, linking her arms around his neck.

"You like that?"

"Uh-huh." As he walked them to the door, their lips met and melted, tongues teased and enticed.

"You're making my legs weak," he said, pressing her against the door. His hands slid up her bare legs, under her skirt to cup her ass.

"Luke," she gasped, tightening her arms around his neck.

Through her shirt, he rolled her nipple between his teeth and pushed his erection against her core.

"Now," she said as he fumbled with the door. It opened abruptly and sent them sprawling into the house.

"Shit," Luke said, laughing as he managed to land them awkwardly on the sofa. "That was graceful."

"And it started so well."

"It'll end even better."

She clutched handfuls of his hair and brought his mouth down to hers. "Promises, promises."

A low-pitched moan stopped them cold.

"What was that?" she asked. "Where's Buddy?" She'd been so absorbed in Luke, she'd failed to notice Buddy hadn't met them at the door. "Buddy?" Sydney disentangled herself from Luke and hurried down the hallway to the bedroom where she found the dog's hind legs sticking out from under the bed. "Buddy? What's wrong? Luke!" She reached under the bed to stroke the dog's body, and he let out another moan. "*What's wrong with him?*"

"I'll call Janey." Luke rushed from the room.

Sydney swallowed the hot ball of panic that lodged in her throat. "Please God," she whispered as she ran her hand gently over the dog's soft coat. "Please don't take Buddy, too. Please."

Luke returned a minute later. "She wants us to bring him to the vet clinic. I'll carry him to the truck. Help me get him out of there."

They tried to be gentle but Buddy's discomfort was amplified by their efforts to get him out from under the bed.

Tears burned her eyes as she spoke softly to Buddy, trying to settle him.

Buddy growled and snapped at Luke, just missing his hand.

"It's okay, boy," Luke said as he lifted Buddy as carefully as he could. "I know it hurts."

Stuck under a tidal wave of fear, Sydney couldn't seem to move.

"Syd." Luke's firm tone snapped her out of the daze she'd slipped into. "Go to the truck. I'll bring him out. Hurry, honey."

The urgency she heard in his voice spurred her to move

on unsteady legs. Her heart beat too fast, and her hands shook as she flew out of the house and into the truck.

Luke followed right behind her, carrying Buddy. He deposited the dog gently onto the bench seat, his head resting on Syd's lap. "There you go, boy," Luke said as he got in and started the truck. "Probably just something you ate that you shouldn't have."

"You really think that's all it is?" Syd asked, blinking back tears as she cradled Buddy's head. This could *not* be happening. "I don't know what I'll do if—"

Luke's hand covered hers. "Don't go there. He's going to be fine."

While Sydney hung on to his reassurances, the speed with which he maneuvered the winding roads where she'd been so frightened the night before told her he was worried, too.

Janey chugged a steaming cup of coffee in the vet clinic break room while Joe massaged her shoulders. She'd been tense from the moment Luke called Joe looking for her.

"What're you thinking?" Joe asked. He'd insisted on coming with her to the clinic.

"That I wish Doc's niece hadn't chosen this week to get married."

"There's nothing he could do for Buddy that you can't do, too."

"What if he needs surgery? Oh my God." She shuddered and fought back the need to puke and hyperventilate at the same time. "I've certainly never done that on my own."

"But you could. If you had to, you could."

"Keep reminding me of that, will you?"

"I'll be right here, baby. Whatever you need, I'm here."

She leaned into his strong embrace. "Thanks."

He turned her to face him. "You've been training for this your whole life, Janey. Whatever Buddy needs, you've seen Doc do it a million times."

"I know." Janey took another deep breath and released it. "You're right. I can do this." She rolled the tension from her shoulders and mentally prepared to fly solo.

"Luke said he's a young golden retriever, so it's probably nothing serious."

"Let's hope not. Otherwise, he's got a second-year vet student on his case."

Before Joe could reply, they heard the clinic's main door push open.

"Janey!" Luke called out.

"Showtime," she whispered to Joe, who squeezed her hand and released it.

"Right in here." She ushered Luke, who was carrying Buddy, and Sydney into an exam room. Janey took one look at the dog, who was clearly suffering, and could tell right away this was no simple case of an upset belly. *Figures*. The dog cried out in distress when she examined his rigid abdomen.

"Oh God. Buddy." Sydney seemed to be trying—and failing—to keep a lid on her panic. "Will he be okay? Janey, please, tell me he'll be okay."

"Let me get some films of his belly so we can see what's causing his pain." Drawing on her years of training and observation, Janey walked through the steps Doc would've taken—exam, X-rays, blood, pain management. She was shakier than she should've been, and it was easier to blame the single beer she'd had earlier than the fact that she had no business handling an emergency of this magnitude on her own.

The X-rays revealed a blockage in Buddy's intestines. She stepped into the exam room to update Sydney and Luke.

Janey pointed to the X-ray. "He swallowed something, and now it's lodged in his lower intestine. It's got to come out. Soon."

"What do we do?" Sydney asked, her face devoid of color.

The arm Luke had around Syd seemed to be the only thing keeping her on her feet.

Janey felt Joe's hand land on her back and was grateful for his support. She squared her shoulders, fortifying herself for what needed to happen. "Here's the thing— Doc Potter is off-island at a wedding. His backup vet was due to arrive today, but he missed the last boat and won't be here until morning."

Sydney moaned, and Luke tightened his hold on her.

"Can Buddy wait that long?" Luke asked.

"This kind of thing can go bad really quickly. He's still strong, and in my opinion, he'd be better able to withstand the surgery now than he will be in eight or nine hours."

"But if Doc Potter is off-island, who'll do it?" Sydney asked, wiping tears from her face.

Janey made an effort to keep her voice strong and confident. "I will. I've seen it done a hundred times, and I've assisted Doc in surgery since I was eighteen." Her stomach surged with nerves and nausea, but Janey kept her expression calm to reassure Sydney. "I'm not yet a veterinarian, but I'm Buddy's best hope."

"Let her do it, honey," Luke said. "She can save him. I know she can."

"Okay," Sydney said with only a hint of reluctance.

"I'll need you to sign a release and fill out some other paperwork while I get him prepped for surgery." Janey took a few steps to close the distance between them and hugged Syd. "I'll do everything I can. I promise."

"Thank you, Janey."

"I'll give you a minute with him." Janey and Joe stepped out of the room. She turned to Joe. "Will you track down Cal Maitland for me?" The island's new medical doctor had replaced Doc Robach when he retired the previous winter. "His on-call number is the same as Doc Robach's was. Should be in the phone book."

"What do you want me to tell him?"

"That I need him to assist in an emergency surgery. Tell him to hurry."

"Could I help?"

"I appreciate the offer, but I need someone who won't pass out cold on me when I've got poor Buddy's guts in my hands."

Joe winced. "When you put it that way, let me find Cal for you."

Janey went up on tiptoes to kiss her fiancé. "Thank you—for all the support. It helps."

He returned her kiss and gave her a tight hug. "I have no doubt you can do this, Janey. No doubt at all."

"Let's hope you're right." While Joe went to get a hold of Cal, Janey called Doc Potter to let him know what she was about to do in his clinic.

Chapter Thirteen

Luke watched Sydney pace from one end of the small waiting room to the other—at least a hundred times. She vibrated with tension and had bitten several of her nails to the quick, a habit he remembered her trying hard to break as a teenager.

"Syd, why don't you sit for a bit? You'll wear yourself out pacing like that."

She shook her head and kept moving.

Luke stood to block her path. He rested his hands on her shoulders, and was surprised when she shook him off.

"Don't." She stepped around him and continued to pace.

"Syd—"

"You don't have to wait. I'd understand if you wanted to get home."

If she'd punched him in the face, she couldn't have hurt him any more than she had with that cold, detached statement, as if he was nothing more than the guy who'd driven her there. Big Mac's warning about handwriting on the wall chose that moment to run through his mind.

Part of him wanted to walk out the door and leave her to deal with whatever might come. The other part of him couldn't bear to leave her alone if the news was bad. He returned to his seat to watch her pace.

Back and forth she went, another hundred times before Janey finally emerged.

Sydney ran to her. "Tell me he's okay."

"He did very well. We removed the blockage, which was a hunk of garbage bag, by the way."

"Oh, he found that on the beach! Remember, Luke?"

Suddenly, she was euphoric again. "I remember," he said.

"Why would he eat something like that?" Sydney asked Janey.

"You'd be surprised at the stuff they eat. Anything that tastes good is fair game."

"So he'll be all right?" Sydney asked.

"He'll be sore and slow for a while, but he should be just fine."

Sydney hugged Janey. "Thank you so much. I don't know what I'd ever do without him."

"No need to worry about losing him anytime soon. Come on back and see him for a minute, and then you should go home. He'll be out of it for a while."

"But I can't leave him alone."

"I'll be with him. He'll be sedated most of the day to keep him still and quiet, so you should get some sleep while you can." Janey led them into the recovery room where Buddy was attached to IVs. His belly had been shaved for the surgery.

"Have you met Dr. Cal Maitland?" Janey introduced Luke and Sydney to the tall, broad-shouldered doctor who offered them a friendly smile.

"Thank you for helping Janey," Syd said.

"She didn't need much help," he said in what sounded like a Texan drawl. "She knows what she's doing."

"Is it okay to touch him?" Syd asked as she tentatively approached Buddy.

"Sure," Janey said.

Sydney bent her head, pressed kisses to his face and ran a hand down his back. "I'll be back in a little while, Buddy. You get some rest, okay?" She kissed him again. "Love you, good dog."

Sydney turned to Janey. "Let me give you my cell number in case you need me."

A few minutes later, Luke followed Sydney out of the clinic to find the sky still dark but rippled with red streaks announcing sunrise. She was rigid with tension as they pulled out of the parking lot. Even though she was seated just a few feet from him, she seemed a million miles away.

"Would you mind terribly if I went home to my place?" she asked.

Luke gripped the steering wheel tighter. "Nope." Whatever she wanted. He certainly wasn't going to force himself on her.

A short time later, he pulled up to the Donovans' yellow house and let the truck idle. He had no idea what to say to her. Apparently, she didn't know either, because she sat there for a long moment before she finally looked at him.

"Thank you for staying all night."

"No problem."

"I'll see you later."

Luke said nothing as she got out of the truck and hurried into the house as if she couldn't move fast enough to get away from him. What the hell was that all about?

* * *

Sydney closed the front door and slid down to the floor. Only now that she was alone could she give in to the overwhelming fear and dread that had gripped her during the long night. Luke had already seen her unglued once. He didn't need to see it again.

Sobs shook her body, making her chest ache and her head pound. She kept telling herself Buddy was fine, the thing she'd most feared hadn't happened, but she'd come so close to losing the last remaining link to her family.

A soft knock on the door had her raising her head from her knees and wiping her face.

"Syd. Let me in. I know you're upset. You don't need to be alone."

Riveted by his voice, she couldn't bring herself to move.

"Come on, baby. Let me in."

Tears cascaded down her face.

"Sydney." His voice was so soft, so tender. "I'm not leaving you alone. I figured out about two seconds after you walked away that you were on the verge of a melt-down and didn't want me to see you that way again. But I'm not going anywhere. You can melt down every day if you need to. I'll be right here with you."

Sobs hiccupped through her, one right after the other. Suddenly, she was on her feet, opening the door. Braced in the doorway, arms over his head, his tall frame took up most of the space. He scooped her up with one arm and carried her into the house.

"Hold on," he whispered. "Hold on to me."

Sydney wrapped her arms and legs around him and buried her face in his neck, comforted by his familiar scent.

He lowered them into a big easy chair, settling her on

his lap. "It's okay, baby. Get it all out. I know how scared you must've been all night long. I was scared, too. Buddy is such a good boy, and he's been right by your side when you needed him most."

All the fear and dread and worry about Buddy melded with the ongoing grief she lived with every minute of every day, making her feel weak and defeated. She'd tried so hard to put her life together again, but two frightening episodes had set her back.

They sat there until long after the sun came up and lit the room. Luke stroked her hair and whispered soft words until no tears were left, until her sobs became an occasional hiccup. Telling her again to hold on, he lifted her and headed for the stairs, going directly to the room he knew was hers from years of throwing pebbles at her window.

He set her down next to the bed and helped her out of her clothes and into the oversize T-shirt she slept in. Next, he led her to the bathroom and waited outside the door for her before he tucked her into bed and stretched out next to her on top of the comforter.

"Come here, Syd."

She turned into his embrace, taking comfort from his strength.

His lips were warm against her forehead. "Sleep, baby. Close your eyes and let it go for a while. I've got you."

Sydney released a long shuddering breath and closed her eyes, relieved to let it all go, relieved to be surrounded by his unconditional love.

Janey found Joe asleep on the sofa in Doc's office. His arms were tossed over his head, and his long body was sprawled awkwardly over the too-short sofa. She delighted at the sight of him. He was always there for her when she needed him, and she couldn't wait to be married to him in two short weeks.

That she'd once fancied herself in love with someone else seemed so foolish now that she was completely, totally and forever in love with Joe.

Approaching the sofa, she bent to kiss his lips.

He woke with a start. "Oh. Hey, babe," he said, rubbing the sleep from his face. "How's Buddy?"

"Having a nice drug-induced snooze at the moment."

Joe reached for her. "You look beat. Can you close your eyes for a minute?"

"Maybe one or two."

Before she knew what had hit her, he had her arranged on top of him, her head tucked into his chest and his arms around her. "Very smooth."

"Why, thank you." He pressed his lips to her forehead. "Get some sleep. I'll listen for Buddy."

"He'll be out for a while yet. You could go home if you wanted to."

Joe tightened his hold on her. "I'm right where I want to be."

Janey let go of the tension from the long, stressful night. "Thanks for being here."

"You did a great job. You saved Buddy's life and Sydney's sanity. I'm so proud of you."

She raised her head to kiss him. "That's sweet of you to say."

He framed her face and held her still for another kiss. "Watching you take control of the situation—even though you had to be panicking on the inside—was very sexy." Another kiss, this one with a touch of tongue thrown in.

Janey smiled at him. "Is that so?"

"Mmm," Joe said as he outlined her mouth with the tip of his tongue. "Very."

Wanting to encourage him to keep kissing her, she squirmed on top of him.

"Watch the merchandise," he muttered.

She ran her hand down his belly to cup his erection. "This merchandise?"

"Is there any other?"

"Not for me."

Laughing, he said, "Good answer. You think Doc Potter has this place bugged?"

Janey took a look around her mentor's office. "I don't think so. Why?"

Joe tugged on the button to her jeans. "Because if he does, he's about to get one hell of a show."

"I thought you wanted me to sleep."

"You will. After."

Grant stood outside Abby's Attic, the downtown store Abby had opened three years ago. She had created an off-beat success of the Main Street boutique that was part gift shop, part toy store, part eclectic antiques. She'd opened the store after she came home from Los Angeles.

They'd moved there together right out of college to pursue his dream of writing movies. But as much as Grant loved the hustle and bustle of the city, Abby never had clicked with the place. She'd yearned for the simplicity of their home island, and nothing he said or did could convince her to stay once she made up her mind to go home. They'd been living together nearly ten years by then, and he couldn't imagine life without her. But more than anything, he wanted her to be happy. That she wasn't happy in LA was clear to everyone who knew her there.

Something she'd said to him before she left had remained with him ever since. "You can write anywhere, Grant. Anywhere in the whole world. Why can't you write in the one place where I want to be?"

Convinced he needed to stay where the work was, he'd let her go. They'd had a bicoastal relationship ever since and had been making it work—somehow—until last summer when he came home for Mac's wedding and Abby issued an ultimatum Grant hadn't seen coming.

She was all done waiting for him. Either he came home to be with her, or she was moving on with her life without him. He'd panicked, of course, and told her he needed one more year to turn things around in LA. Nothing had gone his way since the magical night he'd received the Oscar nearly three years ago—ironically right around the time Abby had left. Lately, it seemed, he couldn't get a job flipping burgers in Hollywood.

As it turned out, winning the big one had been a disaster for his career. He'd become his own worst nightmare: a one-hit wonder. The latest blow had come a week ago when he'd been rejected for a job he'd been promised by a producer friend. "I couldn't get it past the money people," his friend had said when he called to deliver the crushing news.

It was another disaster on top of the one that had come a few days before—news from home that Abby planned to marry someone else.

Grant had been awake all night after the phone call from the producer. At about three in the morning, it dawned on him that he'd had enough of Hollywood. He'd had enough of living without Abby, of pretending he had any kind of life at all without her by his side.

If he had any prayer of convincing her that she was making an enormous mistake by marrying anyone other than him, he had to go home and make things right with her. So he'd packed most of his stuff into storage, put his place in Malibu on the market, left his car with a friend to sell and headed for LAX.

Now, as he studied her storefront from the quiet sidewalk that would soon bustle with tourists, he could only hope he wasn't too late.

At nine o'clock on the dot, Abby appeared at the front door and turned the Closed sign to Open.

Watching her, Grant stood up a little straighter and waited for her to notice him there. But she turned away and went back into the store, leaving him standing there like a lovesick fool hoping the girl he favored would grace him with a glance.

He'd have to go in. For some reason, that frightened him. He'd pictured this playing out differently. She'd see him out there on the sidewalk, her eyes would widen, and she'd burst through the door to throw herself into his arms.

"It's not a movie, you asshole," he muttered to himself. For a guy who fancied himself rather good with words, he had no idea what he planned to say to her. All he knew was he had to say *something* to stop her from marrying the wrong man.

Steeling himself for whatever reaction she might have to his sudden reappearance, he cleared his throat, ran unsteady fingers through his hair and pushed open the door. Jingling bells announced his presence.

"Be right with you," she called from the back room.

Grant was hit right away with her favorite scents—lavender and sage and a hint of vanilla—and a memory of their years in LA when he arrived home each night to one of her favorite scents coming from the candle of the day. God, why hadn't he married her when he'd had the chance? When she'd been living in his house, their two lives entirely entwined? He'd made the mistake then of assuming nothing could ever come between them. He'd made the monumental mistake of putting his ambition ahead of her.

The store was cluttered and cozy and practical, just like the woman who owned it. As he waited for her, Grant's heart hammered in his chest, and his palms were suddenly damp.

"Hi there," Abby said. "Sorry to keep you waiting."

Grant looked up and their eyes met.

Her big brown eyes got even bigger, and she sucked in a sharp, deep breath when she saw him. "Grant."

"Hi, Abs." Her shiny dark hair had gotten long in the year since he'd last seen her, and as he contemplated the mouth that had fueled his fantasies for as long as he could remember, Grant realized he'd played this all wrong. He never should've given her a year to ponder life without him, and he feared he'd regret that for the rest of his days if he couldn't convince her to give him one more chance.

"What're you doing here? Janey's wedding isn't for two weeks yet." She kept her hands busy straightening shelves that didn't need straightening. A flash from the large diamond on her left hand sliced through him like a heated laser, leaving him breathless and anxious.

"I've come home. To stay." As he said the words she'd waited years to hear, he braced himself for her fury. It was the least of what he deserved.

"Is that so?"

Grant took a step closer to her. "I'm home, Abby."

"Your mother must be pleased."

His *mother*? "Is she the only one?"

"Your dad, Janey and Mac, too, I assume."

What the hell was wrong with her? Here he was telling her he'd finally left Los Angeles. He'd finally come home to her, and she didn't really seem to care. How was that possible after the years they'd spent loving each other so passionately?

"What about you?" Another step closer. "Are you at all happy to see me?"

"Of course I am." Her eyes flashed with emotion, which gave him hope. She began refolding a pile of perfectly folded Gansett Island T-shirts.

"I'm sorry for making you wait so long. I know now that was wrong. I shouldn't have gone back last year after you told me how much you wanted to get married and have a family."

"You did what you needed to," she said in a flat, emotionless tone he'd never heard from her before. "I certainly understand that."

Grant reached out to stop her from refolding another shirt. "Abby, what's wrong with you?"

"Nothing," she said, raising her chin defiantly. "Everything is great with me. I finally have everything I've ever wanted."

"But what about us?"

"There is no more us, Grant. I told you that a year ago. You made your choice, and I made mine. It's over."

He heard the words, but everything in him rejected them. "No. It's not over."

The bells on the door jingled again, and Grant bit back a swear of frustration. He wanted to tell whoever it was to get the hell out, but that would hardly help his case.

"Hey, darlin'," a deep voice drawled behind Grant.

"Brought you a caffeine boost. What a crazy night I had operating on a dog! Oh, sorry, didn't see you had a customer."

Right before Grant's eyes, Abby lit up at the sight of the guy who'd brought the coffee. The *fiancé*, he presumed.

Grant pushed back his shoulders and turned to take in the competition. The guy was tall, he'd give him that, with blond hair—long blond hair. Since when did Abby go for the longhaired type? Muscular, blue-eyed and a goofy lovesick smile aimed at Abby that made Grant see red.

"Ahh, Cal. Come meet my old friend, Grant McCarthy. Grant, my fiancé, Dr. Cal Maitland."

As Cal crushed his hand, Grant tried to fathom being introduced as Abby's "old friend" to her *fiancé*. *I was the love of her freaking life!* Had she completely forgotten that?

"Good to meet you, Grant. You in town for a while?"

"Yeah." Grant cast a long glance at Abby, who radiated discomfort. "I'll be here awhile. As long as it takes, in fact."

"For what?" Abby asked, alarmed.

Grant leaned in to make sure only she could hear him. "To fix this." He nodded to Cal on the way by. "You all have a nice day."

Chapter Fourteen

Luke thought he was dreaming when he woke to voices downstairs. He sat up, ran his fingers through his hair and was about to go see who was there, when Sydney's mother appeared at the bedroom door.

She gasped at the sight of him on Syd's bed and scurried away. *Fabulous*. Thank God he'd stayed dressed and on top of the comforter earlier. Could've been worse, he reasoned. While he really wanted Sydney to sleep for a while longer, he needed to let her know they'd been found out.

He leaned over to kiss her cheek and brushed the hair from her face. "Syd." As he waited for her to rouse, his eyes landed on the photo of Seth and the kids next to her bed. Luke wished he had time to study the picture, but he had more pressing concerns at the moment. "Sydney."

"Hmm." Her eyes flew open. "Buddy. Is it Buddy?"

Luke shook his head. "Your parents are back."

"Ugh, tell me you're kidding."

"Wish I was. Your mom saw us."

"Oh."

The single word didn't give Luke much insight into

what she was thinking as urgent whispers from her parents filtered up the stairs.

Sydney groaned. "I'm so not up for dealing with this right now."

"You want me to go?"

"No! I'm not sneaking you out of here like we've got something to hide. I'm almost thirty-six years old, for crying out loud."

Luke grinned at her feistiness, relieved to see a spark of life back in eyes that had gone dull with worry over Buddy. "And you just got caught in bed with your high school boyfriend."

That drew the first genuine smile he'd seen since they came home to find Buddy in distress.

"It's a *scandal*."

He kissed her. "I'll understand if you'd rather deal with them on your own."

"Wimp."

"You betcha."

Laughing at his grimace, she got up to find a robe and stepped into the bathroom. After he took a turn, they met at the doorway to the bedroom. Sydney reached for his hand and held it tight as they headed for the stairs. The gesture warmed something in Luke that he hadn't known was cold.

They descended the stairs as a unit, but Luke's heart pounded with dread and anxiety. Mr. and Mrs. Donovan had never tried to hide their contempt for the lowly dockworker who'd loved their fair-haired only child. Luke wondered if facing them would be any easier as an adult than it'd been as a kid. He doubted it.

The Donovans waited for them in the kitchen, their faces tight with displeasure. Sydney released Luke's hand to hug and kiss her parents. They seemed to soften as they embraced their daughter.

"What're you doing back so soon?" Syd asked.

"We were concerned about you being here alone all month," her mother said with a pointed look for Luke. "But it seems you haven't been alone."

"Luke has been a great friend to me, Mom."

"I'm sure," Mr. Donovan said under his breath.

Luke knew if he didn't get out of there—immediately— he was going to say something he'd regret. Because he was no longer nineteen and easily intimidated, he kissed Syd's forehead. "I'll see you later."

Sydney followed him out of the house. "Luke, wait. Please don't go."

Turning to her, he hated the anxiety he saw in her expression. "It's fine. You need to talk to them, and I need to go before I make it worse."

She put her hand on his arm. "I don't want you to go."

"I know you don't, and that matters, believe me."

"Will I see you later?"

"That's up to you." He ran a finger over her cheek. "You know where to find me."

"I'm sorry about this."

He attempted a wry grin, hoping to boost her spirits. "Some things never change, huh?"

"And other things do. I'm not beholden to them anymore. I love and respect them, and I owe them so much for the way they propped me up after the accident, but they don't run my life."

He glanced at the house to find Mrs. Donovan peeking at them through the blinds. "I'm not the one who needs to hear that."

"I know," she said, resigned.

"This is the last thing you need on top of everything

with Buddy. If you want me to disappear for a while, I can do that. Whatever you need."

"Don't you *dare* disappear on me!"

Her fierce tone drew a smile from him. "I'll see you," he said, stealing a quick kiss.

"Yes, you will."

Sydney stood in the driveway until Luke's truck disappeared from view, then squared her shoulders and went inside.

"Honestly," her mother, Mary Alice, said, "what in the world are you doing with *him*?"

"And where's Buddy?" her dad, Allan, added.

Gritting her teeth to keep from shrieking at them, she said, "Buddy's at the vet clinic." She told them what'd happened the night before, which clearly upset them. "Luke was right by my side through the whole ordeal. He's been very good to me."

"Because he wants you back," Mary Alice said. "Can't you see that?"

"I know he does, because he's told me as much."

"Sydney," Mary Alice said in that disapproving tone that reminded Syd so much of the summer she was nineteen and her parents had convinced her she could do *so much better* than Luke. As if she'd read Syd's mind, her mother added, "You could do so much better."

Furious, Syd threw her hands in the air. "There it is! The famous line! Guess what? There's hardly *anyone* better than Luke. He's one of the kindest, sweetest, gentlest people I've ever known. *He* is too good for *me*, if you want the truth."

"I find that hard to believe," Allan said.

"Is he kinder and sweeter than Seth was?" Mary Alice asked, hands on hips, girded for battle.

The question shocked Sydney to the core, causing her eyes to fill and her throat to close. She ran upstairs and started throwing clothes into a backpack.

One thing was patently clear to her—it was time to take control of her life. And what felt good and right to her at the moment was being with Luke. Whether she was ready to commit to him permanently, she couldn't say, but that didn't need to be decided today or even tomorrow.

Her mother came to the door as Sydney zipped her backpack.

"I'm sorry. I shouldn't have said that about Seth."

"No, you shouldn't have."

"I don't want to see you going backward, Syd. You need to be moving forward."

"That's exactly what I'm doing."

"You're vulnerable, honey. Luke knows that. He's taking advantage—"

Sydney spun around. "Do *not* finish that thought. He has been nothing but patient and accommodating and supportive. I feel better being with him than I have since before my life was shattered. Don't take that away from me by being narrow-minded about who and what you think he is." She zipped her bag. "You don't know him at all because you never bothered to take the time to know him. You were too busy judging him for all the things you thought he lacked."

"We only want what's best for you—then and now."

"If that's the case, then trust me to decide that for myself. I'm not a child anymore, Mom. I won't let you run off the man I love because you fear he won't fit in at the country club."

"Mary Alice," her father said, startling both women. "She has to find her own way, even if we don't approve."

"If you knew Luke at all, Dad, you'd approve. Trust me on that, too."

"The boy never had an ounce of ambition," he said. "He's doing the same job he did as a kid. We wanted better for you than that."

"He was *filled* with ambition," Sydney said. "He earned a scholarship to college that he turned down to stay here to take care of his sick mother. Doesn't he get any credit for that?"

"Why didn't he go after she died?" Allan asked.

"I don't know, but it wasn't due to a lack of ambition. I can assure you of that." Sydney hoisted her backpack onto her shoulder and slid her feet into flip-flops.

"Where are you going?" Mary Alice asked.

"Into town to check on Buddy."

"And then?"

"To Luke's."

"We haven't seen you in weeks," Mary Alice said. "We were hoping to have dinner tonight."

"If that's what you wanted, maybe you could've been a little nicer to my friend." Sydney headed for the stairs, and they followed her.

"When will we see you?" Allan asked.

Sydney grabbed her purse, keys and cell phone off the counter. "I don't know." She headed for the door but stopped herself, knowing she couldn't leave them like this. If the accident had taught her anything, it was to leave nothing left unsaid. Turning to them, she studied their faces, hating how dramatically they'd aged in the last year.

"I love you both very much. I never would've survived everything that happened without your love and support.

A long time ago, I made the mistake of allowing you to tell me how I was supposed to think and feel, and a decent, honorable young man was terribly hurt by my choices. I won't make that mistake again."

The moment she was buckled into her car, all her bravado drained away, leaving her shaken and rattled. She'd just stood up to her parents for the first time in thirty-six years. Declaring her independence should've left her feeling exhilarated. Instead she was sad that she'd needed to do it in the first place.

Ned walked the length of Ocean Road twice before he stopped at the gravel drive that led to the Sturgil place. Old Wendell Sturgil had been a school friend of his a hundred years ago. Now Wendell's son lived in the family home, married to the daughter of the only woman Ned had ever loved.

Francine Tornquist had stolen his young heart the first time he laid eyes on her, fresh off the ferry to work the summer at the Beachcomber damn near thirty-two years ago now. From his perch at the cabstand, he'd seen her struggling with bags and had insisted on walking her and her luggage up the hill and across Ocean Road to the hotel.

She'd had fiery red hair and a figure that made Ned want to drool just thinking about it, even all these years later. That first summer, he'd made it a point to put himself in her path every day until she finally agreed to go out with him. Ned had just about worked up the nerve to ask her to marry him when Bobby Chester showed up on the island with a gang of pals for a bachelor party weekend. Francine never looked at Ned again after smooth-talking Bobby swept her off her feet.

For years after Bobby left her alone with two little girls to care for, Ned had hoped Francine would come to him, but she never had. Now here he was lurking in her driveway wishing he'd had the nerve to approach her after her good-for-nothing husband left her to fend for herself and her kids. Back then his pride had kept him away.

Seeing young Luke Harris together again with the girl he'd once loved had given Ned the courage to take a chance. Well, it had given him the courage to lurk in the woman's driveway anyway. He'd heard through the grapevine that Francine was living above the dance studio where her younger daughter, Tiffany, taught dance classes. Her other daughter, Maddie, was married to Little Mac McCarthy. Happy as clams, the two of them.

"Well," he said, slapping the dust off his best khaki shorts, "here goes nuttin'." He'd even combed his hair and trimmed his beard in honor of the occasion. He couldn't remember the last time he'd done either. Head held high, he marched up the driveway, past the house where Jim and Tiffany lived with their young daughter, to the stairway that led to the apartment.

Ignoring the boogie skip of his heart and the tremble of his hands, Ned climbed the stairs and rapped on the door.

It cracked open and one green eye peered out at him. "What'd you want?"

"It's me, Ned. Saunders." Why should she recognize him? After all, they'd managed to live on the same small island and steer clear of each other for thirty-two years.

The door opened a little farther, and he could see those years hadn't been kind to his poor Francine. Then again, an old codger like him probably didn't set her heart to pitter-patter, neither. "Ned."

"That's m'name. Don't wear it out." *Stupid! What a stupid thing to say!*

She seemed genuinely flabbergasted to see him. "What're you doing here?"

"I, um, I came to see if ya might like to, um, if ya'd consider, that is—"

"Spit it out already!"

"Have dinner with me. Tonight."

Her mouth fell open in surprise. "You want to go out. With me?"

"That's what I said, ain't it?"

"Why?"

Ned stared at her, dumbfounded. Why did he want to go out with her? Because from the minute he met her, he'd never wanted to go out with anyone else. That's why. But he couldn't exactly tell her that, could he? "Because."

"Because why?"

"Look, do ya wanna go or not? Won't hurt my feelings if ya say no."

"It won't?"

He let out a growl of frustration that seemed to amuse her. "Were ya always this difficult and I just don't remember?"

"Perhaps." She studied him for a long, *long* time during which he had no earthly idea what she was thinking. He'd begun to sweat when she finally took a deep breath. "Do you know about my troubles?"

"I know about yer troubles." Who on the island didn't know that writing bad checks had put her in jail for three months last year? How he wished she'd come to him when she'd fallen on hard times. He'd have taken care of her *and* her kids. They wouldn't have wanted for anything. But she hadn't come to him. Someday maybe she'd tell him why. For now, he was just hoping for dinner.

"And you still want to go out with me?"

"Ya've just about talked me out of it," he said in a teasing tone.

That drew an honest, genuine smile that nearly stopped his fragile heart. *There* was the Francine he'd once known, before life and circumstances had stolen her joy. Maybe together they could somehow get it back.

"I'd be honored to go to dinner with the nicest boy I've ever known."

Shocked to his very soul by the compliment, he wondered if that was regret he saw in her expression. Clearing his throat, he said, "Uh, ya wanna go now?"

"But it's only five o'clock."

"I ain't doin' nothing. Are you?"

"No," Francine said, still smiling. "I'm not doing anything at all."

Chapter Fifteen

Sydney arrived at Luke's and was relieved to see his truck parked outside the house. She'd wondered if he had gone to work. Donning the backpack, she stuck her head inside the house and called for him. When she received no reply, she walked across the lawn to see if he was down at the beach but didn't see him there either. Had he taken the rowboat out on the pond?

She turned to look back at the house, and her eyes settled on the barn-shaped garage that had been added to the place since she first knew him. At the garage, she went around to the front. The double doors were open, and Luke was applying a coat of varnish to a staggeringly beautiful vintage powerboat.

"Wow," she said. "That's gorgeous."

He looked up, and she saw surprise and pleasure in his eyes as they skirted over her in a visual inspection that made her tingly in some interesting places.

"Is it yours?" she asked of the boat as she came closer to get a better look.

Shaking his head, he said, "Belongs to a guy in Falmouth."

"How'd it end up here?" She wanted to run a hand over the smooth, glossy surface but was afraid to touch it.

"Something I do on the side. Kind of a hobby."

"What do you do exactly?"

"Restore them." He gestured to the workbench behind him. "Before pictures are over there."

Above the bench a carved sign read Harris Boat Works. Sydney wandered over to view photos of what could only be called a wreck. Next to them was another photo of the boat in its prime. She whirled around. "*That's the same boat?* As the one in the pictures?"

"Uh-huh," he said with a chuckle.

"Oh my God, Luke! It's amazing! How long did it take?"

"Coupla months. I fit it in when I have time. Tough during the summer when I'm working so much at McCarthy's."

"This is really incredible. I'm so impressed."

His lips formed a small smile. "Thanks."

"How did you get into this? When?"

"Let's see, Miss Twenty Questions, must've been about fifteen years ago. Big Mac found an old junker in a boatyard on the mainland and brought it back to the island. Mrs. McCarthy was giving him grief about keeping it in the driveway at the White House," he said, referring to the name the locals had given the McCarthy's home, "so I told him he could bring it over here. I started tinkering with it—"

"Meaning you completely restored it when he wasn't looking."

"Something like that," he said with a laugh. "He was blown away, and in typical Big Mac fashion, he told *everyone*. He keeps it at the marina where he can show it off. Next thing I knew, people were calling me about restoring their old boats. One thing led to another." He shrugged. "Word of mouth."

"How many do you do a year?"

"Three or four."

"They must pay you a boatload—no pun intended."

He snickered at the joke. "I do all right."

"How do they get them here?"

"Some, like this beauty, come over on the ferry. Others come under their own steam, and we haul them out over here."

"I bet you've got people waiting in line for you."

"The list is tacked up over the bench."

Sydney glanced up and found at least thirty names and phone numbers on the piece of notebook paper. "You're gifted, Luke. Truly gifted."

Shrugging, he said, "Don't know about that. Just something I do for fun."

Sydney studied him as he applied the varnish in smooth, even strokes. "Why didn't you tell me about this? When we were talking about your life the other night. You never mentioned this."

"Didn't think of it, to be honest." He stepped back from the boat to study his work. Seeming satisfied, he put the can of varnish on the bench and hammered the cover on. "You going camping or something?"

She realized he meant the backpack that still sat on her shoulders. "Oh, well, I seem to be homeless at the moment. I was wondering if you might be willing to take in a stray."

"Lucky for you, we only accept the finest of pedigrees at this shelter."

Sydney smiled at the compliment.

"Big fight with the folks?"

"Not so big."

"Then how'd you end up homeless?"

Cornered, Sydney winced. "At least I stood up to them this time. That's progress."

"What'd they have to say?"

"Something about wanting me to go forward, not backward."

Leaning against the bench with his arms folded across his chest, he looked powerful and sexy and so perfectly perfect. A man in his prime, from the top of his silky dark head to the bottom of his size thirteen feet. "Do you feel like you've taken a step backward being with me again?"

"No! If anything, I feel like I'm moving forward again. Finally."

"I don't want to come between you and your parents, Syd."

"We'll work it out. Eventually. Don't worry about it."

He tilted his head, beckoning. "Come here."

She dropped the backpack to the floor and walked around the boat to stand in front of him.

Even though he kept his arms crossed, she could tell by the hungry look in his eyes that he was making an effort to keep his hands to himself. "Are you okay?" he asked.

"Strangely enough, I'm quite well, thank you."

His lips quirked with amusement. "And Buddy? How is he?"

"They want to keep him one more night and then maybe let him come home tomorrow. The substitute vet said Janey did an amazing job. He was really impressed."

"I'm glad he's doing so well."

"He was happy to see me but still kind of loopy. They said I could visit him again later, but they wanted him to rest, and having me there got him all excited."

"I know how he feels."

"Luke," she said, her face heating under his intense scrutiny. "Does this mean you're going to take me in?"

Sighing dramatically, he said, "I suppose if I have to." He turned to reach for a can of turpentine and dumped some in a bucket to soak his brushes.

Sydney stepped back from the overwhelming odor of the turpentine but stayed close enough to watch him clean up his bench. "Could I ask you something?"

"Sure."

She hesitated, but curiosity won out over her better judgment. "How come you didn't go to college after your mother died?"

His body went rigid as he stacked paint cans on the bench. He was quiet long enough that she wondered if he was going to answer her. "Who's asking? You or your parents?"

Resting her hand on his back, she discovered tense muscles. "I am."

"My mother was sick for a long time. She didn't have health insurance, so her illness wiped us out. We had to take a second mortgage on this place."

As she let her hand drop to her side, Sydney was already sorry she'd asked. "Oh. I see."

He turned to her. "No, you don't."

She was startled by the bitterness she heard in his tone and saw on his face.

"All you see is a house full of old furniture where nothing has changed since the last time you were here when in fact, a lot has changed."

"That's not all I see, Luke." With her hand on his face, she compelled him to look at her. "That's not all I see."

"I didn't go to college because by the time she died, my scholarship was long gone, and I had a choice of holding on to this place or paying for school. Since I couldn't

imagine living anywhere else, I chose to keep the house."
He finally looked her right in the eye. "I've never regretted
that."

"This is a great place. I totally get why you'd want to
keep it."

"I know your parents think I've been standing still all
this time, working the same job I did as a kid, but that's
not the case. I paid off that second mortgage—and the
first one—years ago. I own this place free and clear."

"That doesn't matter to me."

"It matters to them."

"They just want what's best for me. I told them they
have to trust me to figure that out for myself."

He released a frustrated growl and rolled his hands
into fists that he propped on his hips. "I really want to
touch you right now, but I'm filthy."

"I don't care."

Smelling of varnish and paint thinner, his hands
framed her face and tilted it up to meet his intense gaze.
He kissed her forehead, her nose, and then her lips.
"There's nothing I wouldn't do to ensure your happiness,
to make you smile, to hear the laugh that seems to come
all the way from your toes."

"Luke . . ."

"I don't know if I'm what's best for you. Only you know
that. But I guarantee you no one else will ever want you
the way I do."

Her eyes fluttered closed as his lips found hers in a
hungry, desperate kiss that had her clinging to him. Then,
he slowed it down, softening his lips and teasing with his
tongue.

Sydney dipped her fingers under his T-shirt, finding
the warm skin on his back. A tremble rippled through
him, and she loved knowing she'd had that effect on him.

He tore his lips free and turned his attention to her neck, sucking gently on her skin and running his tongue back and forth. "I want you, Syd." His raspy whisper sent goose bumps down her spine, and she strained against him, needing to get closer. He withdrew from her, grabbed her hand and made for the garage door, stopping on the way by to scoop up her backpack.

Sydney half ran, half walked to keep up with him as he closed the distance between the garage and house. She'd never seen him quite like this before, and her heart beat fast with excitement and anticipation.

"Luke, I—"

The moment they were in the house, his mouth came down hard on hers, stealing the words right off her lips. He moved fast to get rid of clothing until they were both naked and trembling. While his hands moved over her reverently, he kissed her as if he'd never get enough.

Sydney gave herself over to him, willing to go anywhere he wanted to take her.

With his hands on her bottom, he lifted her and drew her nipple into his hot mouth as he walked them into the bedroom. He lowered her to the bed and came down on top of her, feasting on one breast and then the other.

Sydney raised her hips, seeking him.

Suddenly, he stopped, rested his head on her chest and took several deep breaths.

She ran her fingers through his hair. "What is it?"

He didn't say anything for a long moment. "I'm being too rough with you."

"No, you're not."

"I put a mark on you," he said, tracing a finger over a red spot on her breast.

"I don't care."

He followed his finger with his lips. "I do."

"Don't treat me like I'm fragile, Luke. Please don't."

"You're not fragile." Brushing the hair back from her face, he kissed her. "You're the strongest person I've ever known."

She shook her head. "No, I'm not. I fall apart over the slightest thing."

"Coming home to find your dog gravely ill is not a slight thing, and you didn't fall apart. You held it together all night long."

"And then I fell apart."

"Which is perfectly normal."

"If you say so."

"I say so," he said, drawing her into another heated kiss.

"Make love to me, Luke, and don't hold back."

"So you want it hard and fast?" he asked with a sexy grin.

"I'll take whatever you want to give."

He kissed his way from her lips to her neck to the slight abrasion on her breast. "Is that so?"

"Uh-huh."

As he sucked her nipple deep into his mouth, he slid two fingers into her and pressed the heel of his hand against her clit, teasing and pressing and backing off until she was out of her mind.

The combined sensations built and grew and finally burst, sending Sydney spiraling into orgasm, sharp and hot and intense. By the time she returned to earth, he hovered above her, his cock poised at her entrance.

"Welcome back," he said, looking down at her with amusement dancing in his eyes.

Sydney reached for him and tugged his mouth down to hers. "Now, Luke. Please."

"How can I say no when you ask me so nicely?" He flexed his hips and sank into her in one deep thrust.

Sydney gasped and clutched his backside to hold him still as she struggled to accommodate him.

"Babe," he said through gritted teeth.

When she released him, he withdrew and then pounded into her.

Sweat beaded on his brow and his breath came in short pants, but he never let up in the fierce possession.

"Come for me, Syd," he urged. Reaching between them, he coaxed another explosive climax from her before he threw his head back and let himself go.

For a long time afterward, he rested on top of her, breathing hard.

Syd wiped the dampness from his brow and kissed his forehead. "Thanks for taking me in."

He grunted out a laugh. "It's a terrible hardship, but somehow I'll get by."

Chapter Sixteen

Grant knew there was nothing to be gained by drinking himself into a stupor, but that didn't stop him from trying. Whatever it took to find some relief from the relentless pain that had started when he saw *his* Abby with another man who seemed to think he had some sort of *claim* on her.

With the wave of his hand, Grant ordered another beer.

Chelsea, the bartender at the Beachcomber, set the bottle down in front of him. "You're really slugging them back tonight, Grant."

He graced her with his most charming smile. "I'm thirsty."

"How're you getting home?"

Shrugging, he took another big drink of beer. "I'll call a cab."

She scooped up the keys he'd left on the bar—keys to the motorcycle he'd borrowed from Mac. "I'll hang on to these. Just in case you forget." Leaving him with a saucy grin, she moved on to other customers.

Grant ran his fingers through his hair, contemplating the complete mess he'd made of his life. The more he drank, the worse he felt and the more he realized he had no one to blame but himself. He'd taken it all for granted—his career, his relationship with Abby, his future. Everything.

He had no idea how long he sat there staring at his beer bottle before someone slid onto the stool next to him.

Chelsea put a bottle of light beer down in front of the newcomer.

"Thank you, sweetheart."

Jarred by the familiar voice, Grant turned to find his father sitting next to him. "What're you doing here?"

"Heard you were attempting to tie one on over here and figured I'd rather come get you here than bail your ass out of jail."

"You've never had to bail my ass out of jail. That was Mac and Joe."

Big Mac snorted and took a swig of beer. "That's right. You were always my good boy—the smart one."

"For all the good it's done me."

"What the hell's that supposed to mean?"

"In case you haven't noticed, my life has gone to shit."

"How so?"

"Really, Dad, do I have to spell it out for you?"

"I guess you do. Catch me up. Last I knew, you were flying high with an Oscar in one hand and the girl you loved holding the other. What happened?"

"Wish I knew."

"If you don't know, who does?"

"I fucked up, okay? Is that what you want to hear? I'm a total and complete fuck-up." Grant grabbed his bottle, finished off the beer and signaled for Chelsea to bring him another one.

She looked to his father, who shook his head.

"Goddamn it, Dad! You can't do that. I'm not a child!"

"Then quit acting like one."

Grant couldn't remember his father ever using that particular tone with him. With Mac, Adam and Evan, yes, but never with him. Suddenly, he was stone-cold sober, and the pain resurfaced with a relentless disregard for his desire to forget all about what he'd seen earlier—*his* woman with her new man. His eyes burned, and Grant knew he had to get out of there, or he was going to lose it in front of the most important person in his life.

He tossed some bills on the bar and walked out. The cool air blowing in off the ocean helped to further sober him up. Clearly, he hadn't had anywhere near enough to drink if he was still focused on Abby's indifference toward him earlier. After all they'd been to each other for most of their lives, how could she look at him the same way she would a stranger off the street?

A hand on his arm stopped him from staggering down the stairs from the Beachcomber's back porch.

Grant spun around, prepared to do battle, but all the fight went out of him when he saw his father towering over him. "Let me go," he said, attempting to wrench his arm free of his father's grasp.

"What's going on, son? This isn't like you."

"It's more like me than you think." He'd been drinking way too much lately, and he knew it. But he had to so something, *anything*, to numb the pain.

"Come on, pal. Let's go home and get some sleep. We'll figure this out in the morning."

Because he couldn't think of a better plan, Grant allowed his father to propel him to the truck, which was parked on the street.

"I forgot to get the keys to the bike from Chelsea," Grant muttered as they went past Mac's motorcycle in the parking lot.

"I got 'em." Big Mac held the truck's passenger door for Grant and then walked around the front to the driver's side.

Grant tipped his head back, hoping he could make it home without puking. That would be the perfect end to a perfect day. When his father reached across him to buckle his seat belt, Grant felt like a total moron. "Sorry."

"Ain't no big thing."

The sound of laughter outside the truck caught their attention.

Big Mac gasped. "What the . . ."

Grant and his father stared at the duo walking past— Ned, arm in arm with a woman, totally oblivious to anyone watching them as they were deep in conversation peppered with frequent laughter. Grant had never seen his father's best friend looking so animated.

"Is that *Maddie's mother*?" Grant whispered, as if they might hear him.

"Sure is. Well, I'll be damned."

After Ned and Francine were past the truck, Grant glanced over at his father, who looked like he'd been struck by lightning.

"What's going on with them?" Grant asked.

"I have no earthly idea." Big Mac snapped out of his stupor to start the truck. "But let me tell you, if *he's* somehow managed to work things out with *her*, there's certainly hope for you, boyo."

The comment struck Grant's funny bone, and before long, his father joined in. A good laugh with his dad was exactly what Grant needed.

Ned had never been happier than he was during the evening with Francine. Well, that wasn't entirely true. The last time he'd been this happy was the last time he'd been with her. She just did it for him, and she always had. It was that simple.

He'd taken her for a fancy dinner at Domenic's and let her fuss over the prices as he plied her with seafood and wine. Afterward, they came back to town and took a walk along the waterfront. They'd talked about everything— except the one thing Ned most wanted to know. How had Bobby Chester managed to make her forget all about him during the course of one weekend?

He couldn't exactly blurt out the question over clams and white wine. And after such a wonderful evening, he was terrified of scaring her off by reopening an old wound.

They approached the driveway that led to Francine's place, and Ned slowed his steps to prolong their time together. All too soon, they reached the foot of the stairs that led to her place.

"Would you like to come up for a cup of coffee?" she asked

"Sure." Relieved their evening wasn't over quite yet, Ned followed her up the stairs into the small apartment.

"Maddie lived here a few years," Francine said as she measured the grounds and poured water into the coffee-maker. "She was living here when she met Mac."

"I remember," Ned said, amused to realize she was nervous and chattering to fill the empty spaces.

As the coffee began to brew, Francine turned and leaned against the counter. "You haven't asked me about Bobby."

Ned suppressed a gasp at the sudden introduction of the one topic they'd avoided during their hours together. "I don't figure it's any of my beeswax."

"Of course it is."

"How's that?"

"Well, if I hadn't met him, perhaps I would've been married to you these last thirty or so years."

Uncertain of what to do about his sweaty palms, Ned jammed his hands into his pockets. "Ya reckon so?"

Francine tipped her head to study him. "You were going to ask me, weren't you?"

"Mighta thought about it. Once or twice."

Her smile was sad and didn't reach her eyes. "I don't regret marrying him. If I hadn't, I wouldn't have my girls. Even though we had it kind of rough after he left, somehow we made it through, and they're good girls."

"I don't know Tiffany, but Maddie's a lovely gal. She's made my friend's boy very happy, which makes me happy."

Her lips flattened with displeasure. "You're in awfully tight with those McCarthys."

"Big Mac is my best friend. Has been since long before I first laid eyes on ya. His kids are my kids."

"His wife had me thrown in jail."

Ned kept his tone gentle when he said, "Now, Francine, we both know better than that, don't we?" He knew full well that Linda had reported Francine only after she passed a fifth bad check in the bar at McCarthy's Gansett Inn, and that Linda had agonized over the decision. But he kept that information to himself, knowing it wouldn't matter much to Francine after spending three months in jail.

She turned away to reach for coffee mugs. "I should've known you'd side with her."

"I ain't on no one's side. Shit happens. The past belongs in the past."

Facing him again, she said, "If that's the case, why'd you come here today?"

Cornered, Ned had no idea how to answer that. "Well, I, uh . . ."

"Doesn't matter."

Drawing in a deep breath, he closed the distance between them and was gratified when her eyes widened in surprise. "Does matter." He reached out to touch the soft hair she still dyed red. "I came here today because I never stopped thinking aboutcha or that summer we spent together."

"Oh. Really?" That last word came out more like a croak.

"Really."

"Even after I married Bobby?"

"'Specially then. Never could understand what ya saw in that smooth-talking charmer."

"No, you wouldn't. He was the opposite of you in every possible way."

"I know I wasn't as handsome or smooth or full of sweet talk the way he was."

"No, you weren't."

Ned didn't want to be offended, even after all this time, but there it was.

She rested her hand on his chest, and he wondered if she could feel how fast his heart was beating. "You were loyal and faithful and kind. I learned the hard way that those qualities are far more important than handsome or smooth or sweet-talking."

"Why didn't ya come to me? After he left, why didn't ya come?"

"Aw, Ned. I couldn't have done that to you. I walked away—left you without so much as a howdy do. I can't believe you expected me to show up at your doorstep with two little girls in tow after what I did to you."

"I woulda taken ya all. I woulda given you and yer girls everything."

Her eyes sparkled with tears. "Don't say that. You don't mean that."

With his hand on her chin, he compelled her to look at him. "I mean that." Before he could talk himself out of it, he brushed a soft kiss over her lips and drew her into a hug. "I mean it."

"Why didn't you come to me?" she asked, her voice muffled against his chest.

"Foolish pride," he said with a rough chuckle. "Stupid, stupid pride. For all the good it did me."

"I had my pride, too. I was convinced he'd come back. I probably would've sent you away."

"And now?" He drew back so he could look down at her upturned face. "Are ya still waiting for him to come back?"

She shook her head. "Not anymore, but Tiffany has been trying to find him for a while now."

The statement sent a shaft of shock and fear through Ned. "Is that so?" he managed to ask.

"She has no memory of him. I suppose it's natural she'd be curious."

"Does Maddie know she's looking for him?"

Francine shook her head. "Maddie remembers him. She remembers him leaving. The poor thing sat in the window watching the ferry landing for weeks, hoping he'd come back. I don't think she'd be happy to hear her sister is looking for him."

"Do ya hope she finds him?"

"I want Tiffany to get the closure she needs. Beyond that, I don't hope for much of anything anymore."

"It don't have to be that way, Francine. Ya got lots of years left to live yet. No reason they can't be happy years."

"Is that so?"

He nodded and had to fight back the urge to kiss her a second time.

"Will you come and see me again, Ned?"

"I'll come see ya."

She released a long sigh of what sounded like relief. "Good."

Chapter Seventeen

Luke went back to work after two unscheduled days off expecting some major ribbing from the guys at the marina. He had no doubt they all knew what he'd been doing and who he'd been doing it with. Thinking about the time with Syd made him feel giddy and goofy and hopeful. So very hopeful.

They'd spent the entire afternoon and evening in bed and had even eaten dinner in bed. He was stiff and sore and achy from what he'd demanded of his body, and he could only imagine how she would feel when she finally stirred. She'd been out cold when he left for work.

It had become clear to him during the most intense sexual marathon of his life that he'd never get enough of her. No matter how many times he had her, he only wanted her more afterward, and he suspected the same was true for her. After the most amazing night of his life, Luke felt like they'd finally reached a point where he could relax a bit. Even though they'd yet to say the words, he was certain she loved him as much as he loved her. What she planned to do about him—and them—was still up in the air, but he was growing more confident that her future would include him.

Arriving at the marina, he steeled himself for a thorough grilling from Big Mac and the guys but was surprised to find everyone's attention focused on Ned. Even though he was relieved to escape their scrutiny, he couldn't imagine what Ned, of all people, had done to deserve the third degree.

"I *saw* you with her," Big Mac was saying as Luke joined them at the picnic table outside the restaurant where they had coffee and sugar doughnuts every morning.

"I don't know what ya think ya saw, but it might be time for new glasses," Ned fired back.

Mac snorted at the banter between his father and Ned, rolling his eyes at Luke. "Apparently, *someone* at this table had a hot date last night, but he's not talking," Mac said.

Luke's mouth fell open in shock. *Ned? Had a* date?

Ned shrugged. "Wadn't me."

"I gotta get Grant down here," Big Mac said, exasperated. "He saw you, too."

"Two a ya seein' things." Ned shifted his eyes to Luke. "Let's talk about lover boy over there. Ya want a story, there 'tis."

"I'd much rather talk about you," Luke said, and the other guys cracked up. He was still trying to absorb the fact that Ned had been out on a date. He'd never known of Ned to be with *any* woman. Ever.

"I'm sure ya would," Ned said, taking a sip of his coffee.

Stephanie, the waifish young woman who was spending her first summer on the island running the marina restaurant, came out bearing a platter of sugar doughnuts. "Fresh made," she said as she put them down on the table.

"Thank you, sweetheart," Big Mac said, winking at her.

Stephanie's cheeks turned bright red, and she scurried back inside.

"That poor little girl has a crush a mile wide on ya," Ned said to Big Mac. "Speakin' of getting eyes checked, she needs to see an eye doctor stat. Does she know ya're older than dirt?"

"We're not talking about me," Big Mac said. "You oughta tell Mac who you were out gallivanting with last night. I'm sure he'd be very interested."

"Who was it?" Mac asked. "And why would I care?"

"Why don'tcha just shut ya big yap?" Ned snapped at his friend. "Even on this godforsaken island, a man has a right to privacy."

Big Mac roared with laughter, which made Luke smile. It was impossible to be around Big Mac when he was amused and not be sucked in.

"Whatever you say," Big Mac said, wiping tears from his eyes.

Ned scowled at him.

"Now, boys," Mac said. "Let's all get along."

"You shut yer yap, too," Ned said, which set Big Mac off all over again.

"What the hell did I do?" Mac asked Luke.

He shrugged. Clearly, Ned was in a mood, and in some ways Luke could sympathize, since he didn't want his business aired out over coffee and doughnuts any more than Ned did. Still, Luke couldn't deny he was dying to know who Ned had been romancing. He hoped Big Mac would tell them later, when Ned left in his cab to meet the next ferry.

"Hey," Mac said, "check out this dickhead."

The others looked to the pond, where a large power-boat was steaming through the anchorage, making the boats in its wake bob and dip precariously.

Big Mac's brows furrowed with displeasure. "Where's the Coast Guard when you need 'em?"

"Oh great," Mac said. "He's coming here."

Big Mac stood. "Allow me, boys."

"This oughta be good," Ned said as he got up to get a better view of the show.

Mac and Luke followed Big Mac down the main pier, hanging back to allow him to take the lead.

"Whatcha need, skip?" Big Mac called to the boat's captain.

"Looking for dockage for a night or two." He slurred his words, which the women on the boat found hilarious.

"Drunk at nine a.m.," Mac muttered to Luke as they leaned against pilings to watch.

"You're lucky the Coasties didn't see you pouring on the coal in the harbor," Big Mac said, keeping it friendly even though he was pissed. Drinking and driving was a problem on the water, too.

The guy's insolent grin infuriated Luke, who was painfully aware of how much a drunk driver had taken from Sydney. Judging by the stiff set to Big Mac's shoulders, he was none too pleased either. He pointed the forty-foot boat to a dock close to the end of the main pier, away from where he usually put families.

Good call, Luke thought. He'd have done the same, but then he'd learned from the best—party boats at one end, families at the other.

Big Mac loved to say that half these guys probably bought their boats yesterday, and since there was no operating license required, they could take to the water the next day with a hugely powerful machine and no clue how to operate it. This captain was the worst of the worst—all about showing off how much power his boat had.

Luke noticed that the action on the dock had come to a stop, and everyone was watching. Since it was low tide, the boat was far below the standing pier, which made for a more difficult landing. One of the women managed to get a stern line to Big Mac, who wrapped it around a piling while Luke ran up to catch the bow line. It fell short and dropped into the water. The skipper reacted by pouring on the coal. Unprepared for the boat to lurch forward, Big Mac tried to keep a grip on his line.

Luke watched in horror as Big Mac suddenly disappeared off the dock.

Mac let out a scream that chilled Luke to his bones as he watched his friend jump in after his father.

"Someone call 911!" Ned shouted.

"We've got guys in the water!" Luke yelled, but the captain was so caught up in showing off for the women, he didn't hear Luke.

He again threw the boat into gear, engaging the propellers.

"*Shut it down!*" Mac yelled from the water.

Without a thought to possible implications, Luke threw himself onto the boat ten feet below, landing with a great thud on the back deck, which finally got the captain's attention.

"Kill the power, *now*!" Luke lay on the boat's deck, his left ankle at an unnatural angle. "We've got two guys in the water!"

The captain looked down at him sprawled on the deck and finally seemed to get the message. He killed the power, and all Luke could hear in the ensuing silence was Mac screaming for help for his father. Thank God at least one of them was okay.

The boat went silent just as Mac reached his father, who was facedown with a dark slick of blood surrounding him. The back of his head was wide open. With shaking hands, Mac turned him over. "Dad. Wake up." He slapped his cheeks. No response. Mac plugged his father's nose and began rescue breathing, all while treading water to keep them both afloat in water that was cold year round. "Where the hell are the paramedics?" he called to the onlookers above.

"I can hear the ambulance," someone said. "Hang in there, Mac. Just another minute or two."

"Oh my God!" Stephanie cried from the pier above them. "What happened?"

Mac cradled his father's head against his chest. "Don't you dare even *think* about leaving us, do you hear?" he whispered between breaths. "Don't you dare."

"I didn't know he was in the water," the captain said, his words slurred.

"Shut up," Luke said. "Just shut the fuck up."

Mac continued to breathe for his father and went weak with relief when Big Mac finally coughed up a huge load of water and began to breathe again on his own. But he still didn't come to.

"That's it," Mac said, tears streaming down his face. "Nice and easy." He pressed his lips to his father's forehead. "You're going to be just fine." Finally, he could hear the sirens getting closer. "Rescue's almost here."

The next half hour was a blur. Paramedics entered the water, loaded Big Mac on a gurney and lifted him out while a second crew tended to Luke. Chief of Police Blaine Taylor, a high school classmate of Mac's and Luke's, carted the boat owner away in handcuffs. While running after the paramedics hauling his father, Mac asked Stephanie to call his mother.

"I'll find her and get her to the clinic myself."

"Thank you." Even though the morning sun was hot, Mac shivered uncontrollably after spending thirty minutes in the water. He handed Stephanie his ring of keys. "Will you lock up?" As she took the keys from him, he noticed her hands were shaking. "Where's Luke?"

"Cops took him to the clinic. I heard one of them say his ankle is badly sprained, if not broken."

"Shit," Mac muttered. *What a clusterfuck*, he thought as he got into the ambulance to accompany his father to the island's small community clinic. He sure hoped it was equipped for whatever his father needed.

Mac took the blanket the paramedics offered and tried not to focus too intently on his father's gray face as they worked to stem the bleeding on the back of his head. He wanted to call Maddie, but right now all his focus was on his father. "Can you tell if he's hurt anywhere else?" Mac asked.

"His arm is clearly fractured, and his blood pressure is really low, so there could be internal injuries." Mac watched them pull a warming blanket over his father, trying to raise his body temperature.

He squeezed his eyes shut and burrowed into his own blanket, hoping to stop the violent trembling. *Please, God. I'll do anything. Just don't take him from us yet. Not yet.*

Much to Mac's dismay, the clinic's emergency personnel treated him like *he* was the patient. He struggled against their efforts to remove his wet clothes and get him into scrubs. "I'm fine! I don't need to be seen. I have to know what's going on with my father!"

"Mr. McCarthy, you're hypothermic, and your pulse is weak," the nurse said. She examined Mac's eyes with a flashlight. "You might be a bit shocky, too."

Mac's chest began to ache the way it had during an anxiety attack a year or so ago, but he didn't dare tell them that. "I'm not the patient!"

"You are now," the formidable nurse declared after poking a thermometer in his ear. "Your temp is ninety-four." She tugged a heated blanket up over him. "We've got to get you warmed up."

Mac didn't want to admit that the heat felt really good. "Can you find out what's going on with my dad? Please? And Luke Harris? He was brought in, too."

The nurse patted his arm. "I'll go check. Try to settle down."

"I need to call my wife. Can you get me a phone? Mine got ruined in the water."

"I'll see what I can do."

Continuing to tremble under the blanket, Mac waited a long time for the nurse to return. He had plenty of time to ponder life without his father and for the ache in his chest to intensify. The whole thing had happened so damned fast! One minute his dad was standing on the dock, the next minute he was seriously injured and fighting for his life.

Mac shuddered as the images ran through his mind like a horror movie he couldn't escape: his father disappearing from the pier, floating facedown in the water, the pool of blood surrounding him.

The nurse returned. "Since I don't own a cell phone, one of the other nurses is getting hers for you. They're taking your dad for some tests. He's hypothermic as well, so we're warming him up. His arm is definitely broken. That's all I know at the moment."

"Is he awake?"

"Not yet."

"Is that normal?"

"Head injuries run the gamut. We'll know more after we see the scan."

"What if he needs a neurologist?"

She glanced up from his chart. "If necessary, they'll fly one in."

"Can't we fly him to a trauma center?"

"He can't fly if he has a brain injury, but let's not get ahead of ourselves. We need to wait and see what the tests show, okay?"

No, it was not okay. None of this was okay, but what choice did he have but to wait for more information? "How about Luke?"

"Is he a relative?" she asked, raising an eyebrow.

"My, um, brother?"

She gave him a skeptical smile. "I can see the resemblance," she said dryly. "Since he's your 'brother,' I can tell you he has a badly sprained left ankle. But you did *not* hear that from me."

"He probably saved my dad's life—and mine, too."

"Then I guess we'd better take extra special good care of him."

"Please do."

"So," Maddie said as she and Sydney pored over baby furniture catalogs at Maddie's house. They were sitting on the floor while Thomas played with trucks next to them. "Are you going to spill the beans on why you're positively glowing this morning?"

Images from her amazing night with Luke flashed through her mind, heating her face.

"And *blushing*," Maddie said, hooting with laughter.

"It's incredible. I can't believe it's possible, but it's even more intense now than it was before. How can that be?"

Leaning on the coffee table, Maddie rested her chin on her upturned hand. "Wow. As I recall, it was quite something before."

Sydney nodded. "We have this unbelievable connection. I can't even describe it. When you think about it, though, it shouldn't even work between us. We're so different, you know?"

"How do you mean?"

"I'm loud and outspoken, and I need to talk everything to death. He's Mr. One-Word Answer. Less is always more with him." Sydney paused and then added, "Except in bed, of course."

"He can't help that," Maddie said, laughing. "He's a guy."

"True."

"Will less be enough for you over the long haul?"

"That's something I worry about. He's very content with a smallish life on this island. I'm used to much bigger—lots of people and friends and stuff going on."

"You'd definitely be downsizing if you lived here year-round. No doubt about that, but it wouldn't be all bad. There's something very cozy about settling in for a long, cold winter with the one you love to keep you warm."

"You should know." Sydney smiled at the blissful expression on Maddie's face. "I'm tempted to try it for a winter."

"Oh, yay!" Maddie clapped her hands. "We'll keep you entertained. Don't worry."

"What if I try it and it doesn't work out? What if I start to go stir-crazy halfway through the winter?"

Maddie thought about that for a minute. "I suppose you'd have to deal with that if—and when—it happens."

"I'm afraid I'll turn his life upside down—again—if I move out here only to decide later it doesn't work for me."

"No one says the only place you and he can be together is here."

"His whole life is here. He has an amazing side business restoring boats. Did you know that?"

Maddie nodded. "I've been out on the Chris-Craft he did for Mr. McCarthy. It's *gorgeous*. I'm always so afraid Mac is going to crash it or scratch it or something."

"Luke does beautiful work, that's for sure."

"And there's no reason he couldn't do that same beautiful work on the mainland."

"That's true."

Maddie reached over to squeeze her hand. "You're getting ahead of yourself worrying about what *might* happen. All you can do is try it and see what it's like. If you don't like it, you don't like it. I'm sure he wants you to be happy, and if it ends up that he has to move, then I'm sure he would."

"But that would make *him* unhappy."

"If you ask me, you're what makes him happy, and he couldn't care less where he has to live to be with you. Remember what Joe did to be with Janey. He rearranged his entire life, and he's blissfully happy. He loves her, so he did what had to be done so they could be together."

"He hasn't said it, but I know Luke loves me."

"How do you feel?"

"Of course I love him, too. How could I not love him? He's such a great guy."

"Have you told him that?"

"Not yet." Sydney fiddled with one of the catalogs. "I want to say it, but I get to the moment, and I just can't get it out. I guess some part of me knows I'll be making a commitment when I say those words, so I want to be sure, you know?"

"I can see that, but I think you should relax about the details and just go with it. See where it takes you. If anything good has come out of all you've been through, you have the freedom to do whatever you want. If being here with Luke for now feels good, then stay."

"I need to talk to him about this at some point. It would help to know that he would understand if I can't live here full time." She blew out a deep breath. "I can't decide anything until after the sentencing hearing. That's hanging over me like a ton of bricks. Once that's done, maybe I'll feel more ready to make some plans."

"You need closure before you can move forward. I totally get that." Maddie squeezed Syd's hand. "In the meantime, you have to help me decide on this nursery furniture. When I had Thomas, I had to make do with used stuff and hand-me-downs. Mac wants all new stuff for this little one." She rested a hand on her round belly, and her eyes widened when the baby responded with a swift kick.

"Already talking back," Sydney said, laughing. "Has to be a girl."

Maddie chuckled. "Can you even *begin* to imagine Mac with a little girl? The poor thing won't be allowed to date until she's fifty."

"He'll be great with a girl."

"He's so excited about this baby. It's all he talks about."

"That's so sweet."

"It's much different than when I was expecting Thomas and all anyone cared about was who the father was."

"Enjoy every minute. You've got a wonderful son and husband, and another baby on the way."

"You know, as we were talking, I was thinking there's no one here who has your decorating skills. You might find a very satisfying new career right here on the island."

"You drive a hard bargain, Mrs. McCarthy."

Maddie flashed a triumphant grin. "I'm totally biased because I'd so love to have you here year-round."

The house phone rang, and Maddie made a comical attempt to get up from the floor.

"Stop," Sydney said, laughing at the faces her friend was making. "I'll get it."

"It's on the kitchen counter."

Sydney ran for the kitchen and picked up the extension. "Maddie?"

"No, it's Sydney. Let me get her."

"Syd, it's Janey."

Syd's stomach plummeted at the grave tone of Janey's voice. "Is everything okay? Is Buddy okay? I'll be by shortly to pick him up."

"Buddy's fine, but there's been an accident at the marina."

All the air seemed to leave Sydney's lungs in one big whoosh.

"My dad, Mac and Luke were all taken to the clinic." Sydney could hear tears in Janey's voice. "I only know one of them is hurt bad. Stephanie was so hysterical when she called my mother that we don't know anything else. Can you bring Maddie and meet us there?"

"Yes," Sydney said, her hands shaking and her heart beating hard. "We'll be right there." She put down the phone, took a deep breath to calm her rattled nerves and returned to the living room to find Thomas snuggled up to his mother, his eyes heavy.

"Syd? You're totally pale. What is it?"

"There's been an accident."

"Oh God. *No*. Not Mac." In a whisper she said, "Please tell me it's not Mac." Her caramel-colored eyes filled with tears. Somehow she managed to get up and settle Thomas on the sofa.

"Mac, his dad and Luke were all hurt. Janey didn't have any of the details, except that one of them was hurt bad. She said we should meet them at the clinic."

Maddie stood frozen in place, one hand resting on her pregnant belly.

Sydney went to her. "Whatever it is, we'll get through it together, okay?" Sydney had no idea where this calm control was coming from. The idea that Luke could be injured—or worse—made her want to howl. He had promised her nothing bad would happen to her again. He'd *promised*.

Maddie clung to her for a long moment.

"Let's call Tiffany so we can drop Thomas off with her on the way to the clinic," Syd said. "I'll drive." She lifted the sleeping toddler from the sofa and closed her eyes tight against the rush of emotion as he molded himself to her without waking, the way Max used to at that age.

Maddie grabbed her purse and keys and led the way out of the house to the SUV.

Sydney fumbled her way through settling Thomas into his car seat. Her hands shook all the way into town, where they dropped the boy with his aunt.

Tiffany's concern for Mac sent Maddie even further into herself.

As they headed for the clinic, Syd reached for her hand. "He's okay. He has to be okay. They all are." The alternative was simply unimaginable.

Maddie tightened her grip on Syd's hand but didn't say anything.

Chapter Eighteen

As Sydney and Maddie rushed into the emergency entrance, the first thing they heard was Mac bellowing for someone to tell him *something* about his father. At the sound of his voice, Maddie staggered, and for a moment Sydney wondered if her friend was going to faint.

"Oh," Maddie whispered, "thank God." She rushed past the registration desk, following the sound of her husband's voice.

Since Sydney didn't know what else to do, she went with Maddie.

"I'm Mrs. McCarthy," Maddie said to the nurse in the hallway. "I need to see my husband."

"Right in here." The nurse opened the curtain to Mac, who was red-faced and furious. "He's all yours."

Maddie burst into tears at the sight of him.

"Come here, baby," he said, holding out his arms to her. "Sorry I couldn't call you. My phone is toast."

She crawled right onto the bed with him. "What happened?" she managed to ask through her tears.

Even though Sydney felt like she was intruding on an

intensely private moment, she needed to hear what Mac had to say, so she waited.

He told them about the boat and the accident, adding in a much louder voice, "And *no one* will tell me how my father is!"

"We're checking on him for you, Mr. McCarthy," the nurse said in a long-suffering tone that indicated she'd already told him that a few times.

"Are you hurt?" Maddie asked, her hands traveling from his face to his chest.

"I'm fine, but apparently I have to stay here until Dr. Maitland says I can go."

"Should just be a few more minutes," the nurse said.

"What about Luke?" Sydney asked, holding her breath in anticipation of whatever she might hear.

"He sprained his ankle, pretty badly, I guess."

"And that's it?"

"That's all I heard."

"He was waiting to have an X-ray, last I knew," the nurse said. "I could take you to him, if you'd like."

"Yes," Sydney said, sick with relief. "Please." To Maddie, she said, "Will you be okay?"

Snuggled into her husband's embrace, Maddie closed her eyes. "I'll be just fine."

As Sydney followed the nurse, Mrs. McCarthy, Janey and Stephanie came into the ER, looking undone and teary-eyed. Sydney pointed the way to where they could find Mac.

Janey hugged her on the way by.

"I'm praying for your dad," Sydney said.

"Thank you," Janey said as new tears spilled down her cheeks.

"I'll check on you after I've seen Luke."

Janey nodded and followed her mother into Mac's room.

The nurse led Sydney down a long hallway to the X-ray room. "Right in there," she said, pointing.

Sydney's heart raced as she walked into the darkened room to find Luke on a gurney, his foot propped up on pillows and an ice pack covering his ankle.

"Hey," he said, extending a hand to her.

Sydney had promised herself she wouldn't cry, but the instant she saw him alive and well and talking, she lost the battle.

"I'm okay, honey. Come see for yourself."

Just like Maddie, she crawled into his arms.

His lips brushed her forehead. "I'm okay."

"Scared me."

"I'm sorry. I hated knowing how worried you'd be. My phone is in my truck, so I couldn't call you."

"I heard you were quite the hero."

He shook his head. "Mac was the hero. He jumped in after his father and got him breathing again while they were still in the water."

"Mac said his father's hurt bad."

"He hit his head. We think on the boat's swim platform. It looked pretty grim." A shudder rippled through him. Knowing how close he was to Mr. McCarthy, Syd could imagine how concerned he was. "That drunken son of a bitch had no business running a boat, that's for sure."

"God," Sydney said, shuddering. "You all could've been killed."

With his index finger, he tilted her chin so he could see her face. He wiped away her tears and kissed her. "I'm not going to die, Syd. I promise."

"You can't promise that."

"Yes, I can."

She smiled at him, appreciating what he was trying to do. "How's your ankle?"

"It hurt like a mother until they gave me some good drugs."

"I'll take care of you," she said, nuzzling his neck. "For as long as you need me, I'll be there."

He tightened his hold on her. "They said it could take forty to fifty years to heal."

Sydney laughed through her tears and stayed with him until the X-ray technician arrived.

Janey had to get out of there. She couldn't bear to sit in that room watching her father's ashen face, hoping for some sign of life from one who was always so much larger than life. The waiting was simply unbearable.

She left her mother with Mac, Maddie and Stephanie, and went outside to get some air. Joe had been on the mainland for the day, checking on his house over there, which they had closed up when they moved to Ohio for the school year. When she called to tell him about the accident, he said he'd be there as soon as he could. At times like this, living on an island truly sucked.

He'd made so many sacrifices to support her dream of attending veterinary school, and now with their wedding just over two weeks away, she might have to ask him to make another one.

No way could she get married without her dad there to give her away. They'd have to postpone it until he was able to be there with them. That was all there was to it. The thought of putting off a wedding they'd looked forward to for a year had new tears filling her eyes. Once again her entire life had been upended in an instant, and she was reeling.

She thought she was seeing things when a Gansett Island Ferry Company truck came roaring into the parking lot, skidding into the final turn.

"Oh, Joe," she said, running to him.

He met her halfway and lifted her right off her feet.

"How did you get here so soon? I only called an hour ago."

"Slim flew me over," he said, referring to one of the island's pilots and a friend of the McCarthy family. "Faster than the ferry. How is he?"

"I don't know. They won't tell us anything, just that head injuries are hard to predict. He looks awful. You need to prepare yourself."

"Aw, baby, who prepared you?"

A sob erupted from her chest, and she clung to him. "Seeing him in that bed . . ." She shuddered. "I've never been more afraid in my life." The scent of the ocean and Joe's favorite clove cigarettes comforted her as much as his strong embrace. "We'll have to put off the wedding." Saying it out loud seemed to make it real.

"We don't have to worry about that today. Let's see what the next few days bring."

Janey drew back so she could see his face. "I can't get married without him. I just can't."

"Neither can I. He's been a father to me, too."

Relieved that he agreed, Janey kissed his cheek and then his lips. "I should've known you'd get it. Don't you always?"

"We'll still get married, honey, but if we have to wait a bit longer so he can be there with us, then we'll wait."

"Thanks for understanding."

"I love you love you, Janey," he said as he always did. "No matter what happens, I'll be right there with you, okay?"

Nodding, she said, "Put me down so I can take you to see Dad."

"I will." He pressed his lips to her neck. "In a minute."

Grant's pounding head woke him from a sound sleep. Rolling over, he moaned at the shaft of pain that sliced through his skull. He'd awoken in this condition far too often lately. In fact, nearly every day since his mother called to tell him about Abby's engagement.

Since no one had bothered to tell him she'd been dating, the news had caught him completely off guard and totally unprepared. How could she even think about marrying someone else? There was no way she could possibly *love* that guy. Not as much as she loved him.

He sat up and fought back a swell of nausea. The drinking had to stop. It wasn't making anything better. His career and life had gone to shit, and no amount of booze was ever going to change that.

Dragging his aching head into the shower, Grant set the temperature to freezing and was only slightly more alive after five minutes under the icy water. He added some hot water and washed his hair. *I need a plan*, he thought. *Something to get Abby's attention. Something that will convince her to give me another chance*. He'd talk to Janey, who was close friends with Abby. She'd know what he needed to do to win Abby back.

In the bedroom that had been his growing up, Grant reached for his cell phone and was startled to find numerous missed calls from his mother and Janey. As he listened to the voice mail message from Janey, his heart slowed to a crawl as he heard about the accident at the marina.

Appalled that he'd slept through their frantic phone

calls, he got dressed as quickly as his fumbling hands would allow and went into his parents' room, hoping his father had left the keys to Mac's motorcycle where Grant could find them. Finding no sign of them there or downstairs, he ran out the front door, heading for town.

All he could think about was getting to his father. He couldn't die thinking Grant was a drunken loser. Grant would rather be dead himself than have to live with that memory of his final hour with his beloved father.

Despite the painful objections from his head and stomach, Grant kept running until a horn beeping beside him caught his attention. Ned and his cab. Grant had never been happier to see anyone in his life.

"Git in, boy," Ned called.

Breathing hard and sweating, Grant slid into the old woody station wagon.

"Yer mama sent me to find ya when ya didn't answer yer phone."

"Thanks," Grant said, embarrassed again to have slept through their calls. "How bad is it?"

"Pretty bad. Yer daddy was bleeding all over the place. Out cold."

"God," Grant said. "I can't imagine this world without him."

Ned sniffled, and Grant looked over as a tear rolled down a wrinkled cheek.

"He'll be okay," Grant said, reaching out to rest a hand on Ned's shoulder. "He has to be." Grant couldn't conceive of any other outcome.

"I was cranky with him earlier," Ned said, swiping at his face. "He was bustin' my balls like he does. Wish I hadn't sniped at him."

"You two have been sniping at each other for forty

years. He wouldn't want it any other way, and you know that."

"Suppose yer right."

They arrived at the clinic, where the family gathered in a waiting room. His mother was sitting with Mac on one side and Janey on the other. Maddie, her mother, Joe and the new woman from the marina restaurant were with them.

"Oh, Grant, there you are," Linda said. "I was worried when I couldn't reach you."

"Sorry." Grant went to his mother and hugged her. "What're they saying?"

"Cal is in with him now. We're waiting to hear."

Grant went rigid at the news that Abby's so-called fiancé was treating his father. Didn't that beat all?

As if this situation didn't already suck badly enough, Abby came rushing into the ER a few minutes later. Without so much as a glance at him, she made a beeline for his mother. "I came as soon as I heard. How is he?"

His mother hugged Abby and updated her.

Grant couldn't bear to be so close to Abby and not be able to touch her or hold her. When he needed her more than he ever had before, she was unavailable to him.

He turned his back on the group and looked out a window so he wouldn't be tempted to stare at Abby. It seemed like they waited forever before Cal came through the double doors.

Turning in time to notice Cal's pleasure at seeing Abby there, Grant wanted to kill the guy. It was all he could do not to stake his claim on her right then and there. But this wasn't the time or place.

Wearing a white coat over jeans and a button-down shirt, Cal zeroed in on Grant's mother. "Mrs. McCarthy, I have good news," he drawled. Since when was Abby attracted to men who *drawled*? "There's no sign of a brain bleed or anything life-threatening."

An audible sigh of relief went through the room.

"We've stitched up the cut on his head and set his broken arm. He suffered a rather significant concussion, so when he comes to, you can expect him to be confused and in some pain. We'll do what we can to keep him comfortable, but I don't see any need at this time to transport him to the mainland or to bring a neuro over to consult."

"What if we want a second opinion?" Grant asked.

The bastard never even blinked when he said, "I'm afraid I'm all you've got at the moment."

Grant's mother tossed him a dirty look and then returned her attention to Cal. "Thank you so much, Dr. Maitland. May I see him?"

"Of course, right this way." He gestured to the door. "Abby, may I speak to you for a moment?"

His mother, Janey, Mac and Abby followed the doctor into the ward. As much as Grant wanted to see his father, he'd wait until the doctor moved on to other patients.

Joe stood and came over to Grant. "You might want to tone down the violent stares. He's the only doctor around, and your dad is still in a world of hurt."

"I don't know who he thinks he is, stealing *my* girl right out from underneath me."

Joe raised an eyebrow. "Is that how it happened?"

"I don't want to talk about it." Grant was light-headed and queasy and not in the slightest bit interested in rehashing how he'd landed in this boat. "I need some air." He went outside and leaned against the brick building, tilting his face into the sun and breathing in the fresh sea air.

Just when he'd been convinced things couldn't get any more screwed up, here he was relying on his rival to keep his father alive. Even with his vivid imagination, he doubted he could've written such a messed-up scenario.

"He's going to be all right," a small voice beside him said.

Grant opened his eyes and looked down at the woman from the marina restaurant. Her eyes were rimmed with red and puffy from crying.

"He has to be all right."

Grant wasn't sure who she was trying to convince—him or herself. They'd call her a waif in Hollywood, with her tiny frame and big blue-green eyes. She had multi-colored spiked hair that made her look even younger.

"We haven't officially met," she said. "I'm Stephanie. Your dad hired me to run the restaurant this summer."

He shook her outstretched hand. "Grant McCarthy."

"I know who you are," she said, her face flushing. "I mean, I'm familiar with your work."

"Is that so?"

She nodded. "*Song of Solomon* was amazing. It changed my life."

Hearing that never got old. "I'm glad you liked it."

"I was thrilled that you won the Oscar. You totally deserved it."

"Thanks. That's nice of you to say."

"I had no idea you were related to Mr. McCarthy until I heard him telling someone about his son, the famous screenwriter."

Grant winced. "He can be a bit effusive at times."

"He's so incredibly proud of you."

Did she have any idea how badly he needed to hear that just then?

"Are you all right?" she asked. "You look kinda green."

"Few too many last night."

"I have the perfect cure for that."

"What's that?"

"I'll go get it and come back."

"Oh, no. That's not necessary."

She smiled up at him. "It'd give me something to do. I'm madly in love with your dad, and this has been one of the worst days of my life. What happened at the marina . . ." She shuddered, and her face went pale.

Grant reached out to her. His hand landed on her shoulder, but when she flinched, he removed it. What was that all about? "It must've been awful."

"I was so afraid he'd been killed. When they brought him out of the water, he looked bad. Really bad."

Grant swallowed hard. "Sounds like he's going to be okay."

"Thank God."

"Yes."

"You should be in there with him."

Surprised, he stared at her.

"I don't mean to tell you what to do, but why are you out here when your family is with your dad?"

"Because my ex-girlfriend is apparently engaged to the island's only doctor, and I'm better off out here than in there plotting ways to kill the guy who's keeping my dad alive."

"You should act like you don't care that they're engaged."

"Is that so?"

She flushed again. "It's certainly none of my business."

"No, please. Tell me why you think that'll work."

"Because your indifference will bother her more than your anger does."

"Huh," Grant said, pondering what she'd said.

"I'll go get you something to fix up that hangover."

Intrigued, he watched her head for the parking lot. She was nothing like his usual type. In other words, she was nothing like Abby, who was curvy and filled a bra to over-flowing. Stephanie, by contrast, was almost boyish with her spiked hair and lack of curves.

Deciding to take her advice, Grant went back inside to find everyone gone from the waiting room except for Ned, who was sitting next to Maddie's mother. Francine was holding Ned's hand and talking softly to him. They never even noticed Grant as he went to the reception desk to ask for directions to his father's room.

In the hallway outside the room, a crowd had formed.

Luke, propped on crutches, was standing with Sydney, Maddie and Mac, who leaned against the wall, visibly exhausted.

"How is he?" Grant asked his brother.

"Still out cold," Mac said. "But his color seems a little better than it was earlier."

"That's good," Grant said, relieved. The group went quiet, everyone lost in their own thoughts. When the quiet began to grate on his nerves, Grant said, "So what's going on with Ned and Maddie's mom?"

Chapter Nineteen

"What're you talking about?" Maddie asked Grant.

"Dad was ribbing Ned this morning about a hot date he had last night," Mac explained. "But Ned was being tight-lipped about it."

Maddie's mouth fell open. "My mom and *Ned*?"

"She was holding his hand and whispering to him in the waiting room just now," Grant said. "I was with Dad last night when he saw them together."

"Well, I'll be," Mac said, laughing. "No wonder Dad was acting like he'd stumbled upon the hottest scoop on the island."

"My mom and *Ned*?" Maddie said again.

Chuckling, Mac slid an arm around her shoulders and kissed the top of her head. "Take a breath, babe."

"I had an odd conversation with Ned the other night," Luke said. "He was talking about a girl he'd once known who'd left him for another guy. When he said she still lives on the island, I encouraged him to go see her."

"So they were together *before*?" Maddie asked. "*When*?"

"Before she met your dad," Luke said. "I guess she left him for your dad."

"Oh," Maddie said. "Wow. I had no idea." Resting a hand on her belly, she grimaced.

Mac stood up straighter. "What?"

"Nothing."

"That was *not* nothing, Madeline."

"Just some weird twinges today. Probably Braxton-Hicks contractions."

"I want to have you checked," Mac said. His amusement over Ned and Francine had been replaced by intense concern.

"It's fine, Mac."

"We'll let Dr. Maitland decide that."

As Mac took his wife's hand and led her off to find the doctor, Luke noticed the scowl on Grant's face.

"What's eating you?" Luke asked.

"Not a damned thing."

"Whatever you say."

"How's the ankle?"

"I'm told it'll hurt like hell once the pain meds wear off."

"Thanks for what you did. I heard you took a hell of a risk to save my dad and Mac."

Luke shrugged off the praise. "Mac took the bigger risk."

"I need to get you home." Sydney took Luke's arm. "Doctor's orders." To Grant, she added, "They want him off the foot so the swelling will go down."

"With me and your dad both laid up, we might need an extra set of hands around the marina," Luke said to Grant. "Are you willing?"

"Whatever I can do."

"Thanks. I'll talk to Mac and let you know what we need."

"If I can do anything at all for you," Grant said, "just give me a ring."

"Will do. Thanks."

"Let us know how your father and Maddie are, please," Sydney said.

"I'll check in later," Grant said.

Sydney walked slowly along with him as Luke made his way on crutches to the emergency entrance. They'd wanted him to use a wheelchair, but he had refused.

"I don't feel right about leaving while Big Mac is still out of it," Luke said.

"I'm sure he'd want you to take care of yourself."

"Are you okay? You seem worried or something."

"I'm thinking about Buddy. I need to pick him up from the vet." She bit her thumbnail as she thought it over. "I can't lift him on my own, so I'll have to call my dad to help me."

"Sorry to be of no use whatsoever."

She stopped walking and turned to him. "All I care about is you're *alive* and you *only* sprained your ankle."

Luke smiled. She was so cute when her dander was up. "Come here and kiss me."

Glancing around the busy clinic, she took a tentative step toward him.

"A little closer."

She rested her hands on his shoulders and went up on tiptoes to kiss him.

"I know for a fact you can do better than that."

"*Here?*"

"You just said all you care about is I'm alive. Prove it."

Her eyes dropped to his lips, and that was all it took to make him hard as stone. By the time she slid her hand around his neck and gave him a much better kiss, Luke was ready to beg.

"Mmm." He wished he could put his arms around her and hold her close. These crutches were going to be a serious drag. "Now we're talking."

"Can we go home now?"

"How're we getting there?"

"Oh crap. I left my car at Maddie's." She rolled her lip between her teeth. "If you have no objection, I'll call my parents."

Luke wasn't exactly keen on another encounter with the Donovans so soon after the last one. "Or we could ask Ned."

The cab driver was in the waiting room, still holding hands and talking with Francine.

"Nah," Syd said. "Leave them be. They've got a lot of catching up to do." She drew her phone from her shorts pocket and dialed a number as Luke continued toward the door. "Mom? Are you busy?"

Sydney's parents pulled up to the emergency room entrance fifteen minutes later.

"We heard about what happened at the marina," her mother said as she held the back door of the SUV for Luke. "Thank goodness you're all right."

"Thanks," Luke said.

Her father took Luke's crutches and stowed them in the back. "Any word on Mr. McCarthy?" he asked.

"Nothing new," Luke said. "Dr. Maitland said he should be okay, though."

"Well, that's a relief," Mary Alice said.

Sydney appreciated that her parents seemed to be making an effort to be nice to Luke. She directed them to Luke's house and held his hand between both of hers in the back seat. "Dad, would you mind taking me to get Buddy after we get Luke home?"

"'Course not."

"I can't lift him on my own, and I'm afraid of hurting him."

"Why don't we take him home to our house," Mary Alice suggested. "We can look after him, since you'll have your hands full taking care of Luke."

Luke squeezed her hand and sent her a questioning look.

Syd had no idea where this new, agreeable version of her mother had come from. "Are you sure that wouldn't be too much trouble?"

"We'd be happy to have him, right, Allan?"

"Absolutely."

"That would certainly take a load off my mind," Syd said. "Thank you."

When they arrived at Luke's house, Sydney got his crutches and helped him out of the car.

"Where's your car, honey?" Allan asked.

"Over at Maddie's. I'll get it tomorrow."

"I can run you over there on the way home."

"May as well," Luke said. "That way we aren't stranded without a car, since my truck is at the marina."

"Okay," Syd said. "Thanks, Dad."

"Thanks for the lift, Mr. Donovan," Luke said.

"No problem."

"Hope you feel better," her mom added.

Her parents waited outside while Sydney escorted Luke into the house and helped him get settled on the sofa.

He removed the walking boot and propped his foot on a pillow.

Sydney gasped at her first look at his horribly swollen and bruised ankle. "Oh, Luke," she said. "God, it's awful."

"Could've been much worse," he said, but she noticed he was sweating and his lips had gone white with pain.

She got him an ice pack, wrapped it in a towel and brought him two of the pain pills the clinic had sent him home with. Bending to kiss his forehead, she said, "I'll be right back, okay?"

"I'll be right here."

Handing him the remote for the TV, she kissed him one more time and hurried out the door, anxious to get back to him. She climbed into her parents' car and closed the door.

"Is he all right?" Mary Alice asked.

"He's in pain, and his ankle is horrible."

"Will he be able to work?" Allan asked, glancing at her in the rearview mirror.

"Not for a while, I suppose."

"I wonder what he'll do," Mary Alice said fretfully.

"He's not destitute, Mom."

"He'll get workers' comp for an accident at work," Allan, the lawyer, said.

"I suppose," Sydney said.

"Quite a piece of property he's got there," he added.

"Yes." Her mother's worries had Sydney wondering if even with workers' comp Luke could afford to be out of work for several weeks, especially in the summer. "Thanks for the help, you guys."

"We were glad you called," Mary Alice said, turning in her seat. "We feel bad about what happened the other day."

"I certainly don't want to be at odds with you. Not after all we've been through."

"We don't want that either, honey."

"I'd like you to do something for me." She met her mother's gaze. "I want you to get to know Luke so you can see what I see in him. I'm asking you to give him a chance. Can you do that?"

"There's nothing we wouldn't do for you, Syd," Allan said. "You know that."

"Does that include respecting my choices?"

"We want you to be happy again," Mary Alice said. "If Luke makes you happy, then we're happy, too."

"You mean that?"

She nodded. "The last thing we want is for you to suffer any more heartache. You've already had more than your share."

"He loves me," Syd said. "I feel that every minute I'm with him."

"Are you sure it's not too soon to be getting so involved with someone else?" Allan asked. "It hasn't been that long."

Even though she knew it was a reasonable question, it still made her mad. "How long is long enough, Dad? Can you tell me that? Is there a widow rule book I don't know about?"

"Now, honey, I don't mean to upset you. I'm concerned about you getting hurt again."

"Luke would never hurt me."

"Not intentionally."

"Not ever. I'm far more worried about hurting him the way I did before."

"You have to stop blaming yourself for what happened years ago, Syd," Mary Alice said. "You were just a kid."

"I was old enough to know he'd be crushed, but I was too much of a coward to end it the way I should have."

"If you saw fit to end it with him then—"

"I *didn't* see fit to end it! *You* told me he wasn't good

enough for me, and I *believed* you! I let you twist me in knots until I didn't know which end was up."

"But you were happy with Seth. We saw that with our own eyes."

"I was happy with him, but I never loved him the way I love Luke." The words were out of her mouth before she could stop them, filling her with despair. Until that very moment, she hadn't admitted it even to herself.

"Sydney! How can you say such a thing?"

"It's the truth. I can't help how I feel." She swiped at the tears. "I couldn't help it then, and I can't help it now."

"But if you hadn't married Seth—"

"I don't regret marrying him. I don't regret the life we had together or our beautiful children, but I deeply regret decimating someone else on the way to that perfect life you wanted so badly for me."

In Maddie's driveway, her father parked next to Syd's car and turned off the engine. The three of them sat in uncomfortable silence until Sydney took a deep, fortifying breath. "I miss Seth and my children every minute of every day, but I've chosen not to be defined by what I've lost. I simply can't live mired in tragedy and sorrow without joy or hope or a reason to get up in the morning."

Despite her intention to get through this without tears, they came anyway. "Being with Luke brings me joy, and for the first time in more than fifteen months, I'm hopeful again. I'm hopeful that every day of what's left of my life isn't going to totally suck. He's done that for me, so all I'm asking is that you give him a chance. Just give him a chance. Please."

She got out, shut the door and headed for her own car. For a long time, she sat there hoping her hands would stop shaking so she could drive. A tap on the window surprised her. She turned the key so she could open the window.

"I'm okay, Mom."

"If he feels up to it, how about you and Luke come for dinner tomorrow night?"

Looking up at her mother, Sydney nodded. "We'd like that."

Chapter Twenty

While his mother and Janey went to check on Maddie, Grant stayed with his father, staring down at the bed and willing him to wake up. Cal had said he could be out of it for a while, but Grant kept talking as if his father could hear him.

He stopped talking only to answer text messages from his brothers Adam and Evan, who were en route to the island and were looking for updates on their father's condition.

"Adam and Evan will be here later tonight," Grant told his father. "They said to tell you they don't appreciate you scaring them this way." He smiled, imagining his father's response to that.

"How's he doing?"

Grant spun around and found Abby standing in the doorway, looking nervous and adorable. He wanted so badly to feel her arms around him, to hear her say everything would be okay. No one had ever understood him the way she did.

"About the same," Grant said.

"How're you doing?"

"I'll be better when he wakes up."

"Is there anything I can do for you?"

Grant knew she was just being polite, but he couldn't miss the opportunity. "You could tell me what you're thinking, hitching yourself to that overgrown cowboy."

Her expressive eyes flashed with anger. "You have no right to ask me that."

Behind Abby's back, Stephanie appeared, holding a container. Grant shook his head, and she ducked out of sight.

"I have every right to ask that," he said to Abby.

"I waited *years* for you, Grant. I put my whole life on hold hoping you'd get yours together so we could move forward with our relationship. But that never happened, and I got tired of waiting."

"You can't honestly expect me to believe that you love him more than you love me."

"I love him differently than I loved you."

Her use of the past tense was another knife to his heart. "What the hell does that mean?"

"He's *there* for me. He supports me rather than expecting me to support *him* a hundred and ten percent without anything in return."

"I never expected that."

"Oh come on!" Glancing at his father, she lowered her voice. "That's all I was to you—your muse, your enabler, your lover, your housekeeper. It was never, *ever* about me."

"It was *all* about you. You were *everything* to me, Abby."

At that, her cool composure finally began to waver. "You had a funny way of showing it."

Grant went around the bed to get closer to her.

She took a step back, discouraging him from touching her.

"Give me another chance. I've sold my house and car. I've left LA, and I'm back to stay for now."

"For *now*? What does that mean?"

Even though she was sending the "hands off" signal, he reached out to touch her face. "It means I'm making some changes. I'm nothing without you. You can't just walk away like all our years together meant nothing to you."

She took his hand, lowered it from her face and released it. "They meant too much to me. I lost myself in our relationship, and I don't want that anymore. I'm happy with Cal. He *sees* me in a way that you never did. And I'm sorry if it hurts you to hear this, but I'm going to marry him in October."

Grant shook his head. "You can't marry him, Abby. It's all wrong, and you know that."

"I'm asking you to respect my decision."

"How can I do that when you're ruining both our lives?"

She shook her head. "I'm not ruining my life. If yours isn't what you want it to be, I can't take responsibility for that. Not anymore." Glancing at his father, she said, "Please tell your dad I was here and give him my love. I have to go now." She spun around and left the room.

Grant followed her. "Abby, wait! Don't go."

She turned and stopped him with a hand to his chest. Her eyes sparkled with unshed tears as she looked up at him. "I loved you so much," she whispered. "There was *nothing* I wouldn't have done for you, but it's over now. Please let me go."

Stunned, Grant stood in the corridor and watched her

until she was out of sight. He couldn't believe what she'd just said. How could it be over when they were supposed to have forever together? His stomach ached, and his head pounded, but his heart felt like it had been ripped out of his chest and run over by a truck.

Returning to his father's room, he stopped short when he saw Stephanie waiting for him.

She lowered her eyes as if embarrassed by what she'd just witnessed. "So much for acting like you don't care." She thrust a carafe at him. "Drink this. It'll make you feel better."

"As if anything can make me feel better." He took the container from her and opened it. The smell of whatever she'd concocted had his stomach surging. Recoiling, he thrust it back at her. "The cure is definitely worse than the ailment."

She pushed it back to him. "Trust me. It works."

"If I barf all over the place, I'm blaming you."

The frightened look she gave him made Grant feel like he'd kicked a puppy. "I'm just kidding."

"I know that," she said but didn't look convinced.

Mac came down the hallway looking rattled, and zeroed in on Grant. "Oh good. There you are. I need a favor."

"Sure. Anything."

"Turns out Maddie was in preterm labor."

"Oh my God," Grant said. "Is she all right? The baby?"

He nodded. "They managed to stop it, and they're both fine, but Cal put her on full bed rest until she delivers."

Grant choked back a retort about the good doctor. Everyone's hero.

"Wow," Stephanie said. "What a drag."

"Seriously," Mac agreed. "But she'll do whatever's necessary to protect the baby. It's just that she won't be able to handle a toddler on her own, so I'll need to be home a lot of the time. And with Dad and Luke out of commission—"

"I'll take care of the marina. I already told Luke that."

"We'll pay you like we would any other employee."

"Whatever," Grant said with a shrug. "It's the best job offer I've had in years."

"I find that hard to believe," Stephanie said.

Grant sent her a twisted grin. "Believe it." To his brother, he said, "Is there anything special I need to know?"

"I can show you," Stephanie said, adding, "I pay attention."

"That'd be great," Mac said. "Thank you both."

"We'll take care of McCarthy's," Grant said. "You take care of your wife and son."

"I appreciate that, bro. I really do." Mac peered into his father's room. "Any change?"

"Not yet."

"Helluva day around here," Mac said.

"How's Mom holding up?" Grant asked.

"Remarkably well. It's Janey I'm worried about. Ten days until the wedding and the matron of honor is put on bed rest and the father of the bride is out cold."

"It'll all be fine," Grant said. "You can't keep the McCarthys down for long."

Mac cast another wary glance at their father. "Let's hope you're right about that. I sure wish he'd wake up."

"Yeah, me, too. Go on back to your wife. I'll stay with him."

"Let me know the second anything changes."

"Will do. The boys will be in on the eight o'clock boat."

Mac nodded. "I'll recruit them to help out at the marina, too."

"But I'm in charge, right?" Grant asked with a teasing grin, hoping to lighten his brother's mood.

Mac rolled his eyes and went to rejoin his wife.

"You guys are so lucky," Stephanie said with a wistful expression on her face.

Grant had almost forgotten she was there. "How's that?"

"You have a great big wonderful family to lean on when times get tough."

"You don't have that?"

She shook her head and crossed her arms. "Are you going to drink that or carry it around all day?"

Intrigued by how the mention of family had shut her down, Grant lifted the container to his nose and gagged anew. "I really have to drink this?"

"You'll be praising my name in thirty minutes."

"Is that so?"

"Stop being a big baby and just drink it."

"Well, jeez, when you put it like that, here goes nothing." Grant tipped his head back to guzzle it down, and sure enough, it tried to come right back up. Somehow he kept from hurling all over the corridor, but his head spun and his eyes watered. "Holy shit," he sputtered. "What the hell was in that? Kerosene?"

"Just a little lighter fluid to keep things interesting."

His mouth fell open, and judging from the way her concoction was burning its way through his gut, he wasn't entirely sure she was kidding.

"Shut your mouth before you start to drool—or worse."

Unused to a woman talking to him that way, Grant did as he was told but took a more measuring look at the saucy waif with the spiked hair. Her eyes weren't quite green or blue but rather an interesting combination of the two colors. They were framed by extravagant lashes but marred by overly dark makeup. Multiple studs lined both her ears, and he'd caught a glimpse of a stud in her tongue. Grant swallowed hard at the thought of it. As much as the idea of a tongue stud horrified him, it intrigued him, too.

She had high cheekbones and smooth skin, and while she didn't seem to carry an extra ounce of flesh—anywhere— she had full, plump lips that seemed almost out of place on an otherwise spare face.

He let his gaze drop to her chest, where there was nothing at all to look at, and then farther down to long, thin legs encased in black denim.

His eyes flipped upward to find her taking her own measuring look—at him.

Before he could register his surprise at realizing she was checking him out, a moan from inside his father's room caught his attention. He rushed in to find Big Mac struggling against the IV and the restraints the nurses had said would be necessary when he came to. Grant put his hands on his dad's shoulders and resettled him against the pillow.

Big Mac blinked rapidly. "What're you doing here?" he asked, his voice gravelly.

Overcome with relief, Grant said, "I got home a week or so ago, Dad. Don't you remember?"

"Head hurts. What the hell happened? How'd I get here?"

Grant looked over to find Stephanie wide-eyed and teary. "Will you go get the doctor? And see if you can find my mom?"

She nodded and scurried from the room.

Grant gripped Big Mac's much larger hand and brushed at tears, not wanting his father to see them. "Hang in there, Dad. Everything's okay. You're going to be just fine."

Chapter Twenty-One

Sydney returned to Luke's to find him asleep on the sofa and was relieved to have a few minutes to regroup from the emotional encounter with her parents. She couldn't believe she'd blurted out that she loved Luke more than Seth. What kind of monster was she to admit such a thing?

She stood at the kitchen sink and looked out at the water, trying to collect herself. Maybe her father was right and it was too soon to be getting so involved with Luke. *No*, she thought. *It's not too soon. I won't let them fill my head with doubts when I've been feeling so much better about everything lately*.

Folding her trembling hands, she took deep, cleansing breaths the way her counselor had taught her whenever anxiety got the better of her. Funny how she'd never had anxiety issues until the worst possible thing had happened.

She was so focused on breathing that she never heard Luke come up behind her until his chin landed on her shoulder.

"What's wrong?"

Sydney closed her eyes and rode the wave of tenderness and desire that surged through her at the sound of his familiar voice. "Nothing. Everything's fine."

He massaged her shoulders. "Then why are you tighter than a drum?"

"You shouldn't be on your foot."

"I'm not."

She looked over her shoulder to find him propped on the crutches. "How is it?"

"We're talking about you, not me."

Looking out the window again, she said, "I'm a bad person. A truly bad person." The last thing she expected from him was laughter.

"What the hell are you talking about?"

Sydney shrugged off his hands and wiggled away from him, mindful of his precarious balance. "It's not funny."

He grabbed her hand to keep her from getting away. "You're not a bad person, Syd. I'm not sure who told you that, but they're wrong."

"I told me that. It's the truth. You shouldn't even want to be with me. That's how awful I am."

Luke dropped her hand and cupped her face. "What brought this on?"

Sydney couldn't bear to look at him. Just being in the same room with him made her itchy with the kind of all-consuming desire she'd never felt for anyone but him—and that was the problem.

He brought her in closer to him, settling her head on his chest. "I wish you'd tell me what's got you so wound up."

"I can't say it again. It was bad enough the first time."

"What was?"

"I had another argument with my parents," she muttered,

her voice muffled by his chest. "I said something so awful, so monstrous."

"About them?"

She shook her head. "About Seth."

"Aww, Syd. Just because he died doesn't mean he was perfect. Unless he was totally full of himself, which I doubt he was, he'd probably be the first to admit that. I'm not perfect. Are you?"

"Definitely not. I'm horrible."

"You really have to stop saying that stuff. You're starting to piss me off."

Sydney realized she had to level with him, but it was so hard to put it into words again. The first time she'd blurted it out in the heat of the moment. This time she knew exactly what she was saying. "Do you remember when I told you I loved him, but differently than I loved you?"

"Yeah. What about it?"

"The way it was different—"

"You don't have to tell me this. That's your business, and it has nothing to do with who we are now."

"It has a lot to do with who I am now."

He waited for her to continue.

"I knew, even as I was marrying him, that I didn't love him as much as I loved you," she said. "There. See what I mean? I'm a horrible, horrible person to even think that, let alone say it out loud."

"It must've been bothering you if you felt the need to say it at all."

"What was bothering me is my parents refusing to accept how profoundly they influenced me in the past. I won't allow that to happen again."

"Syd, look at me."

She glanced up to meet his intense gaze.

"You don't have to explain yourself to me or them or anyone. And you don't have to justify your feelings, certainly not to me. Because I *know* you, I have no doubt you were a faithful, dedicated, devoted wife to him and a wonderful mother to your children. What else matters?"

"If I'd followed my heart way back when, I never would've given Seth the time of day because I still would've been with you."

"But then you never would've had Max or Malena, and look at what you would've missed. You can't have regrets, Syd. There's just no point to that."

"If I hadn't been such a stupid fool, do you think we would've stayed together? Made it work?"

"I'd like to think so, but we were awfully young. We probably would've made a holy mess of it and proved your parents right. Maybe everything happened the way it did because we weren't meant to get our shot until later in life."

"You're so rational and sane."

"One of us has to be."

That earned him a reluctant smile.

"You're not a bad person, Syd. Being back with me again has stirred up some old crap that has you questioning decisions you made a long time ago. I understand that, but nothing good will come of second-guessing yourself now."

Hadn't she learned there was no point in harboring regrets? That all we have is right now? However, knowing that didn't do much to assuage her guilt.

"Could I ask you something?"

"Sure," she said, unnerved by his serious expression.

"Are you going to be able to get past the guilt and allow yourself to be happy again?"

Sydney stared at him, dumbfounded by the question and how he'd zeroed right in on her thoughts. "I, ah . . ."

"It's a decision you have to make not to let guilt ruin the rest of your life."

He was right, and she knew it. Still, the guilt had been ever-present since she reconnected with Luke. But that wasn't all that had been present. "Since we've been back together, I've been so happy."

"Then hold on to that rather than the guilt. Happiness is a much more productive emotion than guilt." He leaned in to kiss her. "Give yourself permission to be happy, Syd," he said softly. "It's okay. I promise."

"Thank you." She put her arms around him and held on for a long, quiet moment. "You need to get off your foot."

"Come lie down with me."

She followed him into the bedroom and helped to get his injured ankle settled on a pillow. Stretching out next to him, she rested her head on his chest and her hand on his firm belly. "I need to go see Buddy and check on Maddie. And I'm sure you want to know how Mr. McCarthy is doing."

"I'm concerned about all of them, but for right now, this is what I need." He tightened his arm around her. "You're what I need." Tangling his fingers in her hair, he tipped her head back to receive his kiss. "I hate to see you beating yourself up over stuff that doesn't matter. Don't do that anymore."

"Yes, sir," she said, smiling at him. "How's the ankle?"

"Much better since the pain meds kicked in."

"Will you be okay not working for a couple of weeks?"

"I'll be fine."

"I can chip in, since I'm all but living here."

His face lifted into a sweet smile. "I don't need your money, Syd, but thanks for offering."

She raised herself up on an elbow so she could better see his face. "What if—hypothetically speaking—I move here at some point?"

"Don't get my hopes up."

"I'm serious. I'd want to chip in."

He ran a hand over her head and tugged on her hair. "I've got us covered, babe."

"I know you make decent money on the boats you restore, but you can't make all that much at McCarthy's, can you?"

"You'd be surprised," he said with a mysterious smile.

"What does that mean?"

"Does it matter how much money I make? If I can feed and clothe us and provide shelter, what else do we need?"

"Well, there're cars and insurance and vacations and entertainment and household expenses and—"

He rested a finger over her lips. "If you live with me, life will be a lot simpler than what you're used to."

"I know that."

"Do you really, Syd? Because we're talking very simple and very quiet."

"I get it."

"I promise we'd have everything we need." He leaned in to nuzzle her neck. "What other convincing do you require?"

"We'll discuss that when your ankle feels better."

"My ankle is numb at the moment, but another part of me is starting to ache."

Sydney laughed at the face he made and cupped his straining erection.

His head fell back, and his hips surged in encouragement.

"Luke?"

"Hmm?"

"What if I move here and I hate it? What would we do then?"

He reached for her hand. "You have to stop that if you expect me to talk right now."

She shifted her hand to his thigh. "Better?"

"Not really." He sat up and put his arm around her. "I suppose if island life isn't for you, then we'll move."

"You wouldn't mind that?"

"I'd miss it here, but I'd miss you more if you left without me."

Touched by his sweet words, Sydney shifted carefully to straddle him. "I have some things to take care of at home after Labor Day. Then I can make some decisions about what's next."

"Will we make these decisions together?"

"I hope so."

With his hands on her bottom, he brought her in tight against his arousal. "I hope so, too."

She looped her arms around his neck and kissed him.

"Now what're you thinking?"

"What do you mean?"

His finger traced the furrow between her brows. "Dead giveaway."

He read her so well that sometimes it was almost unsettling. "What if we rearrange our lives for each other and it doesn't work out between us?"

"I don't think that'll happen, but if it does, we'll figure it out then."

"I suppose you're right."

"Why don't you look convinced?"

"I want so badly to believe it'll all be fine, but after everything that's happened to me—hell, after what happened *today*—I'm having trouble with the concept of happily ever after."

"All I could think about on the way to the hospital was how freaked out you'd be when you heard about what'd happened at the marina. I wanted so badly to spare you from that."

She combed her fingers through his hair. "It was a good thing I was with Maddie when I heard about it. I had to keep it together for her sake." Remembering that moment of sheer panic, she shuddered. "I was so afraid you'd been badly hurt or worse."

"I'm sorry you were so afraid. I hate that I caused that."

"I hate that you and Mr. McCarthy got hurt."

"It's all over now, baby." Curving his hand around her neck, he brought her in for a soft, sweet kiss that quickly spun out of control.

Sydney drew back from him. "Hold that thought for an hour or two, will you?" As she got up, he let out a tortured moan. Leaning over the bed, she kissed his forehead. "You'll survive."

"Where're you going?"

Sydney ran a brush through her hair. "I need to see Buddy."

"You're seriously choosing a *dog* over me? You know how to wound a guy."

Sydney pulled off her shirt and reached for a clean one. "I'm not choosing a *dog* over you. I'm choosing *Buddy* over you—and only temporarily. I don't want him wondering where I am."

"All right," he said with a long-suffering sigh. "When you put it like that, I guess I can live with it. Of course, I'm recovering, too."

Groaning, Sydney said, "Don't turn into a typical man on me. Please."

Luke laughed. "I wasn't aware I'd been atypical. What would make me typical?"

"Acting like a big baby just because you're a little bit injured."

"A minute ago you were getting weepy because I nearly died. How fast you forget."

"Typical men are also pouty when they don't get their own way."

He reached behind him and pulled his shirt over his head, tossing it across the room and just missing the laundry basket.

Sydney bent to pick it up and put it in the basket. "Also typical." She turned, intending to scowl at him, but the sight of his sculpted chest and ripped abs made her mouth dry and her mind blank.

"Syd?"

"Oh, um, sorry." She couldn't believe she'd been caught gawking at him.

With his hands behind his head and a satisfied smirk on his face, he reclined against the pillows. "It'll still be here when you get back."

"You're being typical again."

"Maybe I can be typical later, too. After all, my kind is known for being after one thing only, right?"

"You're injured."

"All the most important parts still work."

She stopped to kiss him one more time. "Stay off that foot."

"You're turning into a typical woman."
Hands on hips, she worked up a glare. "How so?"
"B-o-s-s-y," he said, accentuating every letter.
"I can live with that. Be back soon."
"Hurry!"

Chapter Twenty-Two

Sydney found Maddie still at the clinic, where she was spending the night for observation, and leaned over the bed rail to hug her. She was surprised when Maddie held on tight.

"I'm going to kill him," she whispered.

"Who?" Sydney asked.

"My husband."

"Oh."

Maddie finally released her just as Mac came into the room, his eyes crazy and his stride determined.

"I contacted the head of obstetrics at Women and Infants in Providence. She said we can come over in the morning, and she'll see you at noon."

"No," Maddie said.

His eyes nearly popped out of his skull. "What do you mean, *no*?"

"Sydney, will you please tell my husband what the word *no* means?"

"Um, I'd rather not get involved. I'll just wait outside."

Maddie's hand clamped down on her arm. "If you

leave, I'll kill you after I kill him," she said through gritted teeth.

Sydney suppressed a chuckle.

"Maddie, listen to me," Mac said, clearly working at keeping his tone calm.

"I'm *not* leaving the island. I'm in perfectly good hands with Cal, and if you don't quit telling me what to do and *relax*, I'm going to lose it. Do you hear me?"

"How can I relax when you almost went into labor three months early and won't let me take you to a specialist to make sure everything is okay with you and the baby?"

"The stress of what happened today triggered the early labor, and avoiding stress will keep it from happening again. So if you don't want more early labor, *stop stressing me out*!"

"Maddie—"

"Mac."

They were so caught up in glowering at each other that Sydney thought she might have a chance at escaping, but when she tried to break free from Maddie's grip, she just tightened her hold. Foiled.

"Fine," Mac said through gritted teeth. "But don't try to tell me—"

"Will you please go pick up Thomas from Tiffany's? I need to see him."

Hands on hips and a stubborn set to his jaw, he said, "I don't want to leave you."

"Syd will be here, won't you?" Maddie asked, looking up at Sydney.

"Of course. I'll stay until you get back."

"If you're sure," Mac said.

"Go!" Maddie said. "See your father and then go get your son."

"You're reminding me of the day I met you," Mac said.

Something about the way he said that told Sydney he wasn't complimenting his wife.

Maddie's eyes narrowed. "Ditto."

He moved to the other side of the bed and bent to give her a lingering kiss.

Feeling like she was intruding, Sydney looked away.

"We'll talk more about this when I get back."

"No, we won't. Subject closed. Now go get our son."

Mac shook his head in frustration and stalked from the room.

"Well," Sydney said cheerfully, "glad everything is going so well for you guys."

Maddie busted up laughing. "I swear to God, I *am* going to kill him."

"No, you're not. You were beside yourself earlier when you thought he might be injured or worse."

Maddie's eyes filled, and she looked away.

Sydney reached for her hand. "What is it?"

Maddie shifted her gaze to meet Sydney's. "I thought I knew how it might feel to lose what you lost. But until that phone call from Janey, I had no idea."

"And I hope you never do. Thank goodness they're all okay."

"How's Luke?"

"Sore but feisty."

"We're all very grateful for what he did. If he weren't already an honorary member of the McCarthy family, he would be now. Ever since Mr. McCarthy made him a partner in the business—"

"What did you say?"

"That they made him a partner? When Mac joined the business, they divided it among the three of them, but Mac and Luke own the majority."

Astounded, Syd dropped into the chair next to the bed. "He *owns* the business?"

"A big part of it. Didn't he tell you?"

Sydney shook her head as she tried to figure out what it meant that he hadn't told her.

"I'm sorry. I thought you knew."

"Why wouldn't he tell me? We just talked about money earlier today, and he never mentioned he's a partner in the marina." She remembered his mysterious smile when she mentioned his income from McCarthy's.

"Why were you talking about money?"

"We were making some tentative plans."

"Oh, does this mean you're staying?" Maddie clutched her hand. "Please say yes."

"We haven't decided anything for sure, but now . . ." She shrugged.

"Oh, Syd, don't go there. He might have a perfectly good reason for not telling you. Give him a chance to explain."

Sydney tried to shake it off to be dealt with later. "Let's talk about you. What can I do? I can help with Thomas and the nursery and anything else you need. Just say the word."

"What I could really use is some help with Janey's shower. It's supposed to be Sunday, and I've been sitting here all day thinking about postponing it—"

"No need. I'll take care of everything. You can direct."

"Are you sure you want to take that on?"

"I'd be thrilled to help you out."

"I feel so bad for Janey—her dad is hurt and her matron of honor is on bed rest less than two weeks before her wedding."

"We'll get a chaise for you for the wedding so you can be right there with her and not exert yourself."

Maddie cringed at the idea of it. "So I'll be like the queen of Sheba laid out at Janey's wedding?"

"She'll be so excited to marry Joe and to have you there with her, she won't care in the least."

"What've you got in your bag of tricks for dealing with overwrought husbands?"

Sydney laughed. "You're on your own there, my friend."

"I was afraid you'd say that."

Maddie and Sydney discussed bridal shower plans until Mac returned with Thomas.

"Mama," he cried, breaking free from Mac's grasp and running for Maddie's bed.

Mac scooped him up. "Easy, pal. Don't forget what we talked about in the car."

Maddie reached for Thomas and hugged him when Mac handed him over. "What did you boys talk about?"

"Mama has to rest," Thomas said. "'Cuz of my baby brother in your belly."

Maddie glanced at Mac, hoping to see amusement but finding none. "Remember when Daddy and I told you it could be a baby sister?"

Thomas shook his head. "No sisters."

Maddie shared a laugh with Sydney, but Mac barely cracked a grin. She could tell by the set of his shoulders that he was still full of tension.

"Did you see your dad?" she asked Mac.

He nodded. "He's awake and cranky and his head hurts, but he's doing better. My mom, Janey, Joe, Grant and Ned are with him. Your mom said she'll be in after a while."

Maddie had a few questions for her mother, who'd yet to come by to see her—probably because she knew

Maddie would grill her about Ned. "I'm so glad your dad is cranky. That's a good sign." To Thomas, she said, "Can you say hi to Mama's friend Sydney?"

"Hi," Thomas said, smiling. "Buddy?"

"That's right. You remembered. Guess what? Buddy has been sick, too."

Thomas's white-blond eyebrows knitted with concern.

"You know," Sydney said, venturing a glance at Maddie, "if it's okay with your mama and daddy, you can come with me to see him. If you want to, that is."

"Can I see Buddy, Mama?" Thomas asked.

"Sure. That sounds like fun. But you have to be very gentle with Buddy, okay?"

His face solemn, Thomas nodded.

To Mac, Sydney said, "Could we trade cars for a little while so I'll have the car seat? I'll take him to see Buddy and then to Luke's for dinner so you guys can have some time."

Maddie wasn't sure if she wanted time alone with her husband when he was in this mood, but she couldn't disappoint Thomas. "What do you say to Syd?"

"Thank you," Thomas said.

"And you'll be a very good boy?"

He nodded.

"Okay, then. Give me another big hug first."

Thomas wrapped his pudgy arms around her neck and squeezed.

Maddie breathed in the scent of little boy and the sunscreen Tiffany had applied so they could play outside in the sprinkler.

Thomas squirmed free.

"Have a good time, buddy." Mac hugged Thomas and traded keys with Sydney. "Be a good boy."

"Does he have any allergies, or anything he can't or won't eat?" Sydney asked.

"Not that we're aware of," Mac said. "He's not a big fan of vegetables."

"Shocker." Syd extended her hand to Thomas. "I bet Luke has some spaghetti we can make."

"Sketti," Thomas said with a bright smile.

"He likes it with butter and cheese," Mac said. "No sauce."

"Got it. Stay as late as you want, Mac. If he conks out, I'll put him down at Luke's."

"Thanks, Syd," Maddie said.

"Yes, thank you," Mac added.

Hand in hand, Sydney and Thomas walked out of the room. Maddie could hear Thomas's happy chatter all the way down the hallway.

"That was nice of her," Mac said.

"Very." Maddie fiddled with the blanket.

"How do you feel?" he asked, vibrating with tension he was clearly trying—and failing—to keep hidden from her. Unfortunately for him, she knew him better than anyone and could see right through his act.

"Fine."

"What's with the one-word answers?"

"Nothing."

"Great," he said with a sharp laugh. "That's perfect. *You're* mad at *me*?"

Maddie shrugged. "You were a little over the top earlier."

Hands on his hips, he said, "At least that's more than one word. We're making progress."

"Mac."

"What?" he snapped.

"Come here."

"I'm here."

Maddie patted the bed. "Here."

Reluctantly—or so it seemed to her—he perched on the bed, arms folded, shoulders set.

"Closer."

"I don't want to. In case you haven't noticed, *I'm* mad with *you*."

"I noticed, but I need you."

Right before her eyes, all the starch went out of him, and he turned to her, one hand on either side of her hips. "What? Is something else wrong? Does something hurt?"

Laughing softly, she extended her arms. "Come here."

"Are you *mocking* me?" he asked as he moved into her embrace.

"Never." Choking back a laugh, she ran her fingers through the thick dark hair she loved so much and held him close until he began to relax—as much as he ever did.

"You're making me crazy," he muttered.

"I know."

"You won't even *think* about going to Providence for a second opinion?"

"Why do we need one? Cal said the early labor was brought on by the stress of what happened today. I need to stay in bed for three months until the baby comes, which totally sucks, but I'll do what I have to."

"Maybe we should just move to the mainland until the baby comes so we're closer to real hospitals. We could stay at Joe's place—"

Maddie pinched his lips closed. "I want to be in our home with our things, near our family."

"But—"

"No buts. I trust Cal, and he sees no reason for me to go to the mainland."

"What about me?"

Once again Maddie found herself biting back a laugh

that she knew her darling husband wouldn't appreciate. "Are you pregnant, too?"

He turned his face so she could see his scowl. "What if I die of a heart attack from the stress of being so far from a hospital if my wife needs more than this Podunk place can provide?"

"That's not going to happen."

"And are you in possession of a crystal ball I don't know about?"

"I've got something better—mother's intuition."

"I can't bear the thought of you needing something that I can't get you."

Maddie cupped his face. "You've already given me everything. You're the best husband and father anyone could ever hope to have, but if you don't *chill out*, I'll have no choice but to kill you. Do you understand me?"

He chuckled. "You couldn't live without me."

"No, I couldn't, but you still have to relax. Your stress is becoming my stress."

"I get it."

"Today was a bad day, but your dad is okay. I'm okay. You're okay. Take a deep breath, will you please?"

Mac did as directed, and a big shudder shook through his muscular frame. "Remember when I said I wanted four kids?"

"Vaguely."

"I don't think I can do it."

This time Maddie couldn't hold back the laughter. "Because it really is all about you."

"No, baby, it's all about *you*. That's the problem. I love you so damned much that the thought of you being in any kind of jeopardy makes me crazy."

"Then you know how I felt today when I didn't know what had happened to you."

"A very bad day."

"Tomorrow will be better." She continued to stroke his hair, which was wild and disheveled from being wet earlier, and pressed her lips to his forehead. "Except for the part about three months in bed."

"With no fun," he said glumly.

"He didn't say *no* fun. He said no to *one kind* of fun. There're plenty of other kinds, as we've discovered."

"And suddenly this bad day is looking up."

"Mac?"

"Hmm?"

"I love you so damned much, too."

He raised his head and shifted on the bed so he could kiss her. "I'll let you call the shots this time."

"Gee, thanks."

"But you'd better not let anything happen to you, Madeline, or you'll deal with me. Got me?"

She clutched his shirt and brought him in for another kiss. "Got you."

Chapter Twenty-Three

Thomas chattered all the way to Sydney's parents' house, where they found Buddy had been given a place of honor on the sofa, wearing what Seth had called "the cone of shame." The poor guy had hated the cone after his neutering surgery, but this time he didn't seem to have the energy—yet—to do battle with it.

When he saw her coming, he raised his head and let out a weak whimper.

She worked around the cone to smooch Buddy's face. "Awww, how's my good boy?"

He licked her cheek.

"Mom? Dad?"

"Be right down," her mother called.

Syd held a hand out to Thomas. "Come say hi to Buddy."

He toddled over to the sofa. "What's smatter wid him?"

Sydney had already grown to love that serious expression of Thomas's. "He had to have an operation."

"How come?"

Syd took the little boy's hand and held it for Buddy to lick. "He ate something he shouldn't have, and it got stuck in his belly."

"What did he eat?"

"A trash bag."

Thomas wrinkled his nose. "Yucky."

"Very," Syd said, laughing. "You hear that, Buddy? Trash bags are yucky."

"Hopefully, he's learned his lesson," Mary Alice said as she joined them.

"Probably wishful thinking," Syd said. "Mom, this is Thomas McCarthy, Mac and Maddie's son. Thomas, this is my mom, Mrs. Donovan."

As they shook hands, Sydney noted the yearning on her mother's face. She missed her grandchildren something fierce.

"What a handsome young man you are."

"He's adorable," Syd agreed. She filled her mother in on Maddie's condition.

Thomas giggled as Buddy continued to lick his hand.

"I can't imagine three months in bed," Mary Alice said, grimacing.

"No kidding. It'll be a challenge with a busy toddler to manage, too."

Thomas was fascinated with Buddy. "Can he play?"

"Not today. He's got to get better first. You can come back next week to visit him. Maybe then he'll be up for playing."

"Why does he have to wear that hat?"

"So he won't pull his stitches out."

"Oh." Thomas bent to press a kiss on the dog's nose. "Get better, Buddy."

"What a sweet boy," Mary Alice said. "The vet said Buddy will be sleepy for the next few days, so don't worry about leaving him with us for now."

"I guess I can live without him for a day or two but not much longer."

"Dad can bring him over whenever you're ready."

"Let me see how Luke is doing tomorrow."

To Thomas, Mary Alice said, "How would you like some cookies and milk?"

Thomas glanced at Sydney, who nodded. "You can have dessert before dinner—but don't tell your mom, okay?"

Delighted by the conspiracy, Thomas giggled. "Okay, Syd."

Mary Alice reached out to Thomas. "Let's get those hands washed."

As she watched them go into the kitchen, Sydney, too, was filled with yearning for her own children who would've loved Thomas. They'd always had an affinity for younger children, and more than once, Sydney had questioned her decision to have her tubes tied after Malena was born. They would've been an awesome big-brother-and-sister team to a younger sibling.

"Looks like you've made a new friend, Buddy." She spoke softly to him and ran her hand over his back until he drifted off to sleep.

Sydney checked her watch and realized she needed to get back to make dinner for Luke. Remembering what he'd failed to tell her had her stomach aching with anxiety. Why hadn't he told her? Should she ask him? Or should she wait for him to tell her himself? Would he ever tell her? It was all so confusing.

She'd always thought of Luke as an open book—what you see is what you get—but she was discovering there was so much more to him. His boat renovation business was a prime example, and it was another thing he'd failed to mention to her.

Still pondering the issue, Sydney went to join her mother and Thomas in the kitchen. Her mom was wiping chocolate from Thomas's mouth and clearly enjoying the visit with the little boy.

"I'd forgotten," she said softly.

"About?"

"How sweet they are at this age. How open to every new experience they are."

"I always thought two got a bad rap," Sydney said. "*Three* was terrible, and four was willful, but two was sweet and cuddly."

"You know," Mary Alice said tentatively, "I'd be delighted to help out with Thomas while Maddie is on bed rest. I could take him to lunch and the park, or he could come over here for an afternoon." Mary Alice stopped herself, maybe not wanting to get her hopes up. "If it would help."

Sydney hugged her mom. "I'm sure Maddie would love that, and how lucky would Thomas be to get a third grandma to dote on him?"

Mary Alice smiled and put another cookie on Thomas's plate.

"One more," Sydney said. "And then we need to go check on Luke. He hurt his foot."

"Papa got a boo-boo on his head," Thomas said.

"Yes, but he's going to be just fine. And so is your mommy and Luke."

"Quite a day around here," Mary Alice said.

"No kidding—and everyone talks about how nothing ever happens on Gansett."

"Plenty happens around here." Syd's parents had become

year-round residents six years ago but retained their Boston-area home and had spent most of the previous winter there so Syd wouldn't be alone. "Stick around for a winter. You'll see."

"I just might do that."

Mary Alice gasped. "Oh, Syd, really?"

"Thinking about it."

"Are you planning to live with Luke?"

"Maybe." Although they'd have to talk at some point about why he felt the need to keep the bigger details of his life from her. "What would you think of that?"

"Well, you know I'm not a big fan of shacking up."

Sydney laughed. "Come on, Mom. It's not 1950 anymore."

"I don't care if it's 2050," Mary Alice said haughtily. "People should be married before they live together."

"We can agree to disagree."

"It's not lost on me that you're nearly thirty-six and can do whatever the heck you want."

"Well, thank you for that, but your approval has always mattered to me—maybe a little too much."

"It's also not lost on me that you seem very happy with him, and your happiness matters more than anything to me. So I'll do my best to keep my opinions to myself from now on."

Sydney rolled her eyes. "That'll be the day."

"Now that's just not nice," Mary Alice said with a grin.

"Truth hurts," Syd said, kissing her mother's cheek.

"I was planning on steak and baked potatoes for dinner tomorrow night. Does Luke like steak?"

"He loves it. That'll be perfect." Sydney scooped up Thomas and wiped the last of the chocolate from his face. "What do you say for the cookies?"

"Thank you."

"You're very welcome, Thomas. I hope you'll come visit me again soon." Mary Alice handed Sydney a baggie full of cookies. "For your patient."

Touched by the gesture, Syd took the bag. "Thanks, Mom. I'll see you tomorrow."

Ned hovered outside Big Mac's room, waiting for the opportunity to see his best friend. What a damned upsetting day this had been! When he'd seen Big Mac in the water, blood pouring from his head . . . Ned shuddered at the memory. For a few minutes there, he was sure his friend was dead. Thank God Mac had acted so quickly—and at his own peril—to save his father. And Luke! What that boy had done! Ned would be reliving the horror of it all for a good long time.

Big Mac was urging Linda to go home. Ned had to agree with his friend—the usually unflappable Linda McCarthy looked to be on her last legs.

"I swear I'll be fine," Big Mac said, drawing his wife into a kiss. His left arm was encased in a cast and resting on a pillow. "Go on now. We can't have you dropping from exhaustion."

Linda was weepy and clingy—two other things Ned had never seen before. The whole scene was only adding to his stress level.

"Come on, Mom," Janey said, putting her arm around her mother. "Joe and I will take you home."

"I'll stay with Dad," Grant said.

"You go, too," Big Mac said. "You look like hell. Get some sleep. Come back in the morning."

"But Dad—"

"Adam and Evan will be here soon. I won't be alone."

"I'll be here, too," Ned said from the doorway.

"If you're sure," Linda said.

"I'm very sure. Go on home, hon. I promise I'll still be here in the morning."

"That's not funny," Linda said, sniffling as she bent to kiss him one last time.

"You kids take your mother home. Make sure she eats and sleeps."

Grant and Janey did as they were told with Joe tagging along with them. On her way by, Linda hugged Ned. "Call me if anything changes."

"Ya know I will, gal. I'll stay 'til the boys get here."

Linda patted his arm and went with the kids.

"Whew," Big Mac said when they were alone. "How's a man supposed to get a minute's peace with all that hovering?"

"Don't try to fool me. Ya love all the attention."

Big Mac snickered and then winced.

"Gave us a helluva scare today."

"So I hear. It's all a blur."

"Let's hope it stays that way. Not worth remembering."

"Perhaps you can help me fill in some of the blanks."

"I don't wanna talk about it. Worst thing I ever seen."

"Not about the accident. I'm having these vague flashes of memory. Something about you and a woman . . ."

Ned looked up in time to see the glint of devil in his old friend's eyes. Even though he was relieved to see the spark of life, he sure as hell didn't want to talk about Francine. "Ya didn't remember yer own son was home from Lala Land, but ya remember that?"

"Funny how the brain works, huh?"

"I still don't wanna talk about it," Ned huffed. Damn if he couldn't feel his face getting red.

"Aw, come on. I almost died today. Least you can do is toss me a little bone."

Ned choked back a burst of temper. "Don't go playin' that 'almost died' card."

"Come on, it's *me*. We don't have secrets. Least I didn't think we did."

"I ain't tellin' ya nothin', 'cuz ya got the biggest mouth on the island. It'll be all over the docks by morning."

"I swear to God I won't tell anyone."

"Since ya owe God a few favors right 'bout now, I'll hold ya to that. Nothing much to tell. We had dinner. Big whoop."

"Tell that to someone who wasn't there that summer she left you for Bobby Chester or who hasn't watched you avoid her for thirty-two years."

"Don'tcha need to rest up so ya can walk yer baby girl down the aisle?"

"I wouldn't miss that for the world, and you know it, so don't try to change the subject."

Frustrated, Ned ran a hand over his wild white hair. "What d'ya want me to say?"

"I want you to tell me you're being careful. That you won't let her do the same thing she did before."

"Ya say that to Luke, too?"

"So what if I did? It's turning into recycle summer around here."

Ned hooted with laughter. "That's a helluva way to put it."

"I'll tell you the same thing I told him—watch yourself. Don't let her do it to you again. It was bad enough watching that the first time."

"I'm older and wiser this time round."

"Let's hope so."

"Even though yer a pain in my ass, I'm glad ya didn't die."

Big Mac laughed and then winced again when his head fought back. "Aww, thanks a lot, old pal."

"Anytime."

Chapter Twenty-Four

Janey told herself if she just kept busy, she could prevent the meltdown that had been threatening all day. She made soup for her mom and ran her a bath. She put fresh sheets on beds for Adam and Evan, and cleaned up the kitchen. As she was putting the last of the dishes in the dishwasher, Joe hugged her from behind.

"You're running at ninety miles an hour, babe," he said, his lips brushing against her neck.

She attempted to squiggle free of his embrace. "I need to toss in some laundry."

"Not tonight."

Janey turned to him, primed for a rare fight. But when she saw only love and concern on his face, she sagged against the counter.

"You're completely exhausted. Let's go home."

"You can go. I should stay here in case my mom needs me."

"I'm not going anywhere without you, and Grant will be here for your mom. You need sleep."

"The boys will need—"

"To fend for themselves. The *boys* are grown men who manage to survive without you the rest of the time."

Her lip began to quiver, a sure sign of impending meltdown. "But I have to—"

He wrapped his strong arms around her. "Stop, Janey. Just stop."

Despite her best efforts to contain it, a sob hiccupped through her, and the floodgates opened.

He ran his hand up and down her back. "It's okay, honey. Let it all out. It's been an awful day."

"I'm sorry," she said, wiping her face several minutes later. "My dad . . ."

"You can't imagine life without him."

Her heart ached as she shook her head.

"Neither can I."

"What happened today was a big reminder that someday we'll have to live without him." She looked up at Joe. "How will we ever do that?"

"I have no idea, but thankfully that's not something we have to think about anytime soon." He wiped the tears from her face. "Let's go home. You need some time with the menagerie."

At the reminder of her beloved pets, she forced a wan smile for his benefit. "And with you."

"And with me."

"Let me tell my mom I'm leaving." Janey kissed Joe and went upstairs, where her mother was getting into bed. "Mom? Are you all settled?"

"Getting there."

"Joe wants to take me home. Will you be okay?"

"I'll be fine. Go on ahead."

Janey perched on the edge of the bed. "Grant will be back shortly. He went to get Dad's truck at the marina."

"Oh good. He and the boys can use it."

"They can fight over it like old times."

Linda offered a small smile as her eyes filled.

"What, Mom?"

"I've been thinking about how you just never know what's going to happen. I was in such a big rush this morning. Late for a hair appointment. Dad was in the shower, and I left without even saying good-bye." She looked up at Janey. "What if that'd been my last chance to see him, to tell him . . ."

Janey blinked back tears of her own. "He's not ready to leave us yet."

Linda sat up to hug her daughter.

"I can stay if you don't want to sleep alone."

"Go sleep with Joe. Make sure you never miss a chance to tell him, to show him."

"I won't." Janey kissed her mother's cheek. "On that note, love you, Mom. Always have—even when it seemed like I hated you."

Taken aback by words they rarely said out loud, Linda said, "I always knew the hate phase was an act."

"You know everything. That's why we call you Voodoo Mama."

Linda scowled. "I hate that name."

"Which is why it's so fun to call you that," Janey said with an evil grin. "I'll see you in the morning."

"Janey?"

She turned at the doorway.

"Love you, too," Linda said. "My little girl who saved me from having five boys and then turned out to be the hell-raiser of the group."

"At least I never ended up in jail like Mac the Golden Child did." None of his siblings ever missed a chance to mention Mac's night in jail after he and Joe got caught flattening mailboxes in Big Mac's truck.

"True," Linda said.

Janey blew her mother a kiss and went downstairs to Joe.

Luke made good use of the time Sydney was gone to make dinner and clean up the kitchen. While the crutches were a pain, they were necessary since he couldn't bear to put an ounce of weight on his injured ankle. Being hobbled this way was going to seriously suck, but Luke refused to lie around and feel sorry for himself.

As he worked in the kitchen, the conversation he'd had earlier with Sydney kept running through his mind. He could feel her edging toward a decision to stay on the island, to stay with him. She said she had things to take care of before she could make a plan for the next phase of her life. Of course he was dying to know what she needed to do, but he didn't want to ask. She had her secrets, and he had his.

He couldn't say, exactly, why he hadn't told her that he now owned part of the marina. It wasn't that he didn't want her to know. Deep inside he suspected his reluctance had something to do with the differences in their social status. Syd and her family had always been well-off, while he and his mother had struggled. Those differences had driven them apart once before, and Luke was afraid it could happen again.

He could level the playing field a bit by telling her about the partnership, but he didn't want to wonder later if that played any part in getting her to stay. Except for during his mother's illness, Luke had never given a shit about money. As long as he had what he needed, what else mattered? He wanted Sydney to stay because she loved him and couldn't imagine life without him, not because she was impressed that he owned a successful business. He wanted them to have a real chance at something meaningful.

A knock on the door had Luke hobbling into the living room. Opening the door, he was surprised to find Grant McCarthy there. "Come in," he said, swiveling on the crutches.

"Hope I'm not disturbing you."

"Not at all. How's your dad?"

"Much better and full of beans. Kicked me and my mom and Janey out. Adam and Evan will be in on the eight o'clock boat, so they're taking the next shift with him."

"Glad to hear he's feisty. That's a good sign."

"How's the ankle?"

"Pretty good for now. I'm told that keeping up with the pain meds will be important the first few days."

Grant winced. "I know you've heard this a hundred times already, but we're all so grateful for what you did. When I think about what could've happened . . ."

"Probably better not to think about it. How about a beer?"

Grant shook his head. "No, thanks."

Luke headed toward the kitchen. "I've got stuff on the stove."

Grant followed him. "I figured your lady would be tending to your every need tonight."

"No such luck. She had to go check on her dog, who had surgery earlier this week."

"Ouch. Second to a dog."

"I know, huh? Such is my luck."

"Must be nice to be back with her again."

Resting on the crutches for support, Luke dumped the pot of pasta into a colander in the sink. "It's amazing—and complicated."

"What happened to her is such a terrible tragedy. How's she doing now?"

"She still has some rough moments, but for the most part, she's doing well."

"I'm glad you're getting another chance with her."

"I just hope it works out this time."

"And if it doesn't?"

The question sent a shaft of fear zipping through Luke. "I don't even like to think about that."

Grant dropped to one of the stools at the counter. "I hope you make out better than I did."

"I take it you talked to Abby."

Grimacing, Grant nodded. "Twice."

"And?"

"She says it's over. She's actually going to marry that guy." He looked up at Luke, devastation marking his features. "Can you believe that?"

"I can't imagine either of you with anyone else."

"Neither can I."

"So what's the plan?"

"Haven't exactly got one."

"You can't just give up."

"She's *engaged*, man. Getting married in October."

"She's not married yet."

Grant crossed his arms. "She was pretty damned clear earlier when she said it's over for us."

"A lot can happen between now and October. You might have to bide your time. Wait for your chance."

"Is that what you're doing with Sydney?"

"I'm trying to give her space to figure things out. Sometimes it's hard to be patient, because I know what I want."

"I hope you get it."

"Back atcha." Luke raised his water bottle in toast to Grant. "It's good to have you home."

"I wish I could say it's good to be here, but between this thing with Abby and what happened to you and my dad, this visit has sucked the big one."

"Nowhere to go but up from here."

"No kidding." Grant took a long look around the kitchen. "This place is exactly as I remembered it."

"It's been brought to my attention that I'm in a time warp. Syd's going to update me."

Grant smiled. "You or the house?"

"Both, I suspect. You know me—if it ain't broke, don't fix it."

"I envy you," Grant said.

Luke snorted with laughter. "*You* envy *me*?"

"You know exactly where you belong in the world. You're doing what you love in a place you love. Must be nice."

"You don't love your work?"

Grant's jaw tightened with tension. "Haven't for a long, long time." He uttered a sharp laugh. "First time I've said that out loud." Shaking his head, he said, "I've spent the last three years spinning my wheels. I kept thinking if I gave it one more year, I could turn things around, but it went from bad to worse. Now my career has gone to shit, and I've managed to lose Abby, too."

"Wow, sorry, man. I had no idea about the career. I figured you were flying high after the Oscar win."

"That's what I wanted everyone to think. It's a heck of a thing to win the big award and feel like such a loser afterward."

"I certainly know nothing about writing screenplays or writing anything, for that matter, but I can't help but think a break from it all might be just what you need. Put it aside for a while, help out at the marina, chill with us, enjoy your sister's wedding. Stop putting so much pressure on yourself, and maybe things will begin to click again."

"That's not *bad* advice," Grant said with the wry grin the high school girls had gone wild over.

"Glad to be of service. You know how it is out here—slow, quiet, peaceful. A few weeks of that and you'll be a new man."

"Or I'll be going out of my freaking mind."

"Mac thought the same thing, and look at him now."

Grant laughed. "As domesticated as it gets."

"Exactly."

"Thanks for listening to me bitch. It's good to be back with my real friends again."

"It's good to have you." Luke heard the front door open, and damned if his heart didn't do a happy dance in his chest.

Sydney came into the kitchen carrying Thomas. Her cheeks were red from the warm summer day, and her eyes were bright and animated. She was so beautiful she took his breath away.

"Oh, hi, Grant," she said. "I wondered whose truck that was."

"Hi, Syd." Grant reached for his nephew, and Sydney handed him over. "Hey, pal. What've you been up to?"

Thomas hugged his uncle. "I saw Buddy, and he has a funny hat on."

"My dog," Sydney said for Grant's benefit. "Cone of shame so he won't pull out his stitches."

"Ouch," Luke said, wincing. "He must love that."

"He's still kind of out of it, but in a day or two, he'll be furious about it."

Thomas squiggled out of Grant's embrace and scooted over to check out Luke's crutches.

"I'm going to split so you guys can eat," Grant said.

"You're welcome to stay," Luke said. "I made plenty."

"Thanks, but I'm supposed to be babysitting my mom tonight, so I'd better get home." When Luke started toward the door, Grant stopped him. "Stay put. I can find my way out."

"Thanks for coming by."

"Thanks for the pep talk."

"Anytime."

After they heard the door close, Sydney turned to him. Something about her seemed different, but he couldn't figure out what. "You're giving pep talks now?"

Luke shrugged. "He's going through a rough patch." He reached down to ruffle Thomas's hair. "How'd we end up with this little guy?"

"Mac and Maddie needed some time to themselves, so I took him with me to see Buddy. I figured we could feed him dinner and give him a bath. Mac is going to pick him up later." She paused and bit her bottom lip. "I hope it's okay I brought him here."

"Of course it is. Everything okay with Maddie?"

"Except for Mac driving her crazy wanting to take her to specialists."

Chuckling, Luke said, "I can only imagine how worked up he must be."

"At times like this, island life is challenging. He wants her near doctors and hospitals."

"I can understand that." Luke took a closer look at her, still trying to put his finger on what was different. "What about you? Everything okay?"

Seeming surprised, she flipped her eyes up to meet his gaze. "I'm fine, why?"

"No reason." Maybe he was looking for trouble where there was none. "I made spaghetti."

"That's perfect—just what I promised Thomas, but you shouldn't be on your foot. I was going to make dinner for you."

Propped on the crutches, he leaned in to kiss her. "Now you don't have to."

Chapter Twenty-Five

Dreaming of home and her big comfortable bed, Maddie fought off sleep as Tiffany related the latest chapter in the ongoing drama of her troubled marriage. Sometimes Maddie felt guilty for being so happy with Mac when her sister was clearly miserable.

"So now *he* thinks *I* have been cheating on him! Doesn't that beat all? When, exactly, do you suppose I have time to have an affair, between taking care of Ashleigh, running the day care and teaching dance?"

"You two need to have an honest conversation about what's really going on," Maddie said.

"There's *nothing* going on! Nothing with him, nothing with anyone!"

"You've told him that?"

"Only a hundred times. Get this—he's made up his mind that I'm having a fling with Rudy from the Beach-comber because he saw me talking to him in the grocery store."

Maddie's mouth fell open. "Short, fat, bald Rudy?"

"I know, right? As if that's the best I could do!" All of

a sudden her sister's eyes flooded with tears. "I'm so tired of fighting with him," she whispered. "It's all we do." She pressed her hands to her eyes, probably hoping to stem the flood. "I can't do it anymore, Maddie. I just can't."

Tiffany and her husband, Jim, had been having problems for years now, but she'd never heard such resignation from her sister before. "What will you do?"

"I think we need to separate."

"Aw, Tiff. What about Ashleigh?"

"I've stayed with him this long because of her, but all the fighting isn't good for her. I can't stand living like this—always wondering where he is, what he's doing, who he's doing it with. And then to have *him* accuse *me*! That was it, you know?"

Maddie took her sister's hand. "I hate to see you so unhappy."

A knock on the door startled the sisters.

Still in uniform, Blaine Taylor, the Gansett Island police chief, stood in the doorway. "Um, hi, Maddie. Sorry to interrupt. Is Mac still around, by any chance?"

"You just missed him, Blaine. He went to pick up Thomas."

"Oh, okay. I'll catch him in the morning."

"He's going to call me when he gets home. Can I give him a message?"

"I wanted to let him know the captain of the boat has been arraigned on operating under the influence, and we discovered an outstanding warrant for failing to pay child support. Officers from the mainland are coming over tomorrow to pick him up."

"Mac and his family will be glad to hear that. Thanks for coming over to let us know."

"I wanted to check on Mr. McCarthy, too. He was my Boy Scout leader when I was a kid. Such a great guy."

"Yes, he is."

"Well, I won't keep you. Hope you're feeling better soon."

Tiffany sent Maddie a meaningful look.

"Blaine, do you know my sister, Tiffany?"

"I don't think we've met," Tiffany said with a smile for the handsome officer.

"Good to meet you, Tiffany. You ladies have a nice evening."

After he walked away, Tiffany made a big show of fanning herself. "If I were going to have an affair, that'd be more like it. Is he single?"

Frowning at her sister, Maddie said, "You need to talk to your husband."

Tiffany sighed. "I know."

"Knock, knock," Francine said from the doorway.

"There you are," Maddie said. "I was beginning to wonder if you'd heard I was in here."

"I heard," Francine said. "Is everything all right with the baby?"

"Just fine."

"That's a relief."

"When were you going to tell us you've gotten yourself a boyfriend, Ma?" Tiffany asked.

Maddie winced. She'd planned to ease into the subject, but leave it to Tiffany to put it right out there.

"I haven't got a *boyfriend*," Francine huffed.

"Sure looked like it to me—and everyone else—when you were holding hands with him."

Francine glowered at her younger daughter. "People on this island need to mind their own damned business."

"When have you ever known that to happen?" Tiffany asked.

"How are you feeling, Maddie?" Francine asked, turning her back on Tiffany.

"I'm fine but on bed rest for the remainder of the pregnancy."

"Don't worry," Francine said. "I'll help with Thomas. We both will, right, Tiffany?"

"Of course we will. Now, tell us about your boyfriend."

Francine threw up her hands and said, "Ugh!"

"Mac thinks the world of him," Maddie said. "He's like a beloved uncle to all the McCarthy kids. In fact, Mac bought our house from him."

Francine's eyes went wide. "He did not own that big house!"

"Mom, he owns half this island."

Francine laughed. "You're mistaking him for someone else. He drives a cab."

"That's only his hobby. Real estate is his business."

Francine had apparently been shocked speechless.

"Way to go, Mom," Tiffany said.

"I, um, I have to go," Francine said. "I'll check on you tomorrow." She rushed out of the room.

"Was it something we said?" Tiffany asked in a teasing tone.

"Go after her," Maddie said. "Make sure she's okay."

"All right, I'm going."

"Thanks for coming, and keep me posted on the situation with Jim."

Tiffany's smile faded at the reminder of her marital problems. "I will."

* * *

Francine found Ned waiting for her in the clinic parking lot, leaning against the dilapidated woody station wagon he used for a cab. Everything about him was dilapidated, so how was she supposed to believe that he actually *owned* half the island?

As she walked toward him, he didn't seem to blink, but he did smile as if delighted to see her. How silly was that? She'd seen him just half an hour ago. But since then, everything had changed, and she was still processing what Maddie had told her.

"Is it true?" she asked, wincing inside because she hadn't intended to blurt it right out like that. But damn it, she wanted to know.

"Is what true?"

"That you own half this island?" In the darkness, she couldn't be entirely sure, but she swore he blushed. "*More than half?*"

He shrugged sheepishly. "I dunno. Hardly keep track."

Francine blew out a long, deep breath. "So then what's all this?" she asked, gesturing to the cab.

"Gets me outta the house. Meet a lotta nice people. Get ta know who's a-comin' and who's a-goin'."

"Did you really sell that big house to Mac?"

"Yep."

"How did you . . . where did you . . ."

"Bought the first one 'bout thirty-five or so years ago. Fixed it up a bit, sold it for a profit. Bought another one. Even rich people who can afford houses out here fall on hard times every now and again. Took a few off their hands like the one I sold ta Mac." He shrugged again. "Didn't plan it. Just kinda happened, 'tis all."

"Who's the real Ned? The cab driver or the real estate tycoon?"

He winced at the word *tycoon*. "Both, I suspect. Ya got a problem with it?"

She was still trying to process it all. "No, no problem."

"Francine," he said, reaching for her hands and bringing her closer to him. "Money is nice to have—"

"I wouldn't know. I've never had any."

"It's nice to have," he continued, "but it can't buy happiness. Being with you again these last coupla days has made me happier than all the money I've made with my houses ever could."

"It has?" she asked, her voice suddenly squeaky.

He nodded. "Come 'ere and gimme a kiss."

Her face went hot, and her mind went stupid. She glanced over her shoulder and saw Tiffany scurrying away.

Ned stood to his full height and gave her hands a little tug that had her almost tumbling into his chest. He caught her, wrapped his arms around her, and before she could anticipate his next move, his lips were on hers, sweet, gentle and persuasive. His beard was soft against her face, and somehow her arms found their way around his neck to encourage him to keep kissing her.

It had been a long, lonely time since a man had kissed her so tenderly. Maybe since the last time she'd kissed Ned.

He finally broke the kiss. Looking as stunned as she felt, he stared at her for a breathless moment. "Let's get you home."

Since Francine didn't trust herself to speak, she let him guide her into his cab for the ride home.

Luke insisted on driving them to dinner at her parents' house. After spending much of the day with his foot elevated and on ice, he was going stir-crazy. But that was the least of his concerns. Ever since the night before when she'd arrived with Thomas, Sydney had been distant. Something was clearly bothering her, but he couldn't get her to sit still long enough to talk to her about it.

She'd fussed over Thomas until Mac picked him up, and then she announced she was tired and went to bed. Even though they'd slept in the same bed, they may as well have been in separate houses. He'd awoken to a note that said she'd gone to check on Buddy and to help Maddie. She had been out most of the day, returning in time to shower and change for dinner. The silence between them was deafening to Luke, and all of a sudden he couldn't take it anymore. He pulled the truck off the road and brought it to a stop.

Sydney looked over at him. "What?"

"I might ask you the same thing. What's going on, Syd?"

"Nothing."

Luke wanted to yell and scream, but that was so not his style. "What happened yesterday that caused you to shut down on me?"

Her eyes widened and her lips pursed, but she stayed silent.

"We're not moving until you tell me what the hell is going on."

"We'll be late."

"If you're worried about that, start talking."

She crossed her arms, and her face was set in a mulish expression he would've found cute if he hadn't been so concerned about what was bothering her.

"Syd. Talk to me."

She spun around in her seat. "Were you ever going to tell me you're a part owner of McCarthy's now?"

Okay, he hadn't seen that coming. "Eventually. I guess."

"No, you weren't."

"Wait, so you've been all frosty to me because you heard that from someone other than me?"

"Why didn't you tell me? We had all those conversations about your life, our possible life together, and never once did you see fit to tell me that you're not exactly what you pretend to be."

"And what is it that I pretend to be?"

"Just a guy who works the docks and fixes up boats. Simple. Uncomplicated."

"I *am* that guy, Syd. I've always been that guy."

"You *own* the business!"

"Only part of it, and only for the last year or so. It's no big deal."

"It's a huge big deal. That you kept it from me makes me wonder if I know you at all."

"Sydney, Jesus, you know me better than anyone else in this world. I've shown you parts of me that no one else has ever seen. How can you say you don't know me?"

"Why didn't you tell me?"

"Because."

"You have to do better than that."

"I didn't want it to be a factor in whether you decide to stay."

"What does that mean?"

"I wanted you to want me for *me*, not because of what I have."

Her mouth fell open. "Oh my God. You haven't forgiven me. All that talk about clean slates, and you're expecting me to do exactly what I did before!"

"That's not true. But money is important to you. You come in my house and all you see is the threadbare furniture and that nothing has changed. You assume it's because I can't afford to get new stuff. But the truth is, I don't care if it's old. It still works, so why would I replace it? I didn't tell you about the business because it hasn't given me anything I didn't already have. For years Mr. McCarthy has paid me a year-round salary to work six months a year because he said he couldn't run the place without me."

"Luke—"

"Who do you think was keeping the business going before Mac came home?" Luke gripped the steering wheel and stared out the window. "I own my house. I own my truck. I live simply. Even before the partnership, I made plenty of money, and I only spend a fraction of it, not because I'm worried about spending it, but because I have everything I need. Last year someone offered me a million dollars for my property—as is. Of course I declined, but he gave me his card in case I change my mind." Looking over at her, he said, "I'm not without means, Syd." He couldn't remember a time when he'd made such an impassioned speech, but for some reason, he felt like he was suddenly fighting for his life.

"I don't know where you got the idea I care about any of that."

"You married the guy who could keep you in the lifestyle you'd become accustomed to. Don't tell me you don't care about money."

"Maybe I used to, but that's not what I care about now. Apparently, you don't think too much of me if you think money matters more to me than you do."

"The thing is, I have no idea what matters most to you. Is it me? Is it what we have together? Is it your life in Boston? I'd really like to know."

Her hands were folded so tightly in her lap that her knuckles had turned white.

He covered them with his hand. "What matters most to

me is you. I'm sorry I didn't tell you about McCarthy's. I should have."

"I'm sorry you felt I was such a money-grubbing bitch that it would matter so much to me."

Shocked, he stared at her. "I never said that! You're twisting my words all around."

"Am I?"

"Yes! I don't think you're a money-grubbing any-thing." He paused for a moment, hoping to contain the swell of fear and despair that threatened to overtake him at the thought of losing her again. "I spent a lot of years living with the knowledge that I wasn't good enough for you the first time around. This time, I wanted to be good enough. Just the way I am. What you see is what you get."

She stared off into the encroaching darkness.

Luke's heart beat hard as he waited for her to say something. Anything. "Syd."

"You've certainly given me a lot to think about."

"What does that mean?"

"Just what I said. I need to think."

"For how long?"

"For as long as it takes."

"Do you still want to go to dinner?"

"Yes, let's go. My parents are waiting for us."

Luke started the truck, but he wondered how he'd manage to eat when all he could think about was the cold block of dread that had settled in his gut. Had he just totally blown it with her? Again?

Chapter Twenty-Six

Sydney's head was spinning during the dinner with her parents. Because they'd obviously gone to some considerable trouble with the meal and were trying to make Luke feel welcome, Sydney was doing her best to remain engaged, even though her heart ached after their roadside conversation.

Maybe they'd been deluding themselves that they could get past what'd happened years ago and make their second chance work out better than the first one did. After what he'd said earlier, it was clear to Sydney that Luke hadn't completely forgiven her for leaving him without a word or for marrying Seth. He was waiting for her to leave him again.

"Syd?" His deep voice interrupted her thoughts.

She looked up at the three faces watching her with concern and realized her best efforts to remain engaged had failed miserably.

"Everything okay, honey?" her mother asked.

From across the table, Luke studied Sydney intently.

She met his gaze when she said, "Yes, everything's fine." Was that relief she saw on his face?

"Sydney's upset with me because I failed to tell her I'm now a part owner of McCarthy's Marina," Luke said, his gaze locked on her.

Well, he was full of surprises tonight.

"She found out from someone else, which was wrong of me. I should've told her myself."

"Oh," Mary Alice said. "Well."

"So you're a partner," Allan said.

Luke nodded. "When Mac came into the business, he didn't want the full responsibility, so Mr. McCarthy made us partners and retained a small share for himself."

"Congratulations," Allan said. "That's a very successful business."

"Yes, it is."

Watching the exchange, Sydney saw her father looking at Luke with newfound respect. Right in that moment, she got why he hadn't told her. He hadn't wanted it to matter to her the same way it clearly mattered to her dad.

Sydney's heart ached as she understood how worried he was that she would leave him again—or that she would stay for the wrong reasons. Everything became crystal clear to her as she studied his adorably handsome face across the table. The minute they were alone, she would put his mind at ease. There was nowhere else she wanted to be than with him. Why bother to fight it anymore?

The phone rang, and her mother got up to answer it, returning a moment later, her face ashen and her eyes large. "Allan, Simone has had a mild heart attack."

"Oh God. Is she . . ."

"She's at Mass General, but she's okay."

Her father took a deep, rattling breath.

"My aunt," Sydney said to Luke.

"I need to go there." Allan checked his watch. "Oh, we won't make the last boat."

"I'll call Slim," Luke said. "The McCarthys' pilot friend. He'll fly you over if he can."

"Oh, thank you, Luke," Mary Alice said.

While Luke went to make the call, Sydney gave her dad a hug. "Simone is still young and strong, Dad. She'll get through this. I know it."

He nodded, but his entire body was rigid with worry over his younger sister.

Luke hobbled back into the room. "Slim said he'll meet you at the airport in thirty minutes."

"Thank you so much, Luke," Mary Alice said. "Come on, Allan. Let's go pack. I'm sorry about dinner."

"Don't worry about it, Mom. Go get ready." Her parents went upstairs, and Sydney turned to Luke. "Thank you."

"Happy to help." Propped on his crutches, he drew her toward him. "I'm sorry about your aunt. If you want to go with them, I'll take care of Buddy. Grant can help me move him to my house."

Sydney rested her head on his chest. "I'll stay for now and see what tomorrow brings, but thanks for the offer."

"What I said before—it came out all wrong."

"No, it didn't. We'll talk about it after they leave."

Her parents departed a few minutes later in a flurry of hugs and promises to call as soon as they knew more about her aunt's condition.

From his pillow on the floor, Buddy watched the goings-on. He'd been up and around a little more that day and was able to go outside when he needed to but was still weak and easily tired.

After seeing her parents off, Sydney bent to press a kiss to Buddy's sweet face and was rewarded with a lick to the cheek. "Aww, you're feeling better, aren't you? I'm so glad." She kissed him again and stood to face Luke.

"When I came out here earlier this month," she said,

hoping she could get through this without becoming too emotional, "I was hoping to make a few decisions about what's next for me. I'd left my job as a teacher because it was too difficult to be around kids that age without constantly being reminded of the children I'd lost."

Propped on his crutches, Luke watched and listened, but he didn't say anything.

"I never could've imagined you and I would reconnect the way we have or that being with you again would make me so . . ."

"What, Syd?" He tucked her hair behind her ear and stroked her cheek. "Tell me."

"Happy," she whispered. "I've been so happy. I didn't think that was possible anymore, and you've helped me see I still have a whole life in front of me, and it doesn't have to be filled with sadness and grief." She ventured a look up at him and found him watching her intently. "Thank you for that."

"Believe me, it's been my pleasure."

She smiled. "Mine, too."

"But?"

Sydney shook her head. "No buts. I love you, Luke. I don't know if I ever stopped loving you or if it was just on hold or what. But I love you, and I want to be with you, whether it's here or on the mainland or wherever—"

He took a step to close the distance between them, letting his crutches fall to the floor in a loud clatter that drew a whine of concern from Buddy. Hooking an arm around her waist, he tugged her in tight against him.

Sydney's hands landed on his chest. "Luke, your ankle!"

"It's fine," he whispered as he brought his mouth down on hers for a devouring kiss.

Having surrendered to the overwhelming love she

felt for him, Sydney threw herself into the kiss, meeting every stroke of his tongue until she was so breathless spots danced before her eyes.

His lips shifted to her jaw and then to her neck. "I love you so much, Syd. Only you. I've loved you for as long as I've known what love is."

Her fingers sank into his hair, anchoring him to her.

"I have a proposition for you," he said.

Sydney tilted her hips into his erection. "So I see."

"Not that kind of proposition," he said, laughing. "Although that one is definitely on the agenda." As if he couldn't resist, he kissed her again.

"I want to hear your proposition," she said against his lips.

He drew back an inch or two so he could look her in the eye. "I'd like to hire you to redecorate my house."

Sydney started to reply, but he stopped her with a finger to her lips.

"Hear me out. It needs everything, so you'd be committing to a project that could take a year or two."

"That's a long time," she said gravely, playing along.

"Hopefully long enough for you to try island life on for size, and while you're at it, you can try me on for size, too."

Sydney reached down to cup his erection, squeezing in the places that made him crazy. "I like your size just fine."

"Syd," he gasped, "quit that. I'm trying to talk to you."

"I'm listening." She smiled up at him, enjoying the tortured look on his face.

He closed his hand around hers to stop her from stroking him. "After you finish the house, you can decide if you want to stay for good. If you don't, we'll go somewhere else."

"And you'd be okay with that?"

"As long as you're with me, I'd be okay anywhere."

Touched by what he'd said, she flattened her hands on his chest and kissed him. "I'll accept your proposition on one condition—you don't have to hire me. I was hoping to use before-and-after pictures of your place in my portfolio to help start my business."

"I suppose I can live with that."

"Then I suppose I can live with you."

"That's the best news I've had in years."

"I have some things to deal with at home after Labor Day." Her euphoria faded a bit at the reminder. "But then I'll be back."

Luke traced a finger over the furrow between her brows. "Every time you refer to the things you need to take care of at home, you lose your sparkle. What do you have to do?"

"The guy who hit us is being sentenced on September fifth." She looked up at him. "I have to be there."

"Maybe so, but you don't have to go alone."

She shook her head. "I don't expect you—"

He silenced her with another kiss. "I'm going with you. What else?"

"Well, if I'm moving out here, there's no reason to keep my house in Wellesley. I'll need to pack up my stuff, the kids' things I want to keep, Seth's stuff." Just the thought of it was enough to make her want to run and hide, but she knew it had to be done eventually.

"Hey," he said, compelling her to meet his gaze. "We'll do it together. Whatever you need to do, I'll be right there with you."

Sydney hugged him, relieved to know she wouldn't be alone when she closed the last door to her former life and stepped forward into a new life with Luke. "Thank you."

"Whatever comes our way, we'll deal with it together, okay?"

Closing her eyes against the rush of emotion, she nodded.

His hands slid down her back to bring her in tighter against his erection. "Now, about that other proposition you mentioned . . ."

Sydney laughed and drew him into another heated kiss. "You need to get off your ankle," she said when they resurfaced many minutes later.

With his arms around her waist, he fell backward onto the sofa, bringing her down on top of him. "There. Happy now?"

Nodding, she brushed the hair off his forehead and leaned in to kiss him, hungry for more of the way he made her feel.

He combed his fingers through her hair and down her back as his lips moved over hers. "I used to think about this all the time," he said. "The way your hair would drape down over me when we made love." Squeezing her bottom, he held her still and pressed his erection into the V of her legs.

"It's not as long as it used to be," she said, breathless with wanting him.

"It's every bit as beautiful as it always was, and so is the rest of you."

Sydney sat up to pull the top over her head and release her bra.

Luke cupped her breasts, running his thumbs over the tight buds. "Come closer." He closed his hot mouth over her nipple, sucking and licking her until Syd was half out of her mind with wanting him. She extricated herself to get rid of the rest of their clothes.

As his erection sprang free from his shorts, Sydney

bent to take him into her mouth, loving the way his legs trembled and his fingers tightened in her hair.

"Syd, baby, wait." He urged her back up and over him. "I need to be inside you. Now."

She'd never heard such urgency in his voice, which made her want him even more.

He arranged her on top of him and surged into her. As her head fell back, her mouth opened in a silent cry of completion. The sliding of his hands from her hips to her breasts brought her back to reality.

"Down here," he whispered. "I want your hair."

Sydney leaned forward and took his mouth, sending her tongue surging.

He shocked her by sucking hard on her tongue as he pinched her nipples.

An orgasm rocketed through her, catching her off guard and unprepared for the swell of emotion that came with it. She glanced down to find Luke watching her with love and desire and infinite tenderness etched into his expression.

"Ride me, Syd. The way you used to on the beach. Remember?"

She nodded and sat up, reaching for his hands to anchor her. Pivoting her hips, she gave him what he wanted and was astonished to feel a second orgasm building.

Luke held her hips in place, pushed hard into her one last time and sent them both spiraling into a powerful release. Slumped on his chest with his heart pounding under her ear and his cock still throbbing inside her, she couldn't have moved if she had to.

"Wow," Luke said, his lips pressed to her forehead. "Are you still with me?"

"Barely."

From his pillow on the floor, Buddy began to whimper.

"Poor guy," Luke said, chuckling.

"We've scarred him for life."

"He'd better get used to it, because once I have you in my bed every night, he can expect a regular show."

"*Every* night?"

"Maybe every morning, too."

Laughing, Sydney said, "Thanks for the warning."

"It's going to be so great, Syd. I promise."

"If it's this great every night, I may not survive."

"Don't worry, I'll take good care of you." With his hand in her hair, he urged her into another sweet kiss. "You sure you're ready for this?"

Looking at his handsome, sincere face, she smiled and ran a finger over his lower lip.

He drew her finger into his mouth and ran his tongue back and forth over the sensitive tip.

That was all it took to start her motor running again.

"I wouldn't have been ready for anyone but you."

"That works out rather well, because you're the only one I've ever wanted." Brushing the hair back from her forehead, he said, "Tell me again."

"I love you, Luke. I can't wait to live here with you."

He gathered her to him, his arms tight around her. "I love you, too. I can't wait for everything with you."

Sydney was filled with bittersweet relief. She'd never imagined her life turning out the way it had, but after the haze of tragedy and heartbreak had cleared, she'd ended up exactly where she belonged.

Epilogue

Luke held Sydney's hand between both of his as they watched Mac carry Maddie to the chaise that had been set to the left of the altar so she could fulfill her matron-of-honor duties for Janey and still follow doctor's orders to stay off her feet. She wore a gorgeous sage gown and positively glowed with happiness as her husband kissed her and went to stand next to Joe.

Across the aisle from Luke and Syd, Grant sat with his brothers, Adam and Evan, as well as Stephanie, who'd dyed her hair a rich red for the occasion. She'd softened her makeup and had worn a formfitting dress that was rather surprisingly sexy. Sydney noticed Stephanie taking furtive glances at Grant, but his eyes were riveted to Abby, who was Janey's bridesmaid. *Very* interesting.

Behind them, Ned and Francine sat close to each other, hand in hand, out of the closet and a couple again. Ned had shaved off his beard and cut his hair short, making him look twenty years younger, in Syd's opinion. She wondered if they'd be the next to tie the knot.

Everyone turned to the back of the church as Janey and her father appeared in the doorway.

"Wow," Luke whispered. "Look at her."

"Gorgeous," Sydney agreed.

Even though he was noticeably thinner and still recovering from his injuries, Big Mac was handsome in his tuxedo and steady as he walked his baby girl down the aisle. Since his left arm was still in a sling, Janey held tight to his right arm, both of them clearly fighting their way through the emotion of the moment.

With Mac by his side, Joe never shifted his gaze from Janey as she came toward him.

Big Mac hugged his daughter and then Joe before joining his wife in the front row.

Listening to Janey and Joe recite their vows, Luke tightened his hold on Sydney's hand.

She smiled at him, dazzled by how handsome he was in a smart dark suit, and once again she was so grateful to have him back in her life and by her side for the difficult days she had to endure before they could move forward.

Syd had no doubt they'd get through it. Together.

Thank you for reading *Ready for Love*!
I hope you enjoyed Luke and Sydney's story.
Join the Gansett Island Reader Group at
facebook.com/groups/McCarthySeries
to chat with other fans of the series.

Watch for the next book in the Gansett Island series,
featuring Grant McCarthy,
coming soon as a Zebra mass-market paperback:

FALLING FOR LOVE

Turn the page to read Chapter One of *Falling for Love* . . .

This whole thing was Janey's fault. If she hadn't gotten married, Grant wouldn't have had to watch *his* woman, wearing a slinky, sexy bridesmaid gown, prance around at the wedding with her new *fiancé* hanging all over her. If it hadn't been for Janey and her stupid wedding, Grant wouldn't have felt the need to make Abby jealous by dancing with Stephanie from the marina.

Too bad it hadn't ended there. No, he'd had to make sure Abby was *truly* jealous by leaving with Stephanie. And now, as the hammer in his head reminded him of how much alcohol it had taken to get through the nuptials, the warm body sleeping next to him was an even bigger reminder of what a disaster last night had been.

Damn Janey and her damned wedding.

Grant was trying frantically to remember just how far things had gone with Stephanie. He was pretty sure there'd been some kissing in the cab on the way to his now-married sister's place. Janey had traded him the use of her house in exchange for pet-sitting duties while she and Joe were on their honeymoon. Since their mother had been driving him crazy with questions about the mess he'd made of his life, it had seemed like a good deal at the time because it would get him out of his parents' house. But now he was mad with his sister for getting married in the first place, and the sweet deal didn't seem so sweet anymore.

He wished he could escape, but he couldn't exactly leave his one-night stand in his sister's bed. What to do?

Then the warm body stirred.

Grant stayed perfectly still, hoping she wouldn't look at him or, God forbid, try to talk to him. He'd been with Abby so long he'd never had the chance to indulge in one-night stands. He had no idea what the etiquette was, and with a thousand hammers at work in his head, he had no desire to figure it out.

Out of the corner of his eye, he watched Stephanie— oh *Jesus*, she was totally naked—slide from the bed and get busy rounding up her clothes. Still pretending to be asleep, he caught glimpses of small breasts and pretty pink nipples that quickly had the attention of a part of him that didn't know enough to fake sleep. As his cock rubbed against the sheet, he realized he was naked, too.

He was desperately trying to remember how he'd ended up naked in bed with Stephanie, but he couldn't recall a single thing after being in the cab. Not that being naked with Stephanie hadn't crossed his mind far too often in the last few weeks . . . He'd even bought condoms, just in case his horny body won the war with his better judgment. But he'd never expected to actually go *through* with it. Maybe he hadn't. Maybe nothing actually happened. That was possible, right? Naked didn't automatically mean sex, did it?

Shit, shit, *shit*! If Abby heard about this, he'd never get her back, not to mention what his father, who'd taken a special interest in Stephanie since she came to work for them, would have to say about it.

Stephanie turned her back to the bed to put on the formfitting black dress she'd worn to the wedding. Her pale skin was creamy white, and his eyes traveled from her shoulders to the two dimples at the bottom of her spine, above her firmly rounded ass. When he first met her, he'd thought she lacked curves. *Boyish* was the word he'd used to describe her. But now that he'd seen her naked, it was clear that her clothes had hidden small but rather interesting curves.

Not that he was interested in her curves. No, the only curves he craved were Abby's, and somehow he had to figure out a way to get her back. First and foremost, he had to stop drinking. Booze—and Janey's damned wedding—had landed him in bed with the wrong woman, and he couldn't let that happen again. If he had any prayer of winning back Abby, he couldn't get caught with another woman. Making Abby jealous was one thing, but his plan had clearly gone awry in a big way.

Stephanie never so much as glanced at the bed as she hooked her high-heeled sandals around her fingers and tiptoed from the room, closing the door behind her.

Grant let out a sigh of relief that he'd been spared the morning-after awkwardness. But then he remembered he was in charge of the family's marina while his father recovered from a recent head injury and his brother tended to his pregnant wife. With Grant stuck running the docks and Stephanie managing the restaurant, he'd have to face her in a few short hours.

Groaning, he turned facedown on the bed and buried his face in the pillow. Something poked his belly, and he fumbled through the rumpled sheet to see what it was.

When his hand landed on a torn condom wrapper, Grant's heart nearly stopped beating.

"Shit, shit, *shit!*"

He'd rocked her world, and Stephanie would bet he didn't even remember it. As she shivered in driving wind and cold rain on her way to McCarthy's Gansett Island Marina, she relived the night with Grant McCarthy. Of course she'd figured out what he'd been up to at the wedding. He'd been using her to make Abby jealous. She'd also known he was drunk when they left and that he probably wouldn't remember much of what happened between them.

Still, that didn't stop her from taking full advantage of the opportunity for one night with the first guy she'd been attracted to in years. She was under no illusions that this was the start of something with him. He was in love with Abby and still hoping to reconcile with her, although Abby and her fiancé, Cal, had looked pretty darned cozy at the wedding.

If Stephanie were one to gamble, she'd bet on Abby being done with Grant, and him being the last one to realize it. But even knowing that, there was no way Stephanie was going to get all stupid over a guy who clearly wanted someone else. So they'd had sex. Big deal. Just because she hadn't been with anyone in ages didn't mean she was going to turn this into something it wasn't and would never be.

A tooting horn caught her attention, and she stopped to find Mr. McCarthy's best friend, Ned Saunders, pulling up to the curb in the beat-up woody station wagon that served as his cab.

"Jump in, gal. I'll give ya a ride."

Since she was soaked to the skin, Stephanie was thrilled to see the older man who hung around the marina every day. "Thanks, Ned," she said as she slid into the front seat. The floor was littered with coffee cups and old newspapers.

"Sorry 'bout the mess," he muttered.

"No problem. I'm happy to get out of the storm."

"'Tis a doozy of a nor'easter. Not seeing the newly-weds makin' it off-island today."

"That's too bad. They'll miss their flight, won't they?"

"Looks that way."

Stephanie appreciated that Ned didn't mention anything about her obvious walk of shame. "How long is the storm supposed to last?"

"Coupla days at least."

"The marina will be slow today," Stephanie said, dreading a quiet day to spend alone with Grant.

Ned took the final turn that led to North Harbor. As they passed the McCarthy home, called the "White House" by locals, Stephanie looked away as memories of the night she'd spent with their son resurfaced. Mr. McCarthy had been so nice to her. She'd hate to do anything to mess that up.

"The boy's confused," Ned said, breaking the silence.

"Excuse me?"

"Smartest kid I ever knew," Ned continued as if she hadn't spoken. "From the time he was first able to talk, he's been asking questions, studying people, filing stuff away to use later in his stories. When it comes to people in his own life, though . . . well, sometimes he ain't the sharpest tool in the shed."

Stephanie's entire body was on fire with mortification as she continued to stare out the window. *How does he know? And what will he tell his best buddy, Grant's dad?*

"Don't think he gets yet that it's really over with Abby. When he finally catches a clue, I suspect it's gonna hurt."

Her mind raced as she hummed with tension. It was like he could see inside her or something!

"A nice girl like you would wanna watch herself in the midst of all that hurtin'."

Her mouth fell open, but damn if she could find the words. Luckily, their arrival at McCarthy's saved her from having to reply.

"Thanks for the ride," Stephanie muttered, reaching for her wallet.

Ned's hand on her arm stopped her from withdrawing money. "My pleasure, honey."

Stephanie was mortified all over again when tears burned her eyes. She made her escape from the car, but the almost paternal way Ned had treated her stayed with her long after his car disappeared from view. It'd been a long time since anyone had showed her that kind of care or concern, and it had felt good.

A ringing cell phone woke Capt. Joe Cantrell the morning after his wedding. He wanted to grab the phone and toss it across the suite where he and Janey had spent their wedding night, but more than that, he wanted his lovely *wife* to sleep awhile longer.

After so many years of loving her from afar, thinking of her as his wife made him smile. He took the phone into the bathroom and closed the door. Seeing the office number on the caller ID further irritated him.

"This had better be good," he grumbled into the phone.

"So sorry to bother you, Cap," said Seamus O'Grady. Joe had hired Seamus to run the Gansett Island Ferry

Company when he and Janey moved to Ohio so she could attend vet school. "Especially this morning."

"What do you need?" Joe asked with unusual brusqueness.

"I wasn't sure if you'd surfaced yet to take a look at the weather. Tropical Storm Hailey arrived overnight, and we've got a heck of a blow going on. I'm leaning toward stopping service for the rest of the day, but I know you and the wife are planning to take the ten thirty boat off the island. Didn't want to screw you up."

As Seamus spoke, Joe went to the window and looked out over South Harbor. The wind and rain had whipped Gansett Sound into a froth of whitecaps, and the rain beat hard against the window. It was the kind of day they referred to as a barf-o-rama in the ferry business because they'd have to hose the vomit from the boats after each trip. "Go ahead and make the call," Joe said.

"You sure about that, Cap?"

"Such is the chance we take making travel plans from an island, right?"

"Right you are. Don't worry about a thing here. I gotcha covered. We'll get you and the wife outta here as soon as we can. By the way, it was a great wedding."

"Thanks, Seamus." Joe ended the call and crept out of the bathroom.

"What's wrong?" Janey asked. Her voice was husky and sleepy—and sexy as hell. She reached out a hand to him.

Joe tossed the phone into his suitcase and went to her.

She gave his hand a tug to draw him back into bed.

Feeling like the luckiest son of a bitch on the face of the earth to finally be married to the woman he'd loved for more than half his life, Joe snuggled into her warm embrace.

"Now tell me what's wrong," she said.

"There's good news and bad news." He kissed lips that were puffy and swollen from a night of passion. "The bad news is they're shutting the ferries down because of the storm."

Janey gasped. She'd been so looking forward to their honeymoon in Aruba, which they'd chosen because it was outside the hurricane belt. So much for that logic.

"How can there be good news after that?" she asked with her lip curling into the same pout she'd sported as a ten-year-old.

Joe maneuvered her so she was under him and brushed tangled blond hair off her face. "The very good news is we don't have to leave this bed today."

Janey smiled up at him and ran her hands from his shoulders down his back and curved them over his ass, a move that always drove him crazy, as she well knew. "That's very good news indeed."

"I'll get you there, baby," he said as he dipped his head for a kiss. "Might take a day or two, but I'll get you there."

"Doesn't matter where we are. As long as it's just the two of us, that's what matters."

"Have I told you yet today that I love you love you?" he asked.

"Not yet," she said, smiling at the reminder of how he'd once told her he wanted her to *love him* love him.

"Well, I do."

"I think you need to prove it." Flashing a coy grin, she lifted her hips against his erection, letting him know what she wanted.

"Again?" he asked, quirking an eyebrow in amusement. "No one told me I was marrying an insatiable wench."

Janey laughed and guided him to exactly where she

wanted him. "Better get used to it, buddy. You're stuck with me now."

He entered her in one smooth thrust. "Thank God for that."

Driving wind and rain woke Mac McCarthy early on the morning after his sister's wedding. His chest tightened with anxiety when it occurred to him that the storm had probably shut down the ferries for the day.

He glanced over at his wife, Maddie, sleeping on her side the way Dr. Cal had instructed to minimize the stress on the baby. The thought of being unable to get her help if she needed it made him crazy. A high-risk pregnancy on an island was a fool's errand, but he'd had no luck convincing her to move their family to the mainland until the baby was born.

Hoping the weather wasn't as bad as it sounded, Mac got up to look out the window. Sure enough, it was every bit as bad as it sounded. In the distance, he could see the ocean whipped into a frenzy. Rain was coming down sideways in the blustery wind. Running a hand over his chest, Mac wondered if he was having a heart attack. The tightness had been ever-present since the accident at the marina that left his father injured.

The accident had briefly put him in the hospital, too, which had stressed out Maddie. After she went into premature labor and was put on bed rest for the remainder of her pregnancy, she'd refused to leave their island home. Mac had no choice but to cede to her wishes.

Mac went to his dresser to retrieve his phone. A text message from the Gansett Island Ferry Company made it official: service was temporarily suspended. With the wind gusting to what sounded like at least fifty miles per hour, the airport would be closed, too. No way out, Mac thought as the pain in his chest intensified.

Nightmare scenarios such as this had driven him crazy for weeks now. Even when the ferries were running, it was a long hour to the mainland and then more time to get to a hospital. In the meantime, what if something happened that Cal couldn't handle? What if Maddie needed something he couldn't get for her? What if something happened to her—

"Mac?"

He turned away from the window and went to her. "I thought you'd sleep awhile yet," he said, smoothing a hand over her caramel-colored hair. "It's early."

"Why are you up?"

"The wind woke me." His chest began to ache again as he wondered how long they'd be without ferry service. He turned on the bedside light so he could see her in the early morning gloom. "How do you feel?"

"Fat. Horrible." Tears filled her golden eyes. "Hideous."

"Aww, baby." He crawled back into bed and drew her—as best he could—into his arms. They hadn't been able to make love in weeks, which wasn't doing much to help his overwhelming anxiety. "Don't say that. You're gorgeous, glowing and radiant." How would they get through two more months of her being stuck in bed all day, every day?

"You have to say that. You did this to me."

She was so petulant and cute that Mac laughed, even though he knew she wouldn't appreciate it.

Fat tears spilled from her eyes and wet her cheeks. "It's not funny."

"I know," he said, kissing away her tears. She'd been

so happy and content yesterday at the wedding, surrounded by family and friends. The thought gave him an idea of how he could lift her spirits a bit before everyone scattered again after the storm let up.

Just as he was about to share his idea with her, the bedside light flickered and died.

**Preorder *Falling for Love*
to read the minute it's released in print!**